The Brotherhood

A Psychological Thriller

Jo Fenton

CROOKED CAT

Discover us online:
www.crookedcatbooks.com

Join us on facebook:
www.facebook.com/crookedcatbooks

Tweet a photo of yourself holding
this book to **@crookedcatbooks**
and something nice will happen.

To Ray,
for inspiring me to start writing,
and for all the support and
encouragement along the way.

Acknowledgements

Huge thanks go to my lovely friend and editor, Sue Barnard; who has been so supportive of me during the many reviews.

Thanks to all my wonderful Writers United friends: Helen Lane, Lucy Goacher, Gareth Hewitt, Libby Carpenter, Sue Burrows, Carol Lucas, Anya Stojanovic Chand, Bean Sawyer, Sam Carrington, Lydia Devadason, Paul Stephenson, Laura Sillett, Joan Bullion El Faghloumi, Susan King, Suzanne Harbour, Lee Sloan and Caroline Harris; for all your support, advice and feedback.

Also thanks to the fabulous Manchester Scribes (previously Crafty Writers): Jayne Fallows (my critique buddy), Lorrie Porter (who taught me the craft of writing), Louise Jones, Helen Copestake, Grant Silk, Karen Moore, Pauline Barnett, Claire Tansey, Awen Thornber – you all provided great support and encouragement with your critiques.
I send heartfelt thanks also to my additional beta readers: Phil Saunders, Neil Burrows, Jo Newland, Gayle Samuels, Julie Rudolph, Tanya Englander and Lucy Mann – your comments and feedback have been taken into account and have shaped the final novel.

Thank you to Jeni Chappelle and Sally Zigmond for your advice and editorial support on my earlier drafts.

Massive thanks to my incredible family: Ray, Michael and Andrew, for putting up with me, and providing me with the time to write; and to the rest of my family for listening to me.

I would like to thank Dawn Stewart and Allan Jordan for their technical expertise when help was needed with a key plot point.

And finally, a huge thank you to Laurence and Stephanie Patterson for taking a chance on me, and to the wider

Crooked Cat Community for all your support and advice during the publication process.

Thanks to everyone mentioned above. I couldn't have done all this without you.

About the Author

Jo Fenton grew up in Hertfordshire. She devoured books from an early age, particularly enjoying adventure books, school stories and fantasy. She wanted to be a scientist from age six after being given a wonderful book titled "Science Can Be Fun". At eleven, she discovered Agatha Christie and Georgette Heyer, and now has an eclectic and much loved book collection cluttering her home office.

Jo combines an exciting career in Clinical Research with an equally exciting but very different career as a writer of psychological thrillers. When not working, she runs (very slowly), and chats to lots of people. She lives in Manchester with her husband, two sons, a Corgi and a tankful of tropical fish. She is an active and enthusiastic member of two writing groups and a reading group.

The
Brotherhood

Chapter One

A lone magpie pecks at the ground. The sound startles me and for a moment I think… but no, I'm being paranoid. My faded black shoes scuff on the paving stones as I rush from the nurses' hostel. It's mid-afternoon, and the area is empty except for me.

I check my watch; I must get a move on. Dominic will be waiting for me by now, and I don't want to disappoint him. The safer route would take an extra twenty minutes, but I can't afford the time. Taking a deep breath, I turn down the dark alleyway – the short cut leading from the hospital to the town centre. Hairs prickle on the back of my neck, though, and the sound of footsteps makes me turn my head quickly. I can't see anyone, but there are lots of bushes, telegraph poles and shadows where a pursuer could hide.

I hurry down the path. My heart's pounding as I approach the entrance to an adjoining alley. Is someone lying in wait for me? The steps came from behind, but maybe he doubled back. I break into a jog, but I'm quickly out of breath. Fitness has not been a priority recently. Changing to a brisk walk, I pass the junction. There's no one there, but I can still hear intermittent thuds – as if someone is treading carefully in heavy boots.

At the end of the path, the high street is bathed in sunlight. It's casting long shadows in this passageway and my nerve is breaking. I have to run. Finally, I reach the bright main road, panting for breath. The street's full of shoppers, and no one notices a breathless young redhead appearing from a gap between WH Smith and the Cancer charity shop. I try to breathe more normally as I walk the last hundred yards to Starbucks.

I'm almost there. I can see the large expanse of glass,

behind which Dominic sits with a newspaper and a large mug. He hasn't seen me yet, but I smile anyway. He's showed up. There's always a bit of me that worries. Have I scared him off? Did I say something stupid? I can't believe it's only a month since I met him – a month since the memorial service for my mum and dad. He showed up, helped me through the service, and has been meeting me for coffee nearly every day since. He's a minister, and has said he wants to help me. In truth, he helps just by being here.

A figure darts into a nearby side street. Not such a strange occurrence, but after my experience in the alley, my nerves are shot. I recognise my pursuer. I dive through the open door, and plunge towards Dominic's table. He looks up as I arrive.

"Melissa! Are you all right, my child?" He calls me that all the time. It bothered me at first – I'm twenty-two – but it seems to be a term of affection, so I accept it now, and it calms me.

"Yes, thank you." I nod and stumble onto the chair. "Just a bit of… a bit of a rush getting here." I decide not to tell him about the stalker. Let it lie for now.

"Let me get you a coffee while you catch your breath. The usual?"

"Yes please." I calm down while I wait for him, and he comes back a few minutes later with a large cappuccino, smothered in chocolate sprinkles. "You spoil me. Thank you."

"It's my pleasure. You've had a bad time, my child. It's time someone looked after you a little."

"You have been looking after me. I don't know if I could have got through the last few weeks without you." Does that sound clingy and desperate? Probably. My cheeks grow hot.

"What will you do now? You've started back at work, haven't you?"

"I've been back a week. It's hard, though. I keep seeing people come in with their parents, and thinking 'that will never be me'. I try not to, but can't seem to help it."

Tears sting my eyes and I blink them away. Learning not

to cry at the slightest thing is essential. I've already had two warnings at work this week. If I get another one, I'll be jobless and homeless.

A shadow falls across the table, and I glance up. My ex-boyfriend, Pete, is standing inches from my shoulder. He's too close to me, and the hairs go up on the back of my neck.

"Can I help you, young man?" Dominic's words are polite, but the tone is frosty.

"Melissa's my girlfriend. She shouldn't be meeting up with strange men, and definitely not old gits like you."

I cringe. Dominic's not old. He must be in his thirties, maybe forty at the most, but he wears it well. And Pete's pushing thirty anyway.

"Pete, can we stop this please? We broke up weeks ago."

"No Lissa, you tried to break up with me. I never said I agreed with the split. As far as I'm concerned, you're still mine."

His possessive tone annoys me, but I daren't be too confrontational. He continues to invade my space. He lays a hand on my shoulder, and pushes his thumb against my neck, half-hidden by my curls. It probably looks like a caress, but the pressure makes the room swim. As a doctor, Pete knows exactly where to press.

"Please, just leave it, okay?" I try to wriggle away from him.

Suddenly Dominic's on his feet. There's a gleam in his eye.

"Enough. You, Peter, or whatever your name is, get away from Melissa. She clearly doesn't want to have anything to do with you. You don't want to get on my wrong side, believe me. Let go of her, and get out of here."

Dominic hasn't raised his voice, but it conveys a threat. Thank goodness someone can stand up to Pete. He's such a bully. Not that most people realise. The handsome blond doctor usually manages to charm everyone into doing what he wants. Only I know the charm is less than skin-deep.

Pete bends down and whispers in my ear, "I'll get you back. You'll not leave me, Lissa, I won't have it." He casts

Dominic a dirty look, and then marches out into the street.

"Sorry about that. I had a feeling he was following me here, but I hoped I was wrong." I can't stop shaking, and Dominic comes round the table and puts his arm around me.

"You'll be fine, my child. Don't worry. Do you want me to drive you home?"

"Yes please." I hate being so pathetic, but feeling so shaken up, I was dreading the walk home. I'm intensely grateful for the offer.

"Finish your coffee. There's no rush." He returns to his chair. I feel colder now he's withdrawn his arm from around me.

"Thank you." Conversation deserts me, and there's a moment's awkward silence.

"How long have you known... whatsisname... Peter?" Dominic asks suddenly.

"About a year. We met at the hospital where we both work, and he was so charming, he swept me off my feet. Then gradually he started making a fuss when I wanted to spend time with friends and family. He'd get violent sometimes." I shudder, and Dominic reaches over and takes my hand.

"Hush now. You don't need to tell me any more. I can see what sort he is. You're better off without him."

"He won't leave me alone though. Last night he knocked on my door at eleven o'clock, and wouldn't go away until I threatened to call the police. He said he'd make me sorry. He scares me, to be honest."

"Which takes us back to my earlier question: what are you going to do?" He's still holding my hand, and warmth travels up my arm.

Then his question penetrates the fog in my head. What *am* I going to do? What are my options? I can stay here and keep running away from Pete, until he catches me and does something awful. Last time he bullied me into being alone with him, he started to strangle me. I came round to find him checking my pulse. He swore it was a joke, but I think he only wants me so he can keep tormenting me.

"Melissa?"

"Sorry. I don't know what to do. Stay here, I suppose, and hope that Pete gets fed up with following me around." I shiver. It's not much of an option. I don't mention the risk to my job if I don't pull myself together.

"How about your parents' house? That's yours now, isn't it? Could you go there?" Dominic's tone is gentle, but there's a strange light in his eyes. Has he got something else in mind?

"Yes, it's probably mine, but I don't think I could stay there. Too many memories. And anyway, Pete knows where it is. He could just follow me there, and it's far more isolated than the nurses' hostel. I'd be terrified." I glance down.

"Have I told you where I live?"

"No, I don't think so. Where do you live?" The words sound husky, as if I've got a bad throat. Does Dominic have a solution to my problems?

"I live in an Abbey. You know I'm a minister; I run a religious community called The Brotherhood. It's a delightful place – a refuge. Everyone watches out for each other. It's like a big family. Maybe you could come and join us?"

Around us, the tables are now empty as coffee drinkers have dispersed. The staff are cleaning tables and bustling about.

"Can you tell me more about it please?"

"Yes, but I think we'd better leave here. They're starting to drop hints." One barista is pulling down shutters on one of the windows outside, and the lights dim. "See what I mean?" He laughs, and pulls me to my feet. "Come on, I'll give you that lift back to the hospital and tell you the rest in the car."

Chapter Two

He's parked round the back in a pay and display car park.

"Which is yours?"

"That one!" He flashes me a boyish grin, and points at a red Porsche.

"Wow, that's cool."

He opens the door for me, and I sink into the most amazing leather seat. It smells new. I feel out of place in my faded, holey jeans and sloppy t-shirt. He jumps in beside me, and turns the key in the ignition. The engine purrs.

"Actually, she's not mine. An old school friend lets me borrow her sometimes. I do love her though." He gives me another of those delighted grins. I've never seen him this excited about anything. He seems vulnerable somehow, like a kid in a sweet shop. I smile back, warmed by his enthusiasm. It's a small ray of light infusing a dull, grey world.

He drives the mile and a half; the long way to the hospital – there's no short cut for cars – and talks solidly about his borrowed Porsche and all 'her' remarkable features. It isn't until we pull into the car park and he turns the engine off, that he turns to face me again.

"So you want me to tell you about The Brotherhood? I didn't want to get distracted while I was driving, and it's important you know what it's all about."

"Yes, please." I half turn in my seat to face him; compelled by the need to see his expression as he describes his home.

His enthusiasm warms me.

The last few weeks – ever since I got the news about Mum and Dad – have been cold and dark. Locked into a nightmare of logistics with no one to help me, no one to advise, and no shoulder to cry on. Except for this stranger who appeared out

8

of the darkness to guide me. Who allowed me to talk. And who is now offering me a home.

"Do you think I'd fit in okay?"

"You'll be fine there, my child. So perhaps next week? I can come and see you again tomorrow, maybe bring some photos?"

"That would be great, thank you." My voice falters though. I have another week to keep Pete at bay? That's going to be challenging.

"It's nearly dark. Do you want me to see you to your room?"

"Yes, please. If you don't mind?"

Dominic gets out of the car in time to help me scramble out of the deep seat. As he follows me down the hedged path to the front door of C block, a rustling in the bushes makes me pause a moment.

"Did you hear that?" I turn my head to see Dominic, but in the dusk, I can't really make out his expression. I wait nervously for his verdict, a huge knot forming in my stomach. The rustling has stopped, but I'm sure I can hear breathing, and it's neither my companion nor me.

"It's either the wind or an animal. Calm down. Come on, lead the way to your flat."

A flat may be a bit of an overstatement. It's just a room, with a bed, a desk, a wardrobe, and a sink. I do as I'm told, and resume the walk up the path. The slightest sound makes me jump, though, and by the time we get to the door my nerves are coiled tight.

I lead the way into the hall, and along the corridor past the bathrooms to my room, tucked away in a corner. Outside my room, I panic. If Pete finds out I've brought another man to my room, he'll be livid. I've got to keep him pacified for another week yet.

"You'd better wait here. Sorry."

"Are you sure, Melissa? I can come in if you want?"

"No please, but would you wait out here for a moment? I need to check my room's okay. I've got a weird feeling, but I'll get into trouble if you come in."

"Very well, if you insist. I'll wait here for a minute, but come back out and let me know you're all right." He nods, looking relieved.

I swallow. My mouth is dry. I take a deep breath, and unlock my door. I take two steps into the room, then stop dead and scream.

I back out of the room, bumping into Dominic. He puts his hands on my shoulders.

"Melissa, what's the matter? Do you want me to have a look?"

Past caring about appearances, I move aside and squat in the corridor. I dunk my head down, afraid that I'll faint. I can't go back in there. No one emerges from the nearby rooms, so they must all be out. It's shift-change time. Just as well.

A moment later, he backs out, a couple of shades paler. Kneeling down beside me, he touches my shoulder.

"I'm sorry my child, I should have insisted, and stayed with you when you went in. Do you think Peter did that?"

I nod, shocked. Who else could it be? No one else is that sick. I sit properly on the floor. My legs feel wobbly. I know Pete's angry we've split up, but I can't quite bring myself to believe he'd do this.

"Who's in charge of the rooms?"

"I suppose the warden."

"Maybe you should leave him a note. I need to get you out of here as soon as possible."

"We can't just leave him to find that." I point back at the room with revulsion. "He's old. He might have a heart attack."

"Fine. Stay here a minute. I'll deal with it."

As he goes into the room, I shudder. When I first went in, I thought there was a dead body hanging from the ceiling. Only my nursing training forced me to take a second look, revealing the body to belong to the resuscitation training dummy – Annie. A kitchen knife protruded from the mannequin's chest.

Dominic must be taking her down – maybe cutting the

10

tights holding her suspended. I try to block the scene from my mind. I'm relieved (obviously) that it's not a real body, but it's a clear threat. Bile rises in my throat.

A minute later he emerges from the room carrying a black bin bag, with Annie's head poking out.

"I'll just dispose of this somewhere no one will stumble on it accidentally." He disappears through the door towards the outside, and returns a few minutes later empty-handed.

"Do you think we should tell the police?" I don't know if I could bear to, but I feel I should suggest it.

"It depends how much trouble you can handle, my child. There would be endless questions and photographs, and possibly the press to deal with. Whereas if we leave quietly, you can leave a letter for the warden saying you're suffering from stress, and have gone to stay with friends. Then we can get away tonight. What do you think?"

The thought of the press convinces me. It would probably be passed off as a prank – in bad taste, admittedly, but still a prank. Nothing would get done about it, but there would be loads of embarrassing publicity, and I've had more than enough of that recently.

"Okay. I don't want to go back in there though. Would you mind… I don't suppose…?"

"I'll clear your room out for you. Have you got suitcases, or a trunk?"

"Suitcases – under my bed. Thank you."

I sit on the floor outside my room, and listen to the sound of cupboards and drawers opening and closing. Still no one passes, and I remember: one of the nurses is leaving to have a baby, and they're all out celebrating. I can't face partying at the moment, but I bought her a gift and card and gave them to her this morning during our last shift together.

Several moments later, Dominic comes out of the room with my two large suitcases and a laptop case. My handbag is still at my side. I nearly dropped it in the room, but kept hold of it somehow.

"That's it now, my child. I think you should take one last look to make sure I've not left anything. Anyway, it will be better for you to remember the room empty. The letters can wait until we get to the Abbey. You can write them in the morning, and I'll post them for you."

"I'm going to need to drop the keys off with the warden, so I'd better scribble a quick note now." As I speak, I remove a pen and a sheet of A4 paper from my handbag. "I always carry pen and paper with me – it's habit."

"Fine, it's up to you. I just thought you'd want to get out of here immediately."

I nod, rest the paper on my handbag, and start to scrawl:

Dear Mr Brown, I've been feeling unwell with stress since the loss of my parents. I've cleared out my room so someone else can use it. I'm going away for a while. I'll write to matron from my new address. Thanks for your kindness. Melissa.

I drop the keys and note through the warden's letterbox on the way out. I don't want a long discussion.

Dominic opens the door to the Porsche for me, and loads in the suitcases himself. Now we're on our way. Dominic drives in silence this time, until I feel obliged to apologise.

"I'm sorry. I didn't mean to back you into a corner. If you don't want me to come yet, maybe I can stay in a hotel or something until you're ready?"

He throws me a quick startled glance, before looking back at the road.

"Nothing to apologise for, my child. The dummy was hardly your fault, and you can't possibly stay there. We'll be at the Abbey in time for you to meet everyone in your group, and then time for bed."

"Oh, okay." I hadn't thought about it, but I guess I'll have to meet a lot of new people. "Sorry, I'm just a bit tired. I don't mean to sound ungrateful."

"You're worn out," says Dominic after a quick glance at me. "I'm tempted to take you straight to the Infirmary for a good night's sleep. You can have a lie in, and meet everyone in the morning, when you're refreshed. What do you think?"

"That sounds great, thank you. I don't think I could remember anyone's name if I got introduced this evening.

The idea of just going straight to bed and to sleep sounds perfect."

We lapse again into silence, but it's more companionable now. Perhaps he prefers to concentrate on the road. It's not easy to see anything on these dark country lanes, and he must be worried about scratching his car on the hedges. I know I would be.

It's pitch black now, and I have no idea where we're going, but about an hour after leaving the hospital, we pull up on a crunchy gravel drive. Dominic turns off the engine.

"Welcome to The Brotherhood, Melissa."

Chapter Three

The next morning, I wake to find myself in a clean, white ward, partly surrounded by white cubicle curtains.

I rub my eyes. Where am I? Oh. The Abbey Infirmary. As memories return, they bring with them the image of the hanging dummy. I wish I could erase that one. It explains why I'm here, though – in the Abbey at least. There's no good reason for me to be in the Infirmary, except for Dominic's kindness.

I smile to myself, as I get out of bed. My suitcases are still in the corner where I left them last night. It was a struggle to get ready for bed before falling asleep, but I feel much stronger now. I open the cubicle curtains. I'm the only occupant of a four-bedded ward. What do they need an Infirmary for? Surely any poorly residents can be sent to the local hospital? It's a question for another time.

I locate a bathroom at the end of the ward, and take my clothes and toiletries there. Showered and dressed, I wander along the corridor in search of some staff. There are half a dozen wards – all empty. Very strange. Finally, there's a door marked *Nurses*. I knock, and a pretty girl of about my own age opens the door.

"Hi, I'm Emily, and you must be Melissa. Shall we go and get your case, and then I'll take you back to the main house. Dominic left instructions that you're to go to see him as soon as you're ready." Her tone and demeanour are friendly, and I relax. I hadn't realised how nervous I was until that tension released in my shoulders.

"Thanks." I want to make conversation, but my wits desert me, and I can't think of a thing to say as we head back to the ward.

Emily fortunately doesn't seem to have any problems with

this, and barely waits a moment before asking, "I believe you're new here?"

"Yes, this is all a bit... well... daunting, really." I glance at her. She's taller than I am, but so are most people. Her blonde hair is tied back in a long plait, and she looks about fourteen. "You can't have been qualified long. Is this your first job?"

"Second. I graduated in September, and worked on the wards at Chester for a while, but the ward sister was, er, let's just say she wasn't my cup of tea. Dominic said last night that he'd just collected you from a nurses' hostel. Are you a nurse as well?"

"Yes, I graduated the year before, but got out of the big teaching hospitals as soon as I could. I much preferred the local district hospital near where I grew up." I await the inevitable question about why I left, but it doesn't materialise. Instead she asks if I'll carry on nursing now I'm here.

"I don't know. I need a bit of a break from it I think." I decide to tell her anyway. "I lost my mum and dad in a plane crash recently. I did start back at work last week, but I've not been coping very well with it."

Emily rests one hand on my arm, in a sympathetic gesture, and then pushes against an oak door. It seems a little incongruous in the hospital setting, but when it's open, I gasp.

Ahead of me is a beige stone passageway, about the width of two hospital beds. It's like stepping back into a much earlier era. I'm no expert with history, but I wouldn't be shocked to see Henry VIII step out to greet me. The large wooden doors are set at irregular intervals along the passage, and are each decorated with black iron. The air is pervaded by a musty smell. My nose wrinkles as we walk deeper into the ancient building. This feels like a set for a period drama, but I'm brought back to reality when we stop at a door somewhere along the middle. Stencilled neatly on to the wood is the name *Dominic*.

A small fluttering in my stomach heralds the return of anxiety. As Emily knocks firmly on the door, I'm torn between the desire to see Dominic, and panic. When the door opens, Dominic stands there smiling, dressed in his usual smart grey suit with a royal blue tie.

"Thanks, Emily. Melissa, come in, my child. Did you sleep well?"

My tongue seems be stuck to the roof of my mouth, so I just nod. Emily briefly squeezes my shoulder and returns along the corridor. I follow Dominic through the door.

His office is in keeping with the area outside. A large mahogany desk takes up about a quarter of the space, and shelves of the same wood line the walls. Dominic takes a seat in the leather chair behind his desk and waves me to a chair opposite. It matches the rest of the furniture, but is cold and hard. Does he not like visitors? The chair doesn't inspire a long stay.

"Welcome to The Brotherhood, Melissa. Sorry I didn't show you round last night. You looked far too tired and upset to be meeting people." His gentle tone warms me, but the word 'upset' conjures a brief image of the hanging dummy, and I shiver.

"Are you cold, my child?" he asks, frowning a little.

"No, sorry. It's just the memory of… of what was in my room." I try to swallow the lump rising in my throat.

"Well, you're here now, and I'll protect you. I'm sure the perpetrator won't find you here, and if he does, he'll come to regret it." A note of steel creeps in to Dominic's voice. A small knot forms in my stomach, and for a second I feel sorry for Pete. But only for a second. As I visualise the horror he left for me, I know he deserves to be punished. I just never want to see him again. He so obviously hates me, and I don't understand why.

I gaze round the office. *Focus. Swallow. Breathe*. Looking back at Dominic, I'm relieved to see he's watching me with a kind smile.

"Trust me, you'll be fine. And now to business. There are a few forms for you to sign. Nothing major: agreements about abiding by the rules, contact details in case of emergency, that sort of thing." He opens a drawer and fishes out a small pile of papers held together with a bulldog clip. He passes them to me, together with a black biro. "Just sign the back page when you've finished reading. Then we'd better get you out to meet your Chapter before prayers. We've not got long now."

"What do you mean by Chapter?" I look up from the first page, which I've started to read.

"All the groups in The Brotherhood are called Chapters, after the monks that used to inhabit the Abbey. I've put you in with the Cistercians, as they have a vacancy, and I think you'll like them. They're a nice set of people." He nods towards the documents. "You really need to get on with reading those, Melissa. As I said, we don't have a lot of time."

I skim through. Legal-sounding phrases cloud my vision. *I pledge to abide...* and *in so much as...* make the document hard to assimilate. Frowning, I try to gauge the meaning of the long and complicated paragraphs, but I feel as though I'm in an exam, with insufficient time and too much at stake. I shut my eyes tight for a moment, then decide to trust Dominic. He's brought me here in good faith. I turn to the back page, pick up the pen, and sign my name.

"Would it be okay for me to write those letters now? I need to write one to the head nurse in the hospital, and I should let my parents' solicitor know where I am in case she needs to contact me while I'm here."

"Why don't you scribble their names down here? I'll get one of the girls who does a bit of secretarial work for me to type them out. You can sign them later, and I'll post them for you. How does that sound?" He passes me a blank sheet of paper, and glances at his watch.

I suppress the urge to ask if I can the write the letters myself. He's a busy man and he's being very kind to me. Writing the names and addresses takes only a moment, and then I pass the paper back to him.

"Good. I'll let you know when they're ready for you to sign. For now, we've just time to introduce you to your fellow Cistercians."

Chapter Four

Dominic leads me from his office, across the hall and into a huge quadrangle – surrounded on all sides by the Abbey. Various sections of the quad are filled with adults in khaki overalls immersed in gardening activities. The group he leads me to is in the far corner. It would be. I didn't spend a lot of time rummaging through suitcases this morning, so I'm wearing high heels that were at the top of the first case I opened. They sink into the soft earth as we make our way across the grass. Vampire bats flap around in my stomach. For a nurse, I'm appallingly shy about meeting new people. The uniform helps, although I've never realised that until now, as I wade into a group of strangers wearing my own clothes and those stupid black heels.

We're almost there, when I stumble as one heel gets stuck. A big man with sandy hair is at my side in a second, steadying me with surprising gentleness for someone of his size.

"Thank you, Jimmy." Dominic looks down at my feet. "Those shoes are not appropriate for work in the Abbey, as I'm sure you realise now. Never mind. We'll get you sorted out very soon. Meanwhile, Jimmy, can you do the introductions? This is Melissa. She's joining your Chapter. Be nice to her. She's been having a bad time."

I shiver. Those few words are an incredible understatement to describe the last two months. But however kind Dominic's been, I've never managed to convey the full horror of being unable to bury my parents – lost at sea forever. The issues with Pete are almost trivial by comparison, although the memory of Resusci-Annie will stay with me for a long time.

"We'll look after you, lass." Jimmy's voice startles me. His accent is deep Glaswegian – he sounds very like a doctor

I'd worked with during my nurse training.

"I'll leave Melissa in your capable care then. Bridget, get Melissa kitted out from the store room before prayers. You've got thirty-five minutes." Dominic gives me a brief smile as he looks up from his watch, and returns in the direction of his office.

The disappearance of the only person I know here leaves me feeling lost. I smile at Jimmy, whose kindness will hopefully fill the gap, and at Bridget, a middle-aged woman with greying hair in a ponytail, and a no-nonsense air.

There's a moment's silence as Dominic retreats out of earshot.

"Well, lass. Welcome to the Cistercians. We really will look after you. Each Chapter is like a family. We sleep in a dormitory together. We work together, and we support one another. You'll get to know us all soon enough, but I'll run through everyone's names in a minute. All you need to know now, though, is that if you're in any bother, come to us. Dominic doesn't have a lot of time for small things."

"Yeah, Jimmy's right. We'll look after you." Bridget tilts her head to one side as she watches me for a moment, then smiles warmly. "Don't worry. You'll fit right in. We're a nice bunch – mostly." She winks and points at Jimmy. "Of course, he can be a pain at times, but…"

"Och, if there's any trouble to be had, you'll know it's Bridget that's the cause." Their friendly banter reassures me more than anything else, and my shoulders relax as the vampire bats go to sleep.

Bridget starts on the introductions. She indicates a pale thin girl of around my own age.

"This is Tina. She's been in The Brotherhood for a couple of years, isn't that right?" Bridget glances questioningly at the girl, who nods gravely. "She only joined us Cistercians last week though, so in a way, she's almost as new as you are."

I smile at Tina, hoping that maybe we can be friends. She curls her lips, but I sense it's only out of politeness.

I pick up a few names as the introductions continue –

Keith, Leonard, Sarah and Ann – but none of the remaining names stick in my brain, and two minutes later the only names I can put faces to are Jimmy, Bridget and Tina.

Bridget takes me back inside and leads me through an extensive and surprisingly modern kitchen to a store cupboard. It's piled high with food provisions, but on a shelf half way along is a big box. Bridget hauls it down and drops it at my feet.

"What's this for?"

"Clothes." She shakes her head at my obvious confusion, and kneels down in front of the box. She delves inside for a moment and retrieves a brown paper bag. "What size are you?"

"Twelve usually. I've probably lost a bit of weight recently though. I've not eaten much."

Bridget looks up at me sympathetically, then down at the bag in her hands. It has *14* scrawled on in black marker pen.

"Come sit down here and have a rootle through. The dresses tend to come up a bit big anyway, and the portion sizes here are a bit… well… it's not easy to put on weight. You might be better with a ten." She digs through again, and finds a bag with *10* on it. She hands it over and I open it curiously.

Inside I find two khaki dresses with buttons from collar to waist, a set of overalls identical to the ones Bridget has on, two white nighties, several pairs of tights and socks, a selection of plain but sensible underwear, and a couple of cardigans. I ask Bridget about shoes, and she finds me two pairs of ugly black loafers from another box.

"Is this all we're allowed to wear?"

"Pretty much," says Bridget. "It's not very exciting, but we're supposed to be above material desires in here. Apparently, wearing plain clothing is good for the soul. It does stop a lot of envy when you see everyone else wearing the same thing."

I'm pondering this, when a loud clanging is heard. Bridget grabs my arm.

"Come on. Time for prayers." She picks up the bag of

clothes and shoes, and thrusts them at me. "You'll have to hang on to them for now. We can't be late."

I follow her into a beautiful Chapel, with stained glass windows all round.

"Where are the pews?"

"Shhh. Keep your voice down. We're only allowed to chat quietly until Dominic comes in."

"Okay." I lower my voice. "So where do we sit?"

"We don't. We stand up. Cistercians are the fifth row back, level with Samson's window." She points at a depiction of Samson holding up a temple, with an angry Delilah off to the side. We walk towards the window and I realise that most of our group are already standing in the row. Bridget and I join them.

I stand quietly, absorbing the hushed chatter around me and watching as the rows fill. When everyone is in place, the front doors open and a dozen men and women file in. They're wearing similar clothes to everyone else, but navy instead of khaki.

"Chapter heads," Bridget mutters into my ear as they take seats at the front, five on either side of the door. "The short fat one on the right next to the door is Thomas – our head." There's a note of irritation in her voice, and I give her a quick glance before trying to get a better look at Thomas. I can't see him very well due to the rows in front, so give up for now. A tall thin man approaches the lectern and bangs on it with a hammer. Silence falls. He returns to his seat.

Dominic enters the Chapel. He looks immaculate as usual, but his white shirt and tie have now been replaced by a black shirt with a clerical collar.

He makes a gesture and an organ begins to play. Startled, I look around until I see the source. A lady in the corner at the back – in dark blue uniform like the heads – sits at a large brown organ.

A number of unfamiliar hymns ensue, and then one that I recognise. Suddenly, I'm back in the church at Mum and Dad's memorial service. My heart is hammering in my ears; tears are pouring down my cheeks. It's been two months since the plane crash, but I still have moments where I can't stop crying. People start to look around for the noise – discordant against the beautiful hymns. I'm torn between grief and embarrassment.

The music stops. I'm standing in the middle of an audience, my cheeks and collar damp from crying. A hiccough escapes. How much worse can this get? Embarrassment is winning. The sobs subside, but the hiccoughs are coming more rapidly, and everyone in the room is staring at me. I'm the odd one out, wearing a white blouse, short black skirt and high heels – the first clean clothes I found this morning – folded neatly at the top of my suitcase. They are now totally inappropriate.

Nausea churns my stomach and the world spins around me. I want to run, but I don't know where to. The spinning gets faster and the Chapel lights go out.

Chapter Five

A blurry face comes into view. Where am I? It's a face I know. There's an expression of concern above a clerical collar. Dominic.

"Melissa. You're awake. Good. How are you feeling?"

"I don't know. What happened?"

"You fainted." A female voice joins the conversation. A name? Bridget.

I turn my head and smile at her. Memories re-surface. An Abbey. Prayers. Grief. There's a constriction in my chest and the world blurs again. Someone takes my hand in a firm grip and pulls me back to reality. I hold on tight.

"I've sent everyone to their common rooms with the Chapter heads. They can have group prayers until dinner. I think you need to rest. Bridget, when Melissa's feeling strong enough, take her to the dormitory and let her have a nap. It seems the shock of the new surroundings on top of everything has been a bit much." The hand is gently withdrawn. "Melissa, I'll check on you later, and get some lunch sent to you. Stay in bed for the rest of the day." Dominic touches my cheek briefly.

"Thank you." A hole forms somewhere in my middle as he leaves. I look up at Bridget, who takes Dominic's place at my side. She sits cross-legged on the floor. My vision has cleared now, but cotton wool has taken up residence in my head and displaced my brain. I try to sit up, and Bridget puts her hand behind my shoulders and helps. I clasp my knees.

"This is all so strange," I say to her.

"Of course it is. Dominic said you'd been bereaved recently. When?"

"March the twentieth. You must have heard about the plane that came down over the Atlantic – no one survived.

My mum and dad were on the way back from their Silver Wedding anniversary trip to New York."

"Holy… shirtsleeves." The expression brings a weak smile to my face. "Sorry, we're not allowed to swear, but it's hard sometimes. Phrases try to escape and we cover up as best we can." There's a brief silence as the humour recedes. "This is all a bit of a shock to you then?"

"Yes. I didn't know this place existed until yesterday."

"Bl… blithering baboons! I don't want to be rude, Mel, but why did you come here with him? Don't get me wrong. I'm pleased you're here. I think we can be good friends. But seriously?"

"It sounds mad, I know. I need a place to stay. Away from a nasty ex-boyfriend. There are lots of reasons – little ones – but that's the main thing. Anywhere else, he'd track me down. I'll do anything to avoid that. He… he left something horrible in my room – a kind of threat. It was awful." I squeeze my eyes shut for a moment – trying to shut away the vision of Annie with a knife sticking out of her plastic chest.

Bridget stands up. She's frowning, but I don't know why. Perhaps at my difficult situation.

"Come on. Let's get you to the dorm. You need food and sleep. I've got your clothes here." She gives me her hand and helps me to stand up. I'm a bit wobbly, but nothing unexpected after all that's happened. "Our dorm's on the ground floor thankfully. Otherwise I'd be calling Jimmy to carry you upstairs. All the stairways are stone. You really don't want to be falling over and hitting your head."

"How come I didn't hit my head when I fainted?" I follow her out of the side door of the Chapel and along a narrow passageway.

"Jimmy caught you, and lowered you to the floor. If it had been left to the row behind, they'd have let you fall, and stood and watched you bleed. Mean and lazy bunch they are. I don't know why Dominic lets them get away with it, but they seem to be devious as well, so maybe he hasn't noticed."

"Do you like it here?"

"Yes, mostly." Bridget turns and smiles at me. "This is our

dorm. Come on in." She opens the door and beckons me through.

The dorm is how I imagined from reading *Malory Towers* when I was young. Long rows of beds up against the walls. Each bed has a small bedside table on one side, and a mahogany wardrobe on the other, and is surrounded by cream-coloured curtains to create an illusion of privacy.

"I don't want to be rude either, but it smells a bit funny – kind of old and musty."

"It *is* old and musty." Bridget pulls a face, then laughs. "You won't notice it after a while. I expect it's all the dust and old wood. Bedding gets washed once a week, so it shouldn't be that, but the men get a bit pongy at this time of year. They're old and musty too."

I join in with her laughter. She's funny, and there's a warm heart underneath that dry and stoic exterior.

"Hang on a minute. Are you saying we share a dorm with the men?"

"Yep. Men are down the far end; we're near the door. That's why we have the curtains round each cubicle. There's a little boys' and girls' room at each end, but the main bathrooms are along the corridor out there." She dumps the bag of clothes on the table by the bed nearest to the main door. "This'll be your bed. It's the only free one. You've got Tina next to you and I'm opposite. I get a window because I've been here for a couple of years. If someone leaves, then the next longest-standing person gets to choose if they want to grab that person's cubicle. Obviously a man can't have a woman's bed, and vice versa, but other than that – it works well."

"Do people leave often?"

"Some people change groups. I don't think anyone's actually left for ages." She indicates for me to sit on my bed, and she perches on the bedside table. "You'll be fine, Mel, honestly. It's quiet here. We do a lot of household stuff – taking it in turns to do cooking, laundry and cleaning duties – but we also spend a lot of time gardening, and just chatting. In between times, we can read, knit, sew or do jigsaws in the common room. Obviously there's prayers twice a day, but mostly it's just a nice community life."

I must look doubtful, because she moves next to me and puts an arm round my shoulders.

"We'll help you get yourself back together again. Trust me, I know how hard it is coming in here when you've lost someone important and have nowhere else to go."

"Why? Is that what happened to you as well?"

"Yeah. We're not really supposed to talk about our pasts in case it stirs things up, but I think it will help you to know. My husband died in a car crash." Her lips form a thin line. "He was speeding, and managed to kill three other people in the other car as well. I loved him, but he died leaving me in a whole load of debt. Dominic came to me after the funeral, and helped me sort out my papers. I declared bankruptcy and he welcomed me into the fold. That was five years ago." Her arm is still round my shoulders, but it seems as though she's the one in need of comfort now. I turn slightly and return the hug.

"Thanks for telling me. It does help to know I'm not the only one."

Bridget stands up and starts emptying the contents of the bag into shelves in the wardrobe.

"Let's get you settled. Get your nightie on – use my cubicle for the minute while I sort your stuff out here. I'll bring you up some food shortly, the bell will go for lunch in about ten minutes," she says, after glancing at an incongruous white plastic clock on the wall above the door.

Once I'm undressed, I get into the bed. It's soft and a bit lumpy, but no worse than the one I had in the nurses' home. It's good to lie down. Exhaustion grips me.

"Bridget, don't bother with food. I think I'm just going to sleep now. I'm not hungry anyway." I haven't eaten since lunchtime yesterday, but so much has happened, the mere thought of food is making me feel queasy.

"You're sure? I'll pull these curtains around you then, so no one disturbs you. Sleep well. We've got a special day tomorrow, so get some rest."

"Why is it a special day?"

"Oh crikey. I don't suppose anyone's told you." She hesitates.

"Told me what? Please, Bridget? What's going on?" I sit up in bed and stare at her. She perches by my knees.

"Okay, here goes. Dominic is not an ordinary guy." She runs her hand through her fringe and it falls back into place exactly as before.

What on earth does she mean? I know he's not ordinary. He's gorgeous, kind, and incredibly charismatic. There's something weird, and she doesn't seem to know how to tell me.

"Just say it. Whatever it is, it can't be that bad."

"It's not bad. It's... oh... Dominic's the Messiah," she blurts out finally.

Chapter Six

"You're joking?"

But I can see she's not. Bizarre though it sounds, my new friend clearly believes it.

"Anyway, tomorrow's the first anniversary of him finding out about it, so there's a big celebration planned, starting with a special breakfast, then something exciting is going to happen in morning prayers, but no one knows exactly what yet." She carries on talking, but I phase out. I'm buzzing with shock.

What have I got myself into? Have I really met the Messiah? Despite my recent experiences, a thrill takes hold of me, starting at my toes and working its way up through my body. I'm going to be part of this.

"Are you going to be okay?" Bridget stands up and prepares to leave, but gazes at me, a concerned expression on her face. "I should probably have waited until tomorrow to tell you, but it kind of slipped out. We've all been really excited all week."

"It's fine. I guess I need to get my head around it, but it can wait until tomorrow. I've got plenty to think about anyhow." I grin. "You get going. I don't want you to miss lunch on my account."

"Thanks, Mel. See you later. Hope you manage a nap anyway."

I wait until she leaves, then lie back on the thin pillow and try to understand what I've just heard. How can Dominic be the Messiah? He's lovely and amazing and incredible and oh… so many wonderful things… but the Messiah? The real live Messiah? The one who's going to save the world from the Apocalypse? It doesn't seem possible.

Maybe this is some elaborate joke they play on all

newcomers. An uncomfortable sensation, like a crawling insect, settles in the pit of my stomach – something between disappointment and betrayal. It's too soon really to feel betrayed – I barely know these people; but I want to trust them, and I want them to like me. The insect turns into a creature with claws, which jab and thrust. The pain feels genuine, and I turn on my side and curl into a ball hoping the creature will go away.

It doesn't, and I lie in that position for ages waiting for the pain to subside. Torn between bewilderment at Bridget's announcement, and fits of wondering if they're either right, or just deluded, it suddenly dawns on me that I'm hungry. Damn. I said I didn't want lunch. Please let someone come back so I can get up at least for dinner. The claws stretch out and have another root around my stomach. The creature groans, emitting weird noises from inside me. I definitely need food. Sitting up, I'm about to get out of bed in search of lunch, when the door opens.

"Melissa, are you awake?" Bridget's voice is low as she pokes her head around the door. A plate appears, bearing two slices of brown bread and a lump of cheese, and the rest of her body follows. "I wasn't sure if you'd had any breakfast, and I figured you might get hungry if you woke up."

"Thank you. You're an angel. I've not eaten since yesterday afternoon, and I'm suddenly ravenous." I start tearing off pieces of the bread and devouring it as though I've not eaten for a month, rather than just twenty-four hours.

My new friend sits on the end of the bed watching me.

"Are you okay with what I told you about Dominic? I realised after I left that it's a bit hard to take in."

"It is a bit."

"Normally we would wait a few days for people to settle in before breaking the news, but obviously with tomorrow's celebrations pending, it seemed to be appropriate to mention it. And of course we're all wildly excited, even though no one knows exactly what to expect."

"I kind of wondered if you were having me on?" I give her a sheepish smile. I don't want to upset her.

"Goodness, I don't blame you. It's not something you get told every day." She takes the empty plate from my knees and places it on a bedside table. "Look, you don't need to worry about it, okay. Just forget about it for now, and concentrate on settling in, and getting to know the rest of us. We'll help you as much as we can."

"Okay thanks. I might be able to have that sleep now."

"Sure." She gets up from the bed, grabs the plate, and gives me a wry grin. "I'm pleased I brought that in for you – can't have you fainting on us tomorrow morning, you know."

As soon as she's left, I hear her telling someone outside the room that she'd been in to feed me. She sounds strangely nervous, but there's no audible reply, and after a moment I hear two pairs of footsteps fading away. Exhaustion overcomes me, and I shut my eyes.

The scene in my room at the nurses' home flashes in front of me, but I dismiss it. I will not let Pete get to me. Not here. Not ever.

***

A ringing noise drags me from sleep. I open my eyes and look around blearily. I'm surrounded by curtains. Where am I?

"Morning, Mel, are you feeling better?" A face appears around the curtain. Memories flood back as Bridget flashes me an excited grin.

"Hi. Yes, I think so. Not properly awake yet. What time is it?"

"Five-thirty. They've given us an extra half-hour's sleep in honour of the occasion. I did tell you yesterday, didn't I? It's Dominic's Messiah anniversary, if that's the proper term."

"Oh, yes. You did say. Hang on. Five-thirty is a lie-in?"

Bridget nods apologetically. "Didn't anyone warn you? Sorry."

I rub my eyes, and crawl out of bed. This may have been a big mistake.

I hate early mornings. But it's only slightly worse than the early shift at the hospital – that starts at half past six, and to get showered, dressed and have breakfast beforehand, anything later than 5.40 is impossible.

With instructions from Bridget, I manage to find the bathroom; where I shower, clean my teeth, and get dressed appropriately. The dress is a bit tight, and the buttons are taut against my bust, but if the food is really that meagre, I expect it will sort itself out. Anyway, maybe Dominic might notice me a bit more…

I brush that thought away – so totally inappropriate if Dominic is really the Messiah – and I still can't comprehend that either. There's a small hand-held mirror in the top drawer of the bedside table. Vanity is obviously not encouraged, but I use it to check the curls aren't looking too unruly, before I run to catch up the rest of the dorm to go for breakfast.

The dining hall is old, with wooden beams all over the place. We sit at long trestle tables in our groups. Bridget and Jimmy sit on either side of me. They're both very kind and seem determined to look after me properly. Tina is opposite, but she is looking down at her plate, focussing intently on buttering her toast.

"Hey, we're honoured today. White toast, butter and strawberry jam! Don't get used to this, lass." Jimmy smiles at me wryly. "It's usually porridge, with a bit of honey on Sundays."

"No bacon and eggs then?" I ask.

"No. We're vegetarian here. We pride ourselves on following *Thou shalt not kill* to the letter. So no meat, no fish. You'll get used to it."

"It's fine. I was joking. I've been veggie for years. I did eat fish, but always felt a bit guilty about it. There just wasn't always a lot of choice."

"There's not a lot of choice here either, lass. You eat what you're given or you go hungry. The food's okay though most days – nine times out of ten." Jimmy and Bridget exchange dark looks. I wonder what it's about, but it doesn't seem to be the right time to ask.

"Bridget, do you always get called that? It sounds very

formal."

"I've not been called anything else since I was here, but when I was younger, friends used to call me Brie."

"I like that. Do you mind if I call you Brie?" I smile at her.

"Not at all. Takes me back, that does. Good times."

The shortening of Bridget to Brie makes a huge difference to me. A load seems to have lightened from my chest, and a friendship has taken root there.

I'm at the tail end of our group as we file in to the Chapel after breakfast. Brie turns round and grabs my arm; that excited grin is lighting up her face again.

"Come on, Mel, get a move on. We don't want to be late. I heard a rumour that we have a visitor."

My heart rate accelerates as if I've been running around the hospital. What have I got into here? What's going to happen? Who's this visitor?

An impatient look from Brie stops the thoughts rocketing around my head. I speed up and follow her to our position next to Samson and Delilah.

As we get into place, the side door begins to close. It's stopped by Tina. She seems flustered as she takes her place next to me. Her hair is coming loose from its clips and a button is undone on her dress. Her breathing is rapid, and her expression anxious. I point at the button, and she sorts it out with fumbling fingers. Tidying her hair will have to wait.

At the front of the hall, the double doors are flung open. The group heads enter first, as they did yesterday, and take their seats on either side of the doors. There's a brief silence – an air of anticipation. Then Dominic arrives, smiling, handsome and immaculately dressed once again in his dark suit and clerical collar. Over the suit is a white robe trimmed with purple and gold. Looking spectacular, he approaches the lectern.

"My children, good morning. Welcome to this assembly. I wondered how to make this anniversary into a very special occasion. So, when the local parish priest approached me last week, and asked if I could help a young man in his care, this seemed to be the answer. This young man, Trevor, was recently blinded in a fire. He is suffering physically and emotionally. I consulted with the Almighty Lord, and he decreed I should help this poor fellow. What better day to choose for a miracle than this: the first anniversary of our Lord's visitation? Before I bring him in, we should prepare ourselves and ask for the Lord's help with this difficult but worthwhile task."

He signals to the pianist and she plays some opening bars. I don't recognise the music. My heart's racing again and my mouth is dry. Where's the water fountain when it's needed?

"The Abbey Prayer," Brie whispers in my ear.

Everyone is joining in around me, but I don't know the words. There's a chorus after every ten lines or so, and after a few repetitions I'm able to sing a few lines here and there. There's a thrill in the air. Anticipation sparks around me.

I can't believe I'm about to witness a miracle. Will he actually be able to cure this man Trevor? Surely it's not real. But then, Dominic's supposedly the Messiah. Everyone here believes it. Maybe it is real.

The thought is interrupted by a small voice at the back of my head: *He can't bring Mum and Dad back though. What use is a miracle if he can't do that?* A lump forms immediately in my throat. I swallow it impatiently. There's another chorus, so I try to join in again, but my throat is too full. The song ends, and I focus on the activity at the front.

A bulky man in a grey uniform comes forward. There are several men in grey standing around the edge of the Chapel. Dominic whispers to the stocky grey man, who then leaves the Chapel. He returns a moment later, leading a short man in his mid-twenties. As he gets closer, I gasp. I can't help it. His face is covered in scars. They're red and inflamed. The fire must have damaged more than just his eyesight.

A shudder runs through me. My face tingles as I imagine the pain he must be enduring.

Please let Dominic help him. Please don't let it be a sham. Please let Dominic really be the Messiah. I can feel doubt running through me, and do my best to exude positivity and belief – in case it helps.

Trevor stands close to the lectern. I try to see his expression, but my view of his face is blocked by a tall woman in front. Tina shifts, and pulls me across to get a better view. We aren't precisely out of line, but it's an improvement.

I glance again at our visitor. Sweat glistens on the right side of his forehead; the only normal patch of skin on his face. The room's hot. It's only May, but temperatures are soaring into the nineties. I don't think he's sweating from the heat though.

"My dear young man," Dominic addresses Trevor, his voice gentle, yet loud enough to be heard at the back of the room. "I have prayed for guidance so I can understand the best way to help you. I believe you are blind and in pain. Is that correct?"

"Yes sir." Trevor's voice sounds thin and feeble. Perhaps it reflects his state of mind.

Dominic rests a hand on Trevor's shoulder. The young man winces. How far does the scarring extend?

"In order to help you, I need to call on the services of The Brotherhood." He raises his voice slightly and turns his face to us. "My children, I must ask you to sing. Please raise your voices and embrace the beautiful and apt hymn, *O What a Miracle, My Lord*."

I know this one. I join in the much-loved psalm, the depth and meaning of the words adding an extra dimension to the singing. Tears fill my eyes as we reach the end. *I want Mum and Dad back. Give me that miracle, and I'll believe everything*. It's not possible though. I push the thought away again, and return my attention to the Chapel.

"That was beautiful. Now we just need an extra rendition of the Abbey Prayer," says Dominic. His hand still rests on Trevor's shoulder.

I try to sing the choruses, but am not yet ready to attempt any of the verses. But I listen to the beautiful harmonies of the rest, and my heart thumps in my chest in time with the beat. Sweat drips from my own forehead, and I reach in my pocket for a tissue to wipe my face.

As the tune ends, I glance again at our guest. The euphoria pumping through me seems to be having an effect on Trevor too. His face is raised towards the ceiling, and the morning sunlight shining through the high window suffuses him with an orange glow.

"And now I call on the Almighty Lord for a cure." Dominic lays his hands over Trevor's eyes and calls out, "Almighty One, help me cure this man. Remove the clouds that blind him. Strike away the pain that encumbers him."

The light streaming through the window appears to brighten further.

"Can you feel it, Trevor?"

"Oh my God. Thank you. Thank you. Thank you. I can feel the heat. I can see the light."

His voice swells with excitement and passion. The thin, reedy tones become strong. Tears pour down his cheeks, and his expression fills with wonder. His gaze lowers, and he faces Dominic.

"I can see you, sir."

He reaches out and grasps our Leader's arm. He repeats, "I can see you. How did you do that? This is incredible."

"It is the gift of the Lord Almighty. He has worked through me to save you. How about your pain, Trevor? Does your face still hurt?"

"No sir, I feel amazing. Oh God. This is a miracle." Trevor touches his own cheek gently. Then he walks tentatively to the front row, and speaks to one of the women there. She hesitates, then reaches out and touches him. He doesn't flinch, but turns back to look at Dominic. "Thank you, sir. I don't know how you've done it, but you've cured me."

"As I said, it was the work of the Almighty One. All praise the Lord."

"Praise the Lord," we all shout. I can see no difference in Trevor's scars, but it's obvious he is now free of pain.

"Lord bless Dominic, the Messiah," someone calls from the other side of the room. The chant is taken up by the assembled members.

"Lord bless the Messiah," we all sing out, over and over

again. All except for one voice.

"It's just a sham," the woman behind me mutters. "Load of rubbish."

I turn and stare at her. She looks down her nose at me and shrugs her shoulders. My gaze returns to the front, and to the ecstatic Trevor. Is she right? All other faces in the Chapel suggest not. Brie and Tina on either side of me are smiling – clearly thrilled by the miracle. I have just witnessed something very special. If not a miracle, then something very close to it.

Dominic approaches the front row, smiling. He holds out his hands to two of the women in the front, who likewise reach out to him. Their hands make contact and hold fast for a moment. There's a sharp wrench in my gut. For a second I imagine it's me in the front row, and my heart races. Oh my goodness. I'm jealous. I've only known this man for a month but his compassion has got to me.

I grit my teeth and take a deep breath. Common sense prevails.

Dominic's the Messiah. I'm inclined to believe that now. Why would he be interested in me? He's probably not interested in those girls either. He's just savouring their adulation for a moment, and why shouldn't he? He deserves it.

I watch as Dominic releases the women's hands and returns to Trevor. He whispers in the visitor's ear, and then summons the grey-clad warden to lead Trevor from the Chapterhouse. As the warden approaches, Trevor turns to us again.

"Thank you all. I'll never forget your kindness."

We return his thanks with a huge round of applause.

***

Now that Trevor has gone, I can hear a faint buzzing. I look round for the source. I've been afraid of wasps for as long as I can remember.

Hovering near Jimmy, on the other side of Brie, is a

massive one – the yellow and black stripes vibrate, threatening. Jimmy notices it at the same time, and colour drains from his face. Dimly in the background, Dominic is addressing the audience, and I want to listen, but my attention is riveted by the wasp and Jimmy's obvious terror. He stands helpless for a moment, eyeing the creature as it flies round the head of a girl in front. He wriggles his foot, and slowly bends down and takes off a shoe. I suddenly remember the discussion about bacon and eggs from this morning, and I realise Jimmy mustn't kill the wasp.

"Don't. Please don't," I mouth at him, but he's staring at the wasp, and doesn't see me. Brie, standing between us, breaks out of her reverie. Her gaze rests on the wasp and turns to Jimmy's shoe, now raised. Her eyes widen in horror; she perhaps has a greater concept of consequences than I have. She grabs Jimmy's arm, but he pulls from her grasp. The wasp darts towards him, and he swats at it. With the fear and adrenaline behind that stroke, the creature doesn't stand a chance. It falls to the floor, dead.

Jimmy sways. He seems to register the enormity of his actions. Brie and I hold onto each other for support. My gaze shifts between Jimmy – as white as hospital sheets – and the dead wasp.

"Stand aside, my children," Dominic thunders as he strides over to us, and the audience parts like the Red Sea to let him through. His gaze goes from Jimmy, still holding his shoe and standing motionless, to the dead insect on the floor.

"Oh, James, what have you done?" the Leader says, his voice now filled with sorrow. He gestures to the warden by the door, who speaks into a black handset, and is joined seconds later by several of his colleagues. Two of them come straight over. Grabbing Jimmy by the arms, they escort him from the Chapterhouse. He manages one faint protest.

"I'm allergic to wasps. It was going to sting me. It was self-defence, I'm sorry." The anguish shows in his face as he throws a pleading look over his shoulder at us.

Dominic returns to the lectern.

"My children, thou shalt not kill. You know this. There is

no excuse for murder, and James has committed murder. He has a stain on his soul, and he must expiate his sin. I ask you to pray for him, but to pray primarily for the soul of that poor wasp. That creature that died before its time, and before it fulfilled its purpose." Our Leader's tone is earnest and gentle, but in the distance, I hear yells. Dominic's pained expression suggests he hears them too. "I ask you all now to stay here for one hour and pray for the soul of the wasp, and for the expiation of sin from James' soul."

With that, he turns and leaves the room.

The room sways, and I have to take a deep breath to steady myself. What have I got into? I've asked myself this several times in the last twenty-four hours, but it seems even more relevant now. I understand the importance of life, and respect it. I'm a nurse, for goodness sake. But surely Jimmy is more important than a wasp? He would have died if that wasp had stung him. I'm afraid that given the choice between saving a human's life or that of a wasp, I would always choose the human.

The wardens take up strategic positions around the hall. There's no chatter, none of the excitement with which the day began. The room is silent, filled only with a hundred bodies breathing and silently praying. I glance down at the wasp, which, by some oversight, has been left on the floor. It seems undignified and disrespectful somehow; discordant with the ideals. Perhaps the corpse should be laid to rest in the garden, where it belongs.

I don't really care about the wasp. I won't admit it to any of my new friends, but a bit of me is relieved it's dead. It was threatening the life of someone I like. And, in the interests of complete truth, I was terrified it would sting me. If it had come near me, I might not have been able to stop myself from screaming, so yes – Jimmy did me a favour as well. There are some strange things about The Brotherhood, but I need to settle here – conform to the rules and ideals – and build on those new roots of friendship. I've left my old life behind. I can't go back to Pete.

Standing here in silence, there's too much time to think

and feel. The loss of Mum and Dad fills me, and perhaps also the loss of the life I've left behind – the good bits – like nursing, and... okay, just nursing... but mostly Mum and Dad. Our relationship has been fraught for the last few years, and that doesn't help. I never got a chance to say sorry, and I grieve for that missed opportunity too.

I'm conscious we're supposed to be grieving for the wasp, but the sharp intensity of real grief clouds my eyes with bitter tears. I want to curl up in a ball and hide away, but Jimmy's distant cry of pain intrudes and drags me back from the precipice. How can they punish him for killing an insect?

I banish thoughts of Mum and Dad from my head, and pray instead for Jimmy.

Chapter Seven

We don't see Jimmy again until the following evening.

"Melissa, do you think Jimmy's okay? He didn't make it back to the dorm last night, and I haven't seen him all day," Tina asks me as we settle in the common room after dinner. It's the first time she's addressed me directly, but I haven't seen her speak to anyone yet, so I don't think it's personal.

I bite my lip. "I hope so. I can't imagine why he's been away so long. Perhaps we need to be patient."

The other members arrive, but no one comments about the missing Scot except for a quiet, middle-aged man. I think back to introductions, and finally his name comes to me. Leonard.

"Jimmy's still not back then," he says, after a quick glance around the room. He frowns and goes to the window, which overlooks some more gardens – not the quad from yesterday.

"What's over there?" I join Leonard at the window and point to an old large two-storey building a short distance away.

"That's the Infirmary," says Leonard with a grim expression.

Of course it is. That's where I spent my first night here. It takes me a moment to get my bearings.

"What do you think has happened to him?" I say.

"I don't know, but I think we'll find out soon." He nods in the direction of the building, and I follow his gaze to see Jimmy staggering in our direction.

"If he's coming from the Infirmary, does it mean he's been badly hurt?" I ask Leonard in a low voice.

"Let's hope not. Come, we should sit down and not embarrass the poor chap."

Jimmy disappears from view, and arrives a few minutes

later in our common room, to find us all sitting in silence. Other members are sewing or reading religious books. I extract the rule book from my pocket, but am too busy watching Jimmy to read.

The big man stumbles through the door. He looks pale, and has an obvious black eye. He slumps into a threadbare green armchair, which someone has vacated for him, then looks around the room and intercepts my gaze. I smile at him. I put down my book, and sit next to him on the arm of the chair.

"Are you okay?" I keep my voice low, so no one but Jimmy can hear.

"Not great, to be honest. I've been told something, and I don't know what to do."

"What did they do to you?"

"A few punches from the wardens." He hesitates, as if about to say something else, then indicates his face. "But then they took me to the Infirmary to sleep it off. I don't remember getting there, to be honest. I woke up in bed, with my arm covered in bruises. The doc told me they'd taken some blood while I was asleep – general health check. They found out I've got diabetes. They've given me some insulin. I'm supposed to take it every night, but I can't bring myself to stick a needle into my own skin. You're going to think I'm pathetic." He gives a wry grin.

"I used to have to inject someone I knew at school. If you want, I'll do your injections for you. When do you need it doing?" Something prevents me mentioning my nursing background – I'm not quite sure why. Also, I don't mention his other injuries. He glossed over them so fast; either he's embarrassed, or he's too worried about the diabetes.

"I'd better check with Dominic if it'd be okay, but that'd be great. You're a sweetheart, thanks. It's supposed to be done at bedtime, so maybe you could do it in the dorm before lights out?"

I smile and nod, then touch his shoulder before returning to my seat to resume my knitting.

Why can't the Messiah cure Jimmy's diabetes? Is it too

complicated? I don't understand the limitations, but perhaps it's more about the nerves rather than curing problems with hormones and chemicals.

Since Jimmy's removal from the Chapterhouse yesterday, I've been worrying about him, and the wardens have obviously been horrible. But because of his injuries, he got a full check-up. The doctors diagnosed a condition he must have had for a while. He's actually benefitted from killing that wasp.

Is it all about tempering justice with mercy? If so, maybe this place is okay after all. As it is, I have nowhere else to go, so focussing on the positive aspects will get me a lot further than worrying about what can't be helped.

***

When the bell rings to send us all to our dormitories, I follow Jimmy to his cubicle.

"You're sure you don't mind doing this?"

"Of course not," I pull the curtains round to allow for some privacy – a habit that kicks in from my nurse training.

"What on earth are you two getting up to?" Brie pops her head in at the same moment I roll up Jimmy's shirt to expose a flabby abdomen. I'm so stupid. Of course it looks suspicious. I glance over at my 'patient'.

"Sorry, sweetheart, my fault." He raises his voice. "Well, you lot. Come away in. I've got diabetes. The sweet Melissa offered to help me with my injections. This is my first one. Why don't you all watch?" The other occupants of the dormitory seem to miss the sarcasm, and the cubicle becomes crowded. I smile wryly as I prepare the special insulin pen, dialling up the dose written on a slip of paper Jimmy shows me.

"You're going to stick that into my belly?" He's ignoring the audience, who seem unwilling to leave. Perhaps they believe we need a chaperone.

"Afraid so. It shouldn't hurt much; maybe a scratch." I stick the pen needle into his tummy and press the button to inject the insulin.

"Oh, is that it?" he says.

"Yep, all done." I withdraw the needle from his skin, pop the pen back in its box and hand it to him to put away in his drawer. "Show's over folks." I flash a shy smile round the cubicle. I understand their curiosity. Most people don't get to see insulin being injected, so this is a novelty.

"Bedtime now," says Brie. "The lights will be going out in about two minutes." I take advantage of her bossiness, and smile at Jimmy again. He seems bemused, and I'm sure a friendly face in the crowd is appreciated.

***

Hours later, a bluebottle flies in and rests on the end of my narrow bed. It crawls along the metal frame before taking wing; I watch curiously as it buzzes against the window for several minutes before finding the opening and flying out. I breathe a sigh of relief. I'm not afraid of insects that don't sting, but I would be reluctant to go to sleep with it still buzzing around. I do not want to become *the woman who swallowed a fly*. I daren't risk killing it, though – not after what happened with Jimmy and the wasp.

I raise my head, and look down the length of the dorm from my bed by the door. A full moon illuminates the eleven other beds. I'm gradually learning the names of my group, or Chapter, as I should say. They seem a nice bunch, but I'm still drawn most to Jimmy, Brie, and (for some reason) Tina, despite her extreme reserve.

In the next bed, Tina throws off her sheets and flings her arm over her head. The odours assault my acute sense of smell. I found out today that we're not allowed to shower before bed. Rules are strict about showering: only once a day, first thing in the morning. This is apparently due to vagaries of the plumbing, but it's not pleasant during a heatwave like this.

I turn over in an effort to untangle my legs from the sheets, and try to throw the blanket off the bed.

The door opens, and the short rotund figure of our group head sidles in to the room. A light from the passage outside casts shadows around the dormitory. Thomas stands near the end of my bed. I shut my eyes, pretending to be asleep, and try to cover myself surreptitiously with the sheet. My skin prickles with the feeling of being watched. I shiver despite the heat, and my mouth goes dry. Then I hear a shuffling sound. I risk opening one eye just enough to see. Thomas has moved to the far side of Tina's bed, and the light from the doorway shows a greedy gleam in his eye as he scrutinises her. A stealthy hand creeps down and draws her sheets further down her legs.

Is he going to touch her? My breath catches, but a cough from the passageway disturbs him. He backs away and out of the dormitory. The door closes behind him, leaving the room in complete darkness, with the moon now hidden behind clouds.

I breathe freely again. Why is he behaving like that? Thomas seems a bit creepy, but nothing specific that I can pinpoint. What does he want with Tina?

Chapter Eight

Weeks pass, and I become more familiar with the routine of The Brotherhood. Thomas' behaviour from that night is not repeated. It seems unreal, and I wonder if I dreamt it.

I still haven't had those letters to sign, and I worry about what will happen to my nursing contract. Hopefully the note I scribbled for the warden will suffice for now. There's not often time to think about it though, and mostly I've settled in well. I have tried on several occasions to catch Dominic to ask him about the letters. Last week, I lingered outside his door in the evening after prayers – supposedly an open house time, when we're allowed to go to Dominic with any problems. He called in the two ladies in front of me, spending quite a while with each one. The second lady appeared slightly dishevelled as she left his office.

"Are you okay?" I asked her.

"Yeah. I… er… lost something, a piece of paper… and Dominic was helping me search."

I was about to ask her if it had been found in the end, when our Leader emerged from the room. He looked immaculate as usual.

"Sorry, Melissa, there's something I need to deal with urgently. Come back another time, okay?" Before I had a chance to respond, he withdrew into his office, and shut the door. I turned to speak to the mussed-up lady, but she'd gone.

Since then, a notice has been attached to the office door:

The Messiah is currently unavailable for one-to-one meetings. Open house sessions will resume when possible.

***

It's now exactly a month since my arrival, and we're all in

the dining room having breakfast. I listen as Brie moans to me about the quality of the porridge. "I can't eat this anymore. The food is such crap!"

I'm surprised, but as I try to think of a diplomatic response, a huge man dressed in grey appears. I recognise him as one of the wardens, and nerves flutter in my stomach. I've had little to do with the wardens so far, but they carry an intimidating aura. I prefer to avoid them.

He hauls both of us from the orange plastic chairs, grabbing the collar of our cotton dresses, and marches us to a small grey-brick room with no windows and a musty smell. Somehow, this cell remains cold. I ought to be pleased about the reprieve from the relentless heat outside, but my goosebumps have little to do with the temperature. The heavy door he shuts behind us looks impenetrable. His grin is demonic in the dim electric light. I have no idea why we're here.

"Well now, and what do you think happens to ladies who don't do as they're told?"

"We weren't doing anything," says Brie. "You let us out of here now!" Even her bossiest voice fails to have any useful effect on the warden though. His grin broadens, and he removes his leather belt.

The original flutter in my stomach has turned into a horde of vampire bats, and I'm unable to voice any protest. What is going on? I hadn't even said anything. My only crime appears to have been sitting next to Brie.

"First offence – ten lashes each I reckon. Oh, and you can scream all you like. The walls in here are very thick. No one'll hear." He laughs and caresses the belt in his massive hands. He reaches out to grab Brie but she steps away from him.

"I don't know what you think you're doing with that, but you can't hit both of us, without the other one escaping, or hitting you back or— Bloody hell, you bastard!" She crouches in the corner and rubs her arm where he whacked her with the belt.

I'm standing stupefied with my mouth wide open. I want

to help, but fear has paralysed my limbs and voice.

He advances on Brie, grabbing her wrist, and belts her several times on the legs. She yells and swears, but he hits her harder. I lose count of the lashes, but there are loads more than the ten he first suggested. I can hardly breathe, let alone do something to prevent this monster beating my new friend. I'm a terrible friend, letting her down so badly. She'll probably never forgive me.

He finally stops, and she staggers, collapsing to the floor. My muscles release and I go to sit next to her, but he grabs my arm, and pulls me up. He swipes, and I cry out, despite my best attempt to keep quiet. I manage not to swear. I don't want him to hit me again. The louder Brie became, the harder he hit her, but however much I try to keep silent, a whimper escapes me each time the belt strikes me. My bottom stings as the belt connects four more times. I feel like howling, but suppress the urge. I got plenty of practice in the days with Pete – yelling always made him hurt me harder and for longer.

I hear the swish of the belt a sixth time, but simultaneously comes the bleep of a walkie-talkie. The belt taps me and falls to the floor. The warden picks up his communicator.

"Yeah… What now? Okay fine… yeah, I'll leave them here for a few hours. Cheers." While he's speaking, I take the opportunity to sink down on my knees on the stone floor beside Brie. I pray he's finished hitting us. "Right girls, you're in luck. I'm needed somewhere else. You'd better not blab to anyone. I'll send someone to let you out later, but for now, you think about what you're going to tell people, 'cos if I hear any little tales, trust me – neither of you will be sitting down for a month. So keep it shut! Ta-ra."

The door slams shut behind him. The key clanks as it turns in the lock. I feel as if I've been locked in prison, but at least I'm not alone. The warden has left the light on, and Brie is still curled up on the floor trembling; although whether in fear or anger, I don't know.

"Brie, are you okay?" I put a tentative hand on her shoulder. She turns over to face me, and I let my hand fall to my lap.

"Holy bloody hell. I'm still alive, if that's what you mean. I could murder that sodding warden. I've never been in so much pain in my life."

"How long do you think he'll leave us here?"

"As long as he can get away with, I expect. God knows what we're going to tell anyone. I don't want another battering like this. Ever."

"Me neither," I say. "I can't believe Dominic would allow this to happen. Do you think he knows?"

Brie gives me a hard stare, and struggles to sit up. She swears again, and giving up on a sitting position, gets to her feet, hobbling gingerly around the room.

"Shit. Need to get things moving again. Bloody sodding hell. What were you saying? Dominic? Yes, love. I would think he condones all of this. He wants rules to be kept so he'll turn a blind eye to how they're enforced."

I stare at her in complete shock and disbelief. What's the point in being here if Dominic won't protect me?

"Why do you stay here?" I ask.

"This is my home. And I've never been hit before. I don't know what the hell is going on. I don't even know what I did wrong." She stops hobbling for a moment and looks down at me still kneeling on the floor. "Maybe I'm wrong. I don't really think Dominic would arrange to have us beaten, but I was a bit shocked at what happened with Jimmy, and perhaps trust needs to be earned back. This isn't the way to do it." She winces again, as she resumes her slow circuit of the room.

I stand up, sore but in a relatively good state. Guilt for not helping gnaws at me. Brie hasn't mentioned it, but I can't let it go.

"Brie, I'm sorry I didn't intervene."

She looks at me in surprise. "Don't apologise. I wouldn't have wanted you to. He'd have hurt us both far worse if you'd tried to stop him. I'm pleased he got called away before he had a chance to get going with you. Bastard."

"Thank you. You're very kind. What do we do now? How

48

do we get out of here?" I'm not sure if I mean the room or the Abbey. I'm beginning to wonder if I've made a huge mistake. The continuing lack of letters to Matron and to Mum and Dad's solicitor takes on a sinister hue.

"We keep moving, and we pray," says Brie grimly.

I suddenly remember the cynical woman who stands behind us in Chapel. This is as good an opportunity as any to find out why she's so stroppy. I've never yet seen her smile. I ask Brie if she knows.

"Oh, her." Brie's mouth curls in a sardonic grin. "She had a bit of a thing for our Leader, and I believe he indulged her for a while. And then he stopped. You see the results on her face every day."

"Did he just dump her? He must have had good reason. I mean, she doesn't seem all that nice. Maybe she was horrible to him."

"Perhaps. Meanwhile, we need to get moving so we don't have to answer any awkward questions."

I take the hint, and we spend the next hour getting ourselves walking as if we haven't been battered. A series of stretches, and some gentle massage, helps, but neither of us can sit on our bottoms with any degree of comfort. As we reach the point of being able to amble with some semblance of normality, the key turns in the lock and the door opens.

"Are you ladies all right?" Leonard pops his head around the door.

I flick a quick glance at Brie. "Yes, thanks Leonard. How did you know we were here?"

"Thomas sent me to get you for prayers. We'd better hurry. They start in five minutes." He holds the door open for us, and we walk through. A wall of stifling heat hits me as I leave the room, but I have no regrets about getting out of there. Brie holds herself regally, and I wonder what Leonard thinks of her posture. I try to emulate her; regal is a huge improvement on the stooped hobble we started with such a short while ago.

We follow Leonard to the Chapel and slot into place, seconds before Dominic arrives.

It's a huge relief that prayers take place standing up. Despite a bone-wearying exhaustion, I force myself to join in with the singing, and a quick glance at Brie shows her to be making a similar effort. I watch Dominic for any signs that he's aware of our predicament, but he leads the prayers with his usual vigour and no signs of self-consciousness.

We spend the rest of the morning cleaning our dorm and then head to the common room for a break before lunch.

Inside, there's a dark-haired stranger up a ladder in the corner. He looks over as I enter, and smiles. I beam back shyly and head for the chair next to Tina. The man returns to his work. He seems to be messing about with a tiny camera. Will he be sticking around? His friendly face would be a welcome addition. I ignore the flutter in my stomach and curl up in the armchair, tucking my legs under me, so I don't have to rest on my rump.

This seems a good time to start befriending Tina. She's been elusive since my arrival, but there's something very appealing about her.

"How long have you been here?" I ask.

"Five years," she says.

"What Chapter were you in before?"

"Benedictine." She looks down at her lap where she's tying her fingers into knots.

"It must be hard for you to get to know another eleven people from this Chapter, when you were all settled in to your other one. I don't know anyone from any of the other Chapters." It feels such an inane comment, but I babble on anyway.

My eyes return involuntarily to the worker up the ladder, who seems engrossed in his task. He suddenly turns and glances at me. I quickly look back at Tina. She appears to be surveying the room, but without much interest. Then she shudders, and I follow her gaze to see Thomas lecturing Leonard in the corner.

"What? Oh, maybe," she says, clearly not engaged in the conversation.

"Why did you change groups?" I persevere despite her

lack of interest, and try not to get distracted.

"What? Oh!" she shrugs. "One morning I got taken to see Dominic and he told me I had been head-hunted." She looks down again and bites her lip. "Except I don't think it's my head Thomas is hunting," she whispers.

I give her a sympathetic smile, and shiver. Perhaps I hadn't dreamt that visitation after all.

I'm saved from replying by the lunch bell. I look back as I leave the room; the man is still absorbed in his work. After lunch, we all get on with our own chores. This includes cleaning the toilets – a punishment the warden mentioned as we left the dining hall. I assume this is to hide the real punishment. After the chores, we have gardening, which I usually enjoy, but I'm so exhausted, I can't wait for bedtime so I could rest my aching head and stinging bottom.

I manage to pull myself together enough to give Jimmy his injection, during which he watches me with obvious concern. I escape before he can ask any awkward questions and collapse on to my thin mattress. The events of the day tumble round my head like smoothie ingredients in a blender.

The blender slows down a little as the most important issues form in my mind. Does Dominic know about the warden's activities? Can I trust him? I admire him so much. He cured that blind man, Trevor, when I'd just arrived. He showed mercy. He's the Messiah. He can't possibly know the wardens are beating his followers for no real reason. Should I tell him? No. How could the new girl approach the Messiah and... and what? Tell tales? Plead with him to listen to a mere mortal? Beg him to get my letters typed so people know where I am?

So, should I stay here? I weigh up those ingredients. Which is worse: risking another beating from the warden, or returning home to no family, and an ex-boyfriend who would beat me up as soon as he saw me anyway? The beating from Pete seems more of a certainty. And that's assuming he'd settle for no more than a beating. I've been waking in a cold sweat two or three times a week, emerging from a nightmare where I've become the resuscitation doll; the noose is round my neck, and I'm falling... Nothing else is required to convince me to stay here.

My decision is made, and the blender stops. Meanwhile, I resolve to avoid the wardens as much as possible.

Chapter Nine

A week later, I've made some progress with Tina. I've been sitting next to her at breakfast every morning. Brie approves of this. She suggested it might provoke the wardens if we're seen together at breakfast again. I hate being afraid of them, but I think she's right. At least I'm doing something useful (I hope) in befriending Tina, rather than just being a coward.

I've tried talking to Tina about the weather – the ongoing excessive heat seems to be the safest topic of conversation. She hasn't responded beyond a brief nod of the head, and since my previous experience with friendships hasn't been inspiring, I could be forgiven for abandoning the project.

Then yesterday I whispered to her that one of the wardens seemed to be wearing odd socks, and I got a tentative smile in reply. It seemed minimal progress towards friendship, but it was a start. The smile appeared more readily every hour. Today, I'm cleaning the toilets, when I hear the door open. I poke my head out of the cubicle to see Tina coming in carrying a cloth and the bleach. She smiles and waves but doesn't say anything; just starts cleaning at the opposite end of the row. I wipe the bowl with a bit more enthusiasm. When she gets to the cubicle next to me, she speaks.

"Nearly finished now." She sounds quite cheerful. My smile of amazement almost cracks my jaw.

"Thanks, Tina, this is so kind of you. I hope you don't get into trouble for helping me."

Her head pops out of the cubicle and she lowers her voice. "It's fine, I told the housekeeper Thomas had prescribed this as punishment." Her voice becomes grim as she mentions the name of the Chapter head.

"Well thanks again. I'm so fed up with these toilets. I offered to swap with Brie; she's been cleaning the ones in the

Infirmary, but she said she's got used to them now and refused to change." I don't mention it to Tina, but I think Brie's now scared to do anything which brings down the wrath of the wardens, and swapping a punishment duty could be seen as rebellious.

When we finish the cleaning, we leave together to put the bleach and cloths in the utility room down the corridor.

There's an awkward silence. Then Tina says, "You've been so nice to me. I do appreciate it, but I'm not much good at the friends thing. I haven't had a proper friend since I turned eight."

We put the cleaning things away, then she gives me a shy smile and disappears, hurrying off in the direction of the common room. My mouth is dry. I should have replied, but she was gone too quickly. I'm left to reflect that I haven't had many real friends either. It's another incentive to stay here. Between Brie, Jimmy and now Tina, I've begun to feel as though I belong.

***

I begin to notice tiny devices near the windows, tucked away so you wouldn't notice them if you weren't looking. It looks as if the attractive guy with the ladder has been busy. I examine one in the kitchen as I put the saucepans away in the overhead cupboard; he's hidden the small microphone under the cupboard door, and my hand brushes against it by accident. Why all this security? We already have the wardens. Is this for our protection?

I also spot a tiny lens in the top corner of our dormitory. When I come in to change after gardening, the sunlight streams through the small window and glints on the glass. I pretend not to notice, and carry on with getting changed, but I draw the curtains more firmly than usual around my cubicle before getting undressed. It seems a very intrusive place to put a camera. What can Dominic be concerned about?

That night, I look across at Tina's thin figure in the next bed, cocooned in the sheet despite the heat. Thomas has resumed his visits, sneaking in several times in the last week; sometimes he just watches, other times he strokes her thigh or arm. So, it's no surprise when the door opens and he sidles in.

He pulls the curtains closed around Tina's bed. My heart hammers against my chest, and I hope he doesn't hear it. Why does he need to shut the curtains? The smell of his stale sweat turns my stomach as he raises his arm to close the final curtain – the one between Tina's bed and my own. The moonlight shining through the window casts shadows through the thin fabric. I see Thomas's shadow bending over and removing the sheet from around Tina. He must have woken her up, because she cries out, but the sound is suddenly muffled. Maybe he's put his hand over her mouth.

I don't know what to do. I don't want anything to go too far, but my recent beating has freaked me out and I'm reluctant to draw further attention to myself. Then I see the shadow of Thomas climbing on to Tina's bed…

"Aarggghhh, noooo…" I half-shout, half-slur – loud enough to wake my near neighbours. I hear Brie spring out of the bed opposite, and she comes over to where I'm waving my arms and thrashing around.

"What in heaven's name is the matter?" She sounds worried but annoyed, and I know by now that being woken in the middle of the night invariably makes her grumpy.

I open my eyes and rub them as if I've just woken up. "What? Oh, bad nightmare. I dreamt strange men were coming into the dorm attacking everyone, and it was my turn." A shuffling sound from the next bed draws my attention. "Tina, are you okay? Why have you closed the curtains?"

Thomas appears from Tina's cubicle. "She wasn't well. I reckoned it would be better for her to have peace and privacy. I was looking after her, like I'm supposed to. It's my job as head of the Chapter." He's over-protesting, in my view; but I have a suspicion of what he's been up to. By now, quite a crowd has gathered. I seem to have woken at least half the dorm.

"Well, I'm awake now. I had a bad dream and it woke me up. I'm sure Tina would prefer me to look after her if she's feeling poorly. You should have woken me anyway. Someone might get the wrong idea." I hope I managed to convey the right combination of innocence and warning, but I can't know for sure.

"You watch what you're saying, Missy. Haven't you been in enough trouble?" He smirks, and then leaves the room. I open the curtains between me and Tina, and everyone else goes back to bed. Tina looks anxious as she returns her nightdress to its proper position.

"Thank you," she whispers. "You weren't asleep, were you?"

"No, but I didn't know what to do." I sit on the edge of her bed.

"You were great. He touched me... everywhere... so horrible." She shudders. I squeeze her hand as she clutches the sheet around her.

"He's gone now anyway. I'm here to look after you. I don't think he'll come back tonight."

I sit up with Tina for the next hour, sitting cross-legged on the end of her bed until she falls asleep. When her gentle snores reach me, I carefully unfurl my legs and put my bare feet on the cold floor, before standing up and padding back to my bed.

I lie down and shut my eyes, but the thoughts of all that has happened over the recent weeks dart round my head with a ferocity that keeps me awake until the early hours. I still miss Mum and Dad horribly, but events seem to have dimmed the grief – for some of the time at least. Tears wait until nights like this, when everything seems too much, and my loss overwhelms me.

***

My friendship with Tina has been developing, and the events of that night have consolidated my earlier efforts. She always sits next to me at meals and prayers now. Dominic remains his charming but distant self. I miss my friend from before I came to the Abbey. He rarely speaks to me now, and the sign is still up on his door. Few people are allowed close to him: just the Chapter heads, and a select group of women who look after his appearance. I've been told that within The Brotherhood, he has his own hairdresser, masseuse and manicurist. They're followed with envious eyes when summoned to Dominic's quarters. My own feelings about him are mixed. I still lurch from conviction of his innocence to a fear he knows about the beatings. He must have known about, and authorised, the new technology around the Abbey. Meanwhile, his effect on me never diminishes.

It's the morning after the disturbance with Thomas. I sing my heart out in prayers; strongly affected by the relief at having been able to thwart our head's abuse, and I give the hymns new energy and meaning. Dominic must have noticed my enthusiasm, because he looks directly at me and smiles. A strange explosion takes place inside my body, with fireworks and symphonies all competing for attention. I carry on singing to the end, and afterwards I struggle to conceal the ridiculous grin that seems desperate to plaster itself on my face for ever.

I guess I'm not successful, because Brie raises her eyebrows and shakes her head at me.

***

Tina still doesn't talk much, but she smiles a bit more, even if only at me. Whenever Thomas appears, though, there are no smiles; her shoulders hunch and she seems almost to hold her breath. A couple of days after I banished him with my supposed nightmares, we're having lunch at the long table when Thomas sits down in front of her. She shivers despite the heat. He watches her chest throughout the first course, flicking his tongue out to lick his lips between mouthfuls of leek and potato soup. He traces patterns on the table with his free hand as he stares and Tina folds her arms across her chest by way of protection.

Thomas sneers at her. "You need to eat, lovey. I'm sure you don't want to be attracting the wardens' attention, do you?" She shakes her head, and picks up her spoon. She takes the tiniest sip, but swallows hard to get it down. For the next ten minutes, she just stirs her soup, brings the occasional half spoonful to her mouth and then returns it straight to the bowl. I give her an encouraging smile, but there are tears in her eyes, and although she looks back at me, it appears to be as much as she can do not to burst out crying.

By the time the meal ends, she's shaking like a washing machine at full spin. Fortunately, Thomas gets called away by Dominic as soon as we finish eating, and I help Tina from the table, with a bit of assistance from Leonard who pulls out her chair and keeps the other group members away. Alarmed by her pallor, I support her to the ladies' and stand behind her, holding her lank pony tail out the way as the poor girl throws up into the toilet bowl.

Eventually she emerges from the cubicle, with little blood spots all around her eyes, standing out as brilliant red against the whiteness of her skin. Escaped wisps from her ponytail are sticking to her sweaty forehead. I take her straight from there to the Infirmary and hand her over to a nurse who welcomes us with a smile.

"Excuse me please. Could you look after my friend? She's been sick, and I think she's caught a chill, because she keeps shivering." I keep explanations to a minimum, and Tina flashes me a grateful smile as the nurse picks up a blanket from a cupboard by the wall.

"All right dear," says the nurse as she wraps the blanket around Tina's thin shoulders. "You come with me and I'll get you a nice quiet room to yourself where you can have a good rest and some peace and quiet. Dr Griffiths will be along shortly. He's a sweetie – he'll look after you well, and so will I." Then she turns to me. "All right, thanks. You can go."

Her tone is abrupt, and the smile now absent, and I hope she'll be as kind to Tina as she first appeared. She's left me with no choice; I have to leave Tina in her care.

I do my best to scramble through the rest of the day with

as much normality as possible. I avoid Thomas. He tries to catch my eye a few times but I don't want him to ask me about Tina's whereabouts, so I busy myself with chores whenever I sense him watching me.

As the day wears on, I wonder how Tina is. I hope they're looking after her and not letting Thomas near her. I want to sneak over there to see her, but given my recent beating, I decide to wait until the following day after dinner. I know the wardens eat their dinner then, so I'll have more chance of getting across without interference. There are no rules against going to see patients in the Infirmary – or none that I know of.

Meanwhile, memories of Dominic's smile keep me going. Each time I think of it, a warm glow spreads through me. I think about asking him if I can visit Tina, but the thought of the smile disappearing, or worse still, of him banning me from seeing her, prevents me. I wonder if I should take the opportunity to ask about my letters now he seems to be more congenial, but maybe if I ask, the smile would disappear and he would get cross. He doesn't seem to like being challenged. I would be better to wait patiently for the right moment.

Three times I find my steps taking me in the direction of his office, but each time, I stop myself. I need to be strong for Tina.

Chapter Ten

I try not to rush dinner, as I don't want to invite too many questions, but there's a definite fluttering in my stomach all through the evening meal, and prayers.

Finally, I'm free. I tell Brie where I'm going, in case I'm missed, and take the inside route to the Infirmary. It's a bit longer, and I have to pass a few small cameras on the way, but the weather has broken, and outside it's pelting down a mixture of rain and hail.

There are other members in the passageways at this time of the evening – on their way between kitchen and laundry duties and the common rooms, so I'm much less conspicuous inside.

Once there, I ask an elderly woman at reception if I can see Tina. I recognise her as the miserable woman who stands behind me in prayers, and who doesn't believe in miracles. She nods, and disappears through some double doors.

I pace the entrance area for several minutes before a stocky man with bushy eyebrows and a moustache appears. Behind the facial hair is a pair of twinkling eyes and a warm smile. Relieved to finally see a friendly face here, I smile back at him.

"Can I take your name, young lady?" he asks.

"I'm Melissa. I'd like to see my friend Tina please." I catch my bottom lip with my teeth. I've given my name to a complete stranger within the grounds of the Abbey. I don't know if I'm allowed to visit Tina, and despite this man's friendliness, I'm not sure if I should trust him.

"Well, I'm pleased you're Melissa. I have explicit instructions from your friend to admit no one but you to see her. I'm Dr Griffiths." He gives me another comforting smile, and my courage returns.

"You won't tell anyone I'm here, will you? I'm not sure if I'm allowed." I speak quietly, looking around at the same time in case there are bugs or wardens in the vicinity.

"You're all right, my dear. There's no one listening and I won't be telling on you. My first priority is always my patients." His smile falters a little, but I'm still inclined to trust him.

"Has anyone else tried to see her?" I say.

The bushy eyebrows draw together in a frown. "One of the heads attempted to bully me in to letting him in, but I don't answer to him. As I said, my main responsibility is to my patients. Your friend was adamant no men should be allowed in."

"You're a man."

"I don't think doctors count. At least I hope not."

"Thank you." We reach the single-bedded room where Tina is lying amidst a sea of spotless white linen. She still looks pale and anxious, but relaxes back against the pillows and beams at me.

"You don't need to talk much. I don't want to wear you out."

"I'm so pleased to see you." Tina gestures to me to sit down.

"Thank you. How are you feeling?" I pull up one of the ubiquitous orange plastic chairs.

"Relieved to be able to relax for a while." She lowers her voice. "While we're here, can I ask you something?"

"Of course."

"What are you doing here? I mean, why are you in The Brotherhood? You don't seem the type." She nods in the direction of the main buildings. "Sorry, I've wanted to ask for a while, but this has been the first chance I've had."

I sit quiet for a moment. In the short time I've been here, I've realised people don't discuss this sort of thing. Dr Griffiths seems trustworthy, but my bottom stings in warning at the thought of breaking rules.

"Please," she says. "I don't want to intrude, but I would like to hear a bit if you don't mind."

I glance over at the Doctor, who now reclines in a comfy-looking armchair in the far corner of the room. "Is it okay?" I ask. "I guess we shouldn't be talking about this stuff."

The doctor smiles. "It doesn't bother me, my dears. I do have to stay here though. There are no means for the authorities to listen in yet, so I'm supposed to oblige when the patients have visitors. But I do seem to be suffering from a touch of deafness today." He rubs his left ear.

I'm a bit shocked. He's just admitted that he's expected to report back if we break the rules, but his honesty convinces me to trust him.

I turn back to Tina. Sweat beads on my forehead and neck, and not all due to the heat. Since telling Brie on the first day, I haven't mentioned Mum and Dad for about six weeks.

"OK then, but I'd better be quick." I know I'll end up crying if I embellish this too much. "I had a bad relationship with a guy from the hospital where I worked as a nurse. Then I lost my mum and dad in a plane crash. I didn't know what to do or who to turn to." I swallow hard, and blink several times to keep the tears at bay. Even with the brief, abrupt *résumé*, my voice cracks. It's too soon, and this is still too raw. "I managed to turn up to the memorial service our vicar had insisted on – with a bit of help from a bottle of vodka, but I was a mess…"

I tail off for a moment as the memories flood back.

"Please carry on with your story." Tina's voice brings me back to the present.

I wipe my damp cheeks with a hankie, take a deep breath and carry on talking.

"I'd broken up with my boyfriend, but I didn't have any other friends as he'd frightened them all away." I decide to gloss over the finer details of my meeting with Dominic. "At the service this stranger approached me and asked me if I was okay. We met up every day for coffee after that and I thought we'd become friends. After about a month, I… er… I needed to leave my digs, and he offered to bring me here."

"Oh my God," says Tina. "That still sounds brave; leaving everyone you know and coming here. You say you'd only known Dominic for a month."

"Yeah. I thought we'd become friends in that time though. I didn't have any concept of how busy he'd be here. Anyway, after losing my parents, there wasn't anyone else I cared about leaving behind." I take some more deep breaths as Tina watches anxiously. I look over at her, suddenly conscious that I should be the one helping her, not the other way round. "Sorry, I think I should go back and get my head together, but I'll come and see you tomorrow if you don't mind." I get a grip on my straying emotions. "Try and get some sleep now anyway. You're looking tired. I hope I've not worn you out." I look across at the medic dozing in the corner with his mouth open. His snores sound like a rhinoceros being strangled, and I'm struck with a strong urge to giggle. I force myself into some semblance of normality, wink at Tina, and then raise my voice.

"So bye then, Tina, see you tomorrow."

The Doctor jerks awake, looking confused for a second as if he's forgotten where he is.

"Sorry," I say. "I didn't mean to startle you."

"Nothing to worry about, my dear. Only rested my eyes for a few minutes. Are you off now then? I'll look after your friend for you. Pop in and see us again tomorrow. About the same time?"

I nod, smiled at them both and leave the room. I'm exhausted from reliving the funeral, and the long-suppressed grief is bubbling far too close to the surface. I barely notice the walk back to my dormitory. I arrive just in time to give Jimmy his injection before bed.

"You're quiet tonight, lass." Jimmy interrupts my thoughts, as I stick the injection into his arm. "Why have you no' injected me in there tonight?" He points at his abdomen, and I give a guilty start.

"Sorry, I forgot. It doesn't matter that much. Anyway, it's good to use different places every now and again. We could use your thigh as well, but people might get the wrong idea if you started pulling your trousers down for me." Despite everything, I giggle.

"Aye, they might! Seriously though, are you okay?"

"Fine, thanks." I touch him on the shoulder by way of apology before putting away the injection pen and leaving the cubicle.

***

It's been strange telling Tina my story, even the abbreviated version. I left out the worst bit: the loss of my sister Jess, who was abducted from our house when I was fourteen and she was ten. My family fell apart, and the guilt has never gone away.

Meeting Tina – who looks so like Jess, with the same blonde hair and pixie-like features – has stirred all that up again. I rarely admit this, even to myself, but guilt has been responsible for so many of my recent mistakes – certainly my relationship with Pete. I always believed it was my fault when he was being difficult. Everything is always my fault.

I shut my eyes and pray for forgiveness, and for the strength to protect Tina, as I failed to protect Jess. I only open them when I hear a buzzing near my bed. Not another wasp? No. A large fly butts its head against the closed window, trying to get out. The room feels too hot and humid despite the rain earlier this evening. I considered getting up and opening the window to let the fly out, but the sound of voices in the passage outside the room keeps me still. I daren't move. This is no time to be getting into trouble.

Chapter Eleven

Outside my immediate group of friends, the one who has impressed me most is Leonard, with his kindness and air of gentle reserve. Jimmy told me that Leonard joined The Brotherhood about nine months ago, and as I'm missing Tina, who's now been in the Infirmary for a full week, I decide to chat to him a bit and see if I can find out a bit more about him. We're in the greenhouses for the morning.

"Morning Leonard, how are you doing?" I look up at him. He's well over six foot.

He smiles and pauses in his task of potting seedlings. "I'm fine, thanks. How's your friend?"

"She seems a little better, thanks." I hesitate. Apart from our initial conversation about Jimmy, and Leonard's polite concern after releasing Brie and me from the cell, we've had little to do with each other.

"Do you like gardening?" I say.

"Not much."

"What did you do before you came here?" Rules are forgotten in my eagerness to find out a bit more about him, but fortunately there are no wardens around at the time.

"I'd rather not discuss it." His smile disappears and his abruptness startles me. I take a step backwards.

"Okay. I'm sorry. Forget I asked."

He backs down. "If you must know, I had to nurse my wife through terminal cancer." His eyes look suspiciously moist as he crushes the brown plastic plant pot in his fist.

"I'm so sorry." Guilt floods through me. "You're right. It was none of my business."

His reaction to my apology is startling. He squeezes his eyes tight shut for a few seconds, then, opening them, he runs from the greenhouse, races to the edge of the garden, and scrambles up the oak tree whose branches overhang the road outside.

We all stand and stare in shock at this impulsive action. He reaches the edge of the tree, and looks about to jump down to the road outside, when wardens suddenly surround him. One of them has a long stick with a strange hook on the end. He yanks at Leonard and pulls him from the tree, causing him to fall on to the grass. As we watch from the doorway of the greenhouse nearby, two more wardens haul Leonard to his feet, and drag him away. I don't see him again until the evening meal.

Distressed and feeling guilty, I speak to him again when we're in the dormitory getting ready for bed. "Are you okay? I'm so sorry – this is all my fault."

He frowns. "Not at all. I adored my wife and I could do nothing to save her. I don't handle that well, and thinking about it sent me a bit crazy I suppose. I needed to get away."

"Did they hurt you?"

Leonard shrugs his shoulders in response, and looks about to answer, when three wardens arrive.

One of them hauls me off to the room with no windows. Without saying a word, he opens the door and shoves me in so hard that I fall to my knees. The door slams, and I turn round. I'm alone. A low-wattage bulb gives sufficient light to see the room is completely empty – except for me, the stone floor and the brick walls.

I shiver and sit on my bottom. My knees are red and sore, and will probably bruise, but at least I'm not getting a beating this time. I hope. But please, please, please – someone come and let me out so I can go to bed and check that Leonard's okay. Guilt at his predicament churns my stomach. It is my fault, all of it. If I hadn't indulged my curiosity, he would never have taken off as he did. And I wouldn't be back in this detestable room. I don't know why the warden threw me in here – maybe he overheard me talking to Leonard – but I guess I deserve it this time.

Knowing that should make it easier. It doesn't.

I hug my sore knees until my eyelids start to droop. I must

have been here for about an hour. I curl up on the cold floor and, exhausted, fall asleep.

I don't know what wakes me – perhaps the unpleasant sensation of turning over on solid stone – but when I open my eyes, I can't see a thing. I fight the urge to scream. Either I've gone blind, or the light's gone off. Praying for the latter, I sit up – my heart pounding – bring my hand close to my face and try to peer at it. I can maybe make out a dim outline, but I'm not sure.

I've hated the dark for ages; ever since Jess disappeared. My nightmares are filled with spectres of her being close, but out of reach. As I put my hand out to touch her, she disappears, and I awake drenched and shivering. I always half-expect her to be there in the next bed, in the room we shared for several years, but the dark room is always empty except for me.

In a strange way, this feels similar. I want to be able to see something – anything – but sight eludes me. I bend my head.

"Please, someone come. Let me out. I can't bear this. Please." As I pray again for someone to come – hoping for anyone but the wardens with their leather belts – tears fall on the stone floor. The pitch-blackness seems to close in on me, and it takes another huge effort not to scream.

I force myself to take some deep breaths. After a while, my eyes become accustomed to the lack of light, and I can just make out the shape of the room. A huge relief swamps me that I've not gone blind, and my heart rate slows by a few beats per minute.

But then the emptiness and fear begin to play tricks with my vision, and the walls seem to approach me, and then recede like the tide. The musty smell, which I thought I would become used to, somehow intensifies each time the walls come closer, and I can almost hear the sound of waves in my head.

Is this how it feels to go mad?

I can't have been here for more than a few hours, and already I'm losing it. Cold seeps into my bones and I shiver. Is no one going to release me? Terror creeps in on another wave, and my meagre courage deserts me. I rest my head on my arms and sob, praying incoherently for help.

Somewhere my fervent prayers must reach their destination, because the clanging of a key in the lock makes me jump. Hope and fear claw my stomach and the tears dry on my cheeks as the door opens, letting in a dim light. Dominic rushes into the room, carrying a portable lantern.

"Melissa, my child, what are you doing here?"

I blink a few times, adjusting to the relative brightness.

"A warden threw me in. I don't know what I did wrong. How did you know where to find me?"

"The Almighty One knew you needed help, and he advised me. Stand up child, and come here."

I do as I'm told, and he comes over and puts his arms around me; just in time, as my trembling legs can barely hold me upright.

"You're freezing! Come, let's get you out of here." He guides me to the door, his arm continuing to support me. His touch and concern warm me a little, and give me strength to walk. I allow him to lead me to his office – and he assists me to another of those hard chairs, opposite his large leather one.

A moment later, he wraps a soft blanket around my shoulders and thrusts a glass of smoky liquid into my hand. Brandy fumes hit me as I bring the glass to my lips, and I lower the glass a little, preparing myself for the potent spirit. He perches on the desk, his informal posture at odds with the immaculate suit and tie.

"You need to drink it all, Melissa. We have to get you warm and calm so you'll sleep and recover. Come now – drink!"

I obey, and try not to gag as the strong drink burns my throat. He waits until I've drained the glass, then sets it down on his desk and watches me as I struggle to stay upright in the chair. He bends and kisses the top of my head, and a thrill runs through me. Heat fills my veins, but I don't know whether it's due to awareness of Dominic or the effects of the brandy.

"Come, I'll take you back to your dormitory, and you can

sleep."

He takes my hand in his larger one, and pulls me to my feet. Once again, his arm slips round my shoulders as he guides me to the dorm and escorts me to bed. The room's in silence except for a few snores and grunts coming from the usual culprits. I climb into bed, and curl up. He strokes my shoulder and kisses me on the cheek before leaving. It exceeds by far the most contact I've ever had from him, and my heart is thumping in a triumphant rhythm. A strange exultation races through my veins, and the earlier traumas in the cell are almost forgotten.

As Dominic shuts the door of the dormitory, a gleam of moonlight from the window reveals that Leonard's bed is empty.

Where is he now? I hope he's okay. Will Dominic save him too?

Chapter Twelve

Leonard isn't at breakfast the next morning, and on the way to prayers, Brie approaches Thomas with an innocent expression on her face.

"So where's Leonard this morning then? He wasn't in his bed this morning. Is he not well?"

Thomas shifts his eyes under Brie's curious gaze. "Taken ill in the night. Very ill. Don't think he's going to make it."

"My goodness me," says Brie. "Can I go to see him? I might be able to make him better!" There's a mischievous glint in her eyes as she tries to pull Thomas in the direction of the Infirmary, although how she expects to avoid prayers is beyond me!

Thomas shakes her hand from his arm, and glares at her in a way that would reduce a lesser woman to jelly.

Brie doesn't seem fazed. "Maybe later," she says, and retreats to a safe distance. I watch her chuckling to herself about her considered victory over Thomas. I don't think she takes Leonard's reported illness seriously right now.

A caterpillar wriggles in my gut, and I get goosebumps. This doesn't feel good.

I don't know why Brie thinks Thomas has anything to do with Leonard's disappearance, but then Thomas is our Chapter head, so maybe it's not that far-fetched. Under the circumstances, I daren't ask anyone anything. I'm still sore and stiff from sleeping on the stone floor, and I need to make sure I can get across to see Tina in the Infirmary. The only thing keeping me calm is the memory of Dominic rescuing me, and his gentleness as he put me to bed. And perhaps calm isn't quite the right word. The caterpillar turns into a butterfly.

At dinner, after we've all sat down, Dominic announces

that Leonard has passed away following a sudden illness.

What? He was fine yesterday. What's happened to him? I didn't know him well, but he was always very kind. Bitter tears blur my vision, and the room fades out for a moment as I struggle to control my emotions.

Several deep breaths help me to calm down – trusted technique I learnt in counselling after Jess disappeared – and I brush the tears from my face with a reasonably steady hand. As my vision clears, I see Brie murmuring under her breath. She looks pale; she must be regretting her earlier teasing of Thomas. I give her a quick warning glance, but she has enough sense to not make a fuss.

The meal is a sombre one. Everyone at our table sits in silence and eats the bland lentil stew, potatoes and cabbage with our eyes fixed on the unappetizing food. I can barely force it down – it's like eating cardboard. Although Leonard was never the centre of attention, he was still part of our Chapter, my new family. It's disconcerting seeing people like Jimmy and Keith keeping their heads down and avoiding eye contact with anyone. They seem so distressed. Is it partly because they suspect Leonard's death might not have been accidental? The timing's too convenient. Were the wardens too rough? I hope Leonard didn't suffer.

After dinner, I realise I'm going to have to break the news to Tina, so as soon as I can, I head over to the Infirmary. Unfortunately, the kind Welsh doctor is not on duty. Instead, I see a tall, sour-faced man, who in a strange way reminds me of Dominic but without the charm or good looks. He's sitting upright on an orange hard-backed chair outside Tina's room reading the *New England Journal of Medicine* when I approach. There's a name badge fastened to the collar of his grey suit: *Dr Harper – Infirmary Director*.

"Er, excuse me," I say. "Please can I go in and see my friend Tina?"

He gives me a scrutinising stare, and my insides seem to wither.

"You have five minutes." He slowly stands, moves his chair aside and opens the door a crack.

71

I enter the ward, but as I try to close the door behind me, he prevents me with a firm grip on the door handle and another of those withering looks.

I mumble, "Sorry," and rush over to Tina, who looks relieved to see me. I give her a quick hug, which seems to startle her, but as I back away, I get a shy smile. I sit on the chair next to the bed, and whisper, "How are you? Are you being well looked after?" I glance at the door, and she follows my gaze. She rolls her eyes and grimaces. I don't think she likes Harper any more than I do.

"One of the other doctors called in sick, so he had to take over. I don't think he's impressed about having to work down here with actual patients, but at least no one has tried to visit me today. Except you, of course, and that's fine." Tina flashes me another shy grin. "You're always welcome," she says.

"I've got some bad news." I keep my voice low, as I don't trust the Infirmary Director. "I'm really sorry to have to tell you, but Leonard…" I break off. How do I say this? "Oh Tina! It's so awful. He's dead."

Tina's brow furrows. "Is that the tall guy who always looks sad? I heard from one of the nurses this afternoon that he tried to get out by climbing the oak tree."

"Yes." I feel guilty for breaking the news, as Tina becomes pale.

"Are you okay?" I ask, after a moment.

"I hate this place sometimes. Do you think we should try and get out?" she says, in such a quiet voice I can barely hear her, although under the circumstances that's wise. "Dominic doesn't seem able to save people any more."

I suppress the tremor that goes through me at the thought of Dominic. Should I tell Tina what happened to me last night? For the moment, I decide not to.

"I'm going to look after you, okay? As long as we keep our heads down, we'll be fine. Leonard made a mistake yesterday. But perhaps him dying was a coincidence. Don't worry; we'll be fine. The wardens are awful, but Dominic *will* look after us." I keep my voice low and Tina has to lean towards me to hear. But it's as well that I did, as a second later, we're interrupted by Harper.

"I think you'll find you've somewhat exceeded your allotted time." The sarcasm is crushing. "Don't even think of coming tomorrow."

Two days later I return, to find Dr Griffiths back on the ward. He remains in the room at all times though, so our conversations are innocuous, discussing the oppressive heat, and Tina's enforced bed rest.

Then, as I'm getting ready to leave, she announces, "I'm coming out tomorrow." The defiance in her voice tells me she's not happy about it.

"You'll be okay. I won't let Thomas near you." I speak quietly, and glance over at the doctor, but he's busy with some empty sample bottles and appears not to be listening.

"You might not be able to stop him. Thank you for offering though."

"It's not an offer. I swear, he won't stand a chance." I take her hand and give it a squeeze. She squeezes back and shrugs her shoulders.

When I get back to the common room, I start making her a little soft dog out of fuzzy felt. Craft materials are always available, but I don't usually do anything except knitting.

The soft toy is no work of art, but I look forward to giving it to her as a welcome back gift. I want her to understand the underlying message – I'm her watchdog and will look out for her – a friend in need. A tiny niggle at the back of my brain reminds me I haven't been very good at this in the past. Hopefully this time will be better.

***

The rest seems to have been good for Tina. She has more colour in her cheeks and walks out of the Infirmary with her head held high. We arrive back in the Abbey just in time for lunch. The little felt dog is lurking in Tina's dress pocket where she put it for safekeeping. Every now and again, her hand goes to her pocket and clutches the toy. It seems to give

73

reassurance, particularly as we sit down to lunch with Thomas three seats away at the head of the table.

However, whether it's because of my watchful eye or because he's been warned by higher authorities, Thomas avoids Tina as much as possible throughout the meal, chatting lightly to Keith on his right and Jimmy on his left. How long this remission will last remains to be seen, but Tina's definitely more relaxed now she can see Thomas is ignoring her. She seems content to chat to me about the weather and gardening.

This evening she and I go for a short walk in the grounds, knowing that if we speak quietly we have a reasonable chance of a private conversation. There are no listening bugs outside. Many other members are taking advantage of the lovely evening, so we're reasonably inconspicuous – a state I'm doing my best to maintain.

As soon as we reach a spot in the garden where we can be seen but not heard, we sit on the lawn and I say, "Why do you stay here? I know why I'm here, but I've no good reason to leave. You have now."

She thought for a moment. "I suppose you told me your reasons the other day. I guess it's my turn."

"Not if you don't want to say. I'm happy to have you here either way."

"Thanks. I ran away from home. My dad was... doing stuff to me and I couldn't take it anymore. My mum threatened to kill herself if it came out – she said the shame would kill her anyway. The realisation that Mum loved her reputation more than me... well... there was nothing left to stay for. Dominic took me in. I was only fifteen at the time."

I lapse into silence for a moment as I try to digest what she's said. She's gone from abuse at the hands of her father, to abuse by Thomas. How horrible! I understand now why she's so shy. She's like me in so many ways – nowhere to go in the wide world out there, but now she's not even safe here.

I'm about to ask her how she copes, but one of the wardens comes into view and she bends to pick some of the long grass from around a nearby apple tree. She begins playing with the grass, plaiting it in silence, as the warden approaches. I look round and realise that everyone else has gone in.

"Oy, you girls. Get inside. It's getting dark – you can't stay out all night you know!"

Tina drops the grass and we both run towards the house. As we come level with the warden, we slow down and I ask, "What... time... is... it?" as I try to catch my breath.

"It's nine-thirty – past your bedtime, love," he says.

Tina and I look at each other in horror. Everyone has to be in the dormitory at nine, as we're up at five in the morning. If we're late we'll be in deep trouble.

The warden laughs at our shocked faces. "Got you going didn't I?" he says. "You're ok, but you better be quick. It's quarter to nine. Go on with yer."

We arrive at the door next to the kitchen, and I push it to let Tina through before me. Thomas is waiting at the door, and leers at Tina as she passes. She still seems a bit shaky from the fright the warden gave us. She looks at me with a plea in her eyes as she tries to edge through the small gap Thomas has left between himself and the wall. He puts his hand out to stop her getting past.

"In a hurry, are we?" He smirks as Tina stands helpless in front of him.

I glare at Thomas. "Come on – just let us through please?" I'm as polite as I can manage in the circumstances. "We need to be in the dorm in a few minutes."

"You can go. I don't want you here anyway! It's my little Tina that I want to have a chat with."

"Just leave her alone." I push him away from her, catching a whiff of the combination of cheap aftershave and sweat. I grimace in disgust, as I grab Tina's hand and pull her along with me.

I hear a bang and look back. Thomas has slammed the outer door shut and is muttering something to the warden, who's now joined him in the passageway. Taking advantage of his distraction, I turn to Tina.

"Come on, let's run." We make it to the dormitory just as

Brie arrives from the direction of the common room.

"What's got you two so hot and bothered?"

"Long story." I shake my head apologetically. "Good night, Brie."

"Fine. If you don't want to tell me... Night then, girls." Her tone of disgust shows her disappointment at not hearing all the gossip, and I feel a pang of guilt. Brie is still a close friend, and I've been neglecting her recently.

Tina and I head to our beds. We had a move round last week, and Brie relocated us to the far end of the room.

"What am I going to do about Thomas? I can't bear it." Tina gives me a look filled with the level of anxiety that landed her in the Infirmary.

"I'll look after you, I promise." I give her a hug.

I climb into bed deep in thought. Tina's history is repeating itself. After all our earlier hopes that Thomas would ease off a bit, this evening proved he's still watching and waiting. I have to find a better way of helping her. I caught him off guard by the door, but I won't always be able to push him out of the way.

Chapter Thirteen

The latest hot spell has ended with a crash of thunder. At about one in the morning it woke me up, and I watched the fork lightning flash through the thin curtains. So, this morning, we're having breakfast in the Chapel, as the refectory's flooded.

The wooden tables are saturated. I dread to think how long it will take them to dry out. The temperature has dropped several degrees, and it's now raining steadily. The wardens have been given the task of repairing the roof. They grimace as they pass by in hard hats and waterproof jackets. I don't think they're impressed with their new role. I just hope they don't decide to take it out on us.

After sitting on the Chapel floor eating toast and drinking tea, the group heads assign cleaning duties. Thomas has provided us with cheap plastic mops and red plastic buckets and sent us to mop up the water from the refectory floor. At least two inches of water covers the floor, and we're getting nowhere. It's still raining in and the water is up to our ankles. Suddenly, Tina ditches her mop and starts using the bucket to scoop up the water.

"Oh, what a great idea. Clever you!" I smile at her, and follow suit.

A few minutes later, and the whole group is copying Tina. We're getting in to a rhythm when Dominic walks in wearing green wellies (which don't quite go with the pin-striped suit, white shirt and grey tie). He's escorting a man of about my own age who's wearing similar green wellies (probably from the store room – we're all wearing them) but more sensibly with jeans and a dark blue shirt. He looks straight at me and smiles.

The world stands still. It's the man from the ladder! My

heart is pounding in my ears, but I take some deep breaths. Get a grip, Mel!

"Right. Stop work a moment, everyone. This is Mark. He's joining your Chapter." Dominic turns to Mark. "They can introduce themselves. Jimmy, take Mark to the stores after this and get him kitted out. Can't have him wearing his own clothes, but he might as well stay and help clear up this mess first." Dominic looks around the room where we're now making good progress – there's only about half an inch of water left. "You're doing a good job. Keep it up." He then comes over to me. "Melissa, are you all right now?"

I nod and drop my bucket. "Yes. Oh, I'm sorry." Some of the water has splashed above the wellies onto Dominic's immaculate suit. My mouth goes dry, but he pats my shoulder.

"Not to worry, child. It's fine. Carry on with your work now, and make your new friend welcome."

"Yes, thank you. I will do." I pick up the bucket and grip the handle firmly. What must they both think of me? Probably that I'm a clumsy idiot. And they're right.

Mark grabs a bucket from the pile on the table in the corner, and starts work as Jimmy does the introductions.

"Okay laddie? I'm Jimmy, as I'm sure you gathered. The bonny lassie with the curly hair is Melissa; Mel to her friends. Thin blonde lass next to her is Tina. That's our Brie over in the corner, with the long grey mop – sorry lass – silver blonde isn't it?" He winks at Brie, and carries on before she can retaliate, although she shakes her fist at him threateningly. "The tall laddie over there is my pal Keith, then from left to right over there we've got Alison, Dave, Geoff, Chris and Roger. They're the quiet ones in the Chapter – you'll no get trouble from them. The other members of our lot are cleaning the dorm – that's Ann and Sarah – you'll meet them later." This is Jimmy's most jovial speech since we lost Leonard. Even our chats while I give him his injections have been subdued. He must be looking forward to having another man back in the group.

Mark looks at each of us as though trying to commit our

names to memory. He smiles at me as we're introduced, but says nothing. My stomach does a leap in the air, but by the time I remember to smile back, he's looking at Brie.

When Jimmy finishes the introductions, Brie interjects, "You've yet to meet Thomas as well. He's our Chapter leader." Her tone is neutral, but I know her well enough now to recognise the signs. She clearly doesn't like Thomas, and I wonder how much she's noticed his behaviour towards Tina.

We work until lunchtime, and then have cheese sandwiches on the floor of the Chapel. It looks as though this method of eating will last a while. After lunch, Mark chats to Jimmy and Keith as we head into the greenhouses for gardening. It's still raining too heavily to garden outside. I pair up with Tina again. Since she came out of the Infirmary we've been inseparable, like proper best friends, but I do worry that I'm abandoning Brie.

Thomas has avoided Tina since the previous evening when he stopped us at the door, but I see him watching her from afar. He has a brooding look that bodes ill, although I don't mention it for fear of worrying her.

I get Tina to myself for a moment on the way back across the now soggy garden.

"What do you think of Mark?"

"He seems okay. I didn't pay him much attention." She shrugs "I don't usually like men. The closest I get to trusting any of them is that Doctor in the Infirmary – you know – the one with the bushy eyebrows."

"Dr Griffiths, you mean? Yeah, he's sweet." I hesitate. We're on the verge of gossiping – another banned activity. As we're about to re-enter the house, it's definitely time to stop. I walk inside and glance up. The warden holding the door open for us is the same one who threw me into the cell such a short time ago. He smirks.

"Behaving yourself, I hope?"

I swallow hard and keep quiet. Hairs prickle at the nape of my neck. I shuffle past him, dripping from my walk across the grounds.

"Pick your feet up, love. Didn't your mum used to tell you

that?" I gulp and run to the common room. That was one of Mum's many sayings; at least until Jess disappeared. After that, Mum rarely spoke. Not to me, anyway. After all, it was my fault. I'd rushed out to a friend's house to talk about a boy, and left my 10-year-old sister by herself with the door unlocked.

Once in the common room, I slump into an armchair and stare out of the window at the relentless rain. Tears mingle with the water dripping from my fringe. After a moment, my view gets blocked as Mark sits himself on the arm of my chair.

"You should get yourself into some dry clothes," he says.

I nod but don't move.

"Come on, Mel, or you'll catch a chill."

I turn my head and see the kindness and sympathy in his eyes. It undoes me, and I burst into sobs.

He gathers me against a warm dry chest, a big hand alternately patting and stroking my back. This treatment eventually calms me, and I force the competing thoughts of my mum, my sister and the dark cell back into the dim corners of my memory where they belong. As the crying subsides to an occasional sniff, Mark releases me and hands me a spotless and beautifully ironed white handkerchief. I look up at him. His regulation grey polo shirt is now damp and crumpled, but he still watches me with that gentle sympathy. I blow my nose hard on his lovely hankie, and hand it back to him.

"You keep it." His sympathy turns to mock horror. "You weren't honestly planning on giving it back to me, were you?"

"It's such a lovely hankie. I wouldn't want to deprive you of it."

"Don't worry, Mel, I've got others. Come on, let's get you back to the dorm, and you can get some dry clothes on and tidy up a bit before dinner."

***

80

At prayers, I'm between Tina and Mark as we head in to the Chapel, grateful to the two of them for their support as I avoid the gaze of the wardens. Chairs have been set out for a change, and after the hymns Dominic signals for us to sit down. He waits for complete silence before speaking.

"As you all know, I hear news from the outside. I choose to shield you from much of this so you do not spend all your time worrying. Far better for you to live life in peace and tranquillity here in this beautiful Abbey of ours. However, today I heard some very disturbing information. Just half a mile from here, three men were shot in a gunfight. Two miles in the other direction, an elderly woman was stabbed and robbed in broad daylight. And our newest member, Mark, has joined us in part to escape pursuit of some rogues who recently assaulted him for doing his job. It was I who interrupted the beating some weeks ago, and he has now come to us to receive protection, and to join in our peaceful and safe community." Dominic nods his head graciously to Mark, who shifts in his seat, and goes red as several people (me included) turn and look at him.

Our Leader continues, "There is evil around us, my children. Only I can protect you, with the help of the Almighty One, but you have to trust in me. Obedience and devotion are all I ask from you. In return I shall love, cherish and protect you all from the evil outside. I am sad to tell you that the Apocalypse threatens. Whether it will begin this week, next week or next year, is still unclear. Only time will tell. I say once more: trust me, pray to the Almighty One, and do your duty. Then you will be safe and happy. Now goodnight, and God bless you all."

This speech meets with a hearty cheer and a spontaneous burst of the Abbey Prayer. Dominic smiles and basks in the apparent adoration of the masses in front of him, before dismissing us to bed. Amidst the loud chatter from the members, my silence seems to go unnoticed. I've not heard Dominic mention the Apocalypse until now. It seems unreal and almost farcical. I came here to escape. I've found friends and a new family (albeit not a replacement), but this new development is unsettling.

My trust in the Leader drops a notch.

***

A short while later, I lie awake thinking about our new addition. It's not worth getting myself into a state worrying about outside events, and Mark is a far more pleasant subject. I felt a connection with him immediately, and his kindness has given me confidence that this will be a friend worth keeping. I don't dwell on the possibility of anything other than friendship. Relationships, unless arranged by Dominic, are frowned upon, and a part of me still yearns for the closeness I felt with the Leader after he rescued me – even after this evening's comments.

Finally, sleep creeps up on me and with it, dreams of strong arms drawing me into a passionate embrace. The only difficulty is that the face keeps switching between Mark and Dominic.

Chapter Fourteen

As we leave the Chapel after morning prayers, Tina pulls me to one side.

"I wish Thomas would stop staring at me. I think it's all going to start over again."

"Do you mean like your dad?" I ask.

She flushes. "Not just that. You already know I got moved into your Chapter because of Thomas. He's been watching me for months, and he started to make excuses to be nearby. Whenever he had a chance, he would brush past me, touching me. I knew what he was after, but I thought I would be okay until I got the order to move Chapters. I think now he's fed up. Thanks to you, he hasn't had a chance to get near me for ages, except the other night, and not even properly then. He's not happy!"

"I can live with his misery. Come on, we'd better catch up with the others."

We walk across to our greenhouse, where we're working this morning due to the rain. It's pelting down, and if we weren't so keen to talk about the situation, we'd run for it. But heavy rain is good cover for any dangerous conversation, so we get wet. But when we reach the enclosure, the conversation has to end. We get our heads down and concentrate on the job of planting seeds in pots. Thomas comes over, stands right behind Tina and puts his hand on her hip. She tries to move forward away from him, but is trapped by the bench.

"Leave her alone, can't you?" I raise my voice to make sure that the other men hear. Jimmy immediately comes over to our bench.

"Come on Tina, can you give me a hand? I'm rubbish at this potting stuff. Hey laddie," he says to Thomas, "back off a bit and give the lass some space. She can't get past you."

Thomas moves away glowering, and I smile at Jimmy. He winks at me behind Thomas' back.

When we return to the house to get changed, Thomas stops Jimmy at the door to the dorm.

"You're needed to help with some testing in the cellars." Thomas smirks.

The ruddiness drains from Jimmy's face. My heart sinks. This is my fault again. Jimmy only interfered because I alerted him to Tina's predicament. After all that happened with Leonard too. I should have learned by now.

Neither of them are seen for several hours. At dinner, Thomas sits next to Tina, on the other side from me. Jimmy is conspicuous by his absence.

My stomach cramps in fear. What have I done? Will they kill Jimmy too? Just because I interfered? Mark and the other men in the Chapter who might have helped out are seated on another table. We're all in the Chapel and it's been filled with the kind of plastic tables you find in camping shops. Dominic must have been able to get them cheap at short notice, and as they're foldable, they can easily be moved to adapt the room between dining and prayers.

I make sure the wardens are out of sight then give Thomas a hard stare. He's done this on purpose. The other three people at our table are quiet shy women. They sit looking at the food, and not one of them raises their head throughout the whole meal. Thomas must have set the room up in advance, as the adjacent chairs on each table are linked together. Tina tries to move her chair away from him but it's stuck, so she wriggles across instead so that she's almost on the edge of the seat.

"Stop your bloody wriggling, you stupid bitch," Thomas says in a low voice. "Just sit there and shut up. No one's coming to save you now. Your pal Jimmy wasn't looking very well when I last saw him. A few hours on the rack didn't agree with his constitution!"

"I'll save her," I say defiantly. I won't let him get away with this. He's such a bully.

"Just you try. You're in enough trouble. Big Les has been watching you. Ever since you interfered with Leonard. Do you fancy joining Jimmy in the cellar? I know about that little room you spent the night in. Trust me, bitch, that's nothing on my cellar!"

Bile rises in my throat, and I reluctantly stop protesting. At least it sounds as though Jimmy is still alive.

Tina shakes her head at me, and immediately sits still in the centre of her chair allowing Thomas to do with her as he pleases – or as much as is possible in the middle of the Chapel. I see him touching her thigh a few times with his right hand whilst using his left to eat, but she's very brave, forcing herself to concentrate on her food and trying her best to ignore his stroking.

The women opposite keep their eyes on the vegetable stew and potatoes and continue to pretend nothing's happening, although their faces are several shades paler. Dominic glances over at our table once or twice. I try to catch his eye, desperate for a smile or some reassurance that he'll protect us, but he seems preoccupied.

I wish I could just get up, take Tina and run away. Where would we go? Could I take her to my family home? It's not quite the same with no family, but it would be somewhere to live. An image of Pete and of the stabbed dummy stops this train of thought. I couldn't go back to that. And what if he decided to have a go at Tina? It could be a case of frying pans and fires, and I don't think Tina needs things to get any hotter.

No, fleeing isn't an option. I sit, forcing myself to eat, conscious that this monster is harassing my best friend next to me. I don't know how much longer I can take this, and it's so much worse for her.

By the time we get to the dorm for bed, Jimmy still hasn't returned. He'll have to go without his insulin. It's unlikely that missing it will send him into a coma, but it might make him very unwell, particularly if he's been hurt as badly as Thomas hinted.

Unable to sleep, I lie listening to Tina's steady breathing in the next bed, but after about half an hour, I hear the curtains rustle. Through the dim light, I can make out a Thomas-shaped shadow through the curtain between the cubicles. He smells as if he hasn't washed for a week, and I gag as the stench of his sweat hits me.

He whispers to Tina, "Got you now, haven't I? Your friend isn't here to help you this time. We're going to have such fun – at least I am!"

I fling back the blankets and dive into Tina's cubicle, just as Thomas prostrates himself on top of her.

"You think?" I don't bother to lower my voice. "Guess you forgot I was in the next bed. How dare you take advantage of her, you bastard!" In my rage, I forget about the embargo on swearing. My helplessness from dinnertime has turned to fury, and his taunts trigger a rush of adrenaline, enabling me to drag Thomas from the bed.

I pull him onto the floor, and start battering him with my bare fists. He lies there looking at me initially in surprise, but as I continue to hit him, a knowing smirk dawns on his face. A flutter of fear jolts my stomach at the consequences implicit in his grin. My punches lose some of their ferocity. By now, the whole Chapter are gathered round the bed, and gentle but firm arms surround me, preventing me from any further attack on the creep who assaulted my friend. Mark guides me away and into another cubicle. He motions for me to keep quiet.

Meanwhile, it sounds as though Keith is helping Thomas to his feet, reassuring him in an attempt to calm him down. Mark stands close to me with an arm around my shoulder. Unusual behaviour, perhaps, given we've only just met, but under the circumstances it seems very appropriate. The contact cools my temper, but as I become more rational, my fear of the inevitable repercussions overcomes me and I start to tremble.

Mark puts his other arm around me and gives me a big hug. I can smell The Brotherhood's soap on him, a lovely clean scent. I begin to relax, until a tingling ripples through me with a sudden awareness of his masculinity. I have to ignore it, and take strength from his presence. I can't risk ruining our growing friendship.

Gradually the noise subsides, Thomas returns to his own bed and Mark releases me with a gentle smile to return to my cubicle. I go via Tina's. She's lying huddled in a ball shaking under the bedclothes. I put my hand on her shoulder and say in a quiet voice, "It's okay now. He's gone. Try and get some sleep."

I'd like to say more, but one of the wardens walks in. I just make it back to my own bed where I huddle under the sheets lying very still and almost holding my breath until I hear his heavy boots stomping away to the other end of the room. I wait until I hear the door shut, and breathe a sigh of relief. He missed all the action.

Thank goodness. I dread to think of the outcome if he'd arrived ten minutes ago. Exhausted, physically and emotionally, I immediately fall asleep.

Chapter Fifteen

I'm woken from a deep sleep by the bell. Dazed, I think for a moment that it's a fire alarm and scramble out of bed. I'm pulling on my clothes before I realise it's just the morning wake-up call. I look at Tina, ready to share a laugh at my confusion, but seeing her miserable expression reminds me of the events of the night before. The words die in my throat.

Judging by the quiet tables where our Chapter is sitting, I suspect everyone is tired from the night's disturbance.

After breakfast, we're rearranging the room for prayers when my two least favourite wardens come over.

I throw Tina a glance intended to be reassuring, but my own insides have suddenly acquired butterflies the size of elephants, and it's a struggle not to throw up the small amount of porridge I forced down my throat for breakfast. Mark looks across at me. He seems concerned, but must realise it would be better not to intervene.

Terror sharpens my observational powers, and I notice discreet name badges tucked above their breast pockets. The warden who threw me into the cell is called Geoff; the huge one who beat Brie and me has *Dennis* printed on his badge. The other members of our Chapter withdraw from the area, as Geoff and Dennis stand still, waiting in silence, menacing.

Mark casts me another of those worried looks as he retreats, and Jimmy (once again battered and bruised) and Keith both look sympathetic. Brie stalks past me and Tina without looking at us, and if I didn't see the tears glistening in her eyes, I would be upset that she seems so angry. Her angst gets to me almost more than the horror of the wardens. The Chapel completely empties, leaving only Tina, myself and the two awful wardens. Geoff grabs my arm, whilst his colleague pulls Tina away from the orange chair she's holding, and then drags her to the door. Thomas is standing in the doorway. Meanwhile, I'm held back in the Chapel as Thomas picks up Tina and throws her over his shoulder in a fireman's lift.

"You're to join them in a few minutes. I'll take you." Geoff grips my arm as we remain in the Chapel for about five minutes. Then he produces a blindfold from his pocket, and covers my eyes before turning me round three times. It's like a dreadful parody of blind man's buff, but it's not dizziness that makes me feel sick. Fear numbs me, and I'm powerless to resist. I feel myself being lifted in the air, and I must be thrown over the warden's shoulder, but I can't see anything through the blindfold. I'm being taken somewhere – the sound of his heavy boots on the floor changes after a few moments; are there cobblestones underfoot?

We end up somewhere cold with a musty smell, like mothballs. Is it the cell I was in last time? He dumps me on hard ground – fortunately from not too great a height – and removes the blindfold to reveal another dim cellar-like room – smaller than the other one. There are still no windows, and the brick walls are bare. I shiver, and not just from the cold. Anything could happen here and nobody would know. There are two grey metal doors, side by side – one of which we must have come through. Geoff leaves through the one on the left.

Left alone, I look around the dimly-lit cell. I try the handle of each door, but twist the knobs in vain. I slump on to the cold concrete floor and hug my legs against my chest, as much for comfort as for warmth. No noise reaches me for several minutes, and the silence grates on my nerves as I wait for something to happen. Only the sound of my rapid heartbeat dominates the room. Where has Thomas taken Tina?

I lose all track of time, and hope that my friend has been deserted in a similar room; so much better than the alternative. Then I hear a muffled clanking of chains and a scream. An aggressive voice is giving orders, judging from the tone, but it's too distorted for me to make out the actual words. My pulse begins to race again. I continue to sit on the floor, and wrap my arms around my head, in a futile effort to drown out the noise.

More screams follow, and my imagination runs riot. Oh God. Poor Tina. What is he doing to her?

She's endured abuse before, so this must be really appalling to elicit that response. I can scarcely breathe. Is it going to be my turn next?

Where's Dominic? Why can't he rescue us?

Tina's cries begin to fade. Is she being taken further away? Or is she getting weaker, and less able to scream? I raise my head, now trying to listen, and to work out what's happening. All sound has gone now, and I'm left with nothing but the fear.

Suddenly, the door on the right opens and Thomas appears. He grabs my wrist and hauls me up and through the doorway. The sight that meets me in the next room almost stops my heart.

I struggle for a moment to breathe. Tina is naked, lying on a narrow plank of wood, suspended by chains from the ceiling. Blood spatters her thin body, and red weals cut deep in to the skin of her chest, abdomen and legs. She looks over at me, desperation in her eyes, and her face streaked with tears.

I pull my wrist from Thomas' grasp and run across to her. I stroke her forehead and wet cheeks, before he seizes me under the arms and yanks me away from my best friend.

"Get over here, bitch!" he snarls.

I try kicking him, my fury at Tina's state momentarily overriding all common sense. He kicks me back, and then restrains my wrists in some rusty metal things attached to the wall and drops the key out of my reach on the floor. Dodging quickly out of the way of my feet, Thomas picks up a whip and slashes at my legs. Stinging pain brings me back to my senses, and I look across at Tina to see a scared look in her eyes. She shakes her head slightly, and I assume she's begging me to be careful. I nod a tiny fraction and drag my gaze back to Thomas, who's raised his whip again.

"How many more times do you want me to do that, bitch? Or do you want me to hit her a dozen more times instead? No? Right, well you'd better watch and learn. If I hear a sound out of you, you'll both be beaten to death. I've done it before, it's a doddle. Dominic doesn't care, as long as I clean up properly. He'll say a few prayers over your souls. Just for the sake of his."

I shiver and struggle to breathe. I can't believe Dominic would condone this, but he's not here. Will he come and stop this? Will he rescue us?

Thomas gives a self-satisfied smirk. "That's better. Remember: if you both die, it's fine by me." He goes over to a crank and turns it, lowering Tina's plank to the floor.

She whimpers, and my throat constricts. As she lies on the floor, I see more clearly that she's bound to the plank by ropes, but her legs are tied to iron rings protruding from the wooden beam. There seems to be some leeway and she can move her legs a little, but her arms are bound tightly above her head. I want nothing more than to go and release her ropes and run for our lives, but we're both captive, and it's totally impossible.

Chapter Sixteen

Thomas drops his trousers, and I shut my eyes, dreading the inevitable scene to come. But a second later, they're wide open.

"Thomas, what do you think you're doing? How dare you? Get out of here, and go wait in my office."

Dominic goes to Tina first, and releases her from the plank. He wraps a blanket around her and helps her to stand, but she's far too weak and shaken, and slides to the floor. "All right, my child. I'll get you some help in just a moment."

He comes to me next. Thomas has made a quick exit, fear on his face. I wonder what punishment awaits him, but don't really care. He deserves all he gets.

Dominic picks up the discarded key to my restraints, and releases me quickly. I'm sore from being whipped, but it's all I can do not to throw my arms round him in gratitude and relief.

"Thank you, thank you. I don't know what we'd have done if you hadn't arrived." I rush to Tina's side, but trip over one of the chains. I feel myself falling.

***

I try to sit up, but the room spins, and Mark gets a basin in front of me in time for me to throw up. I rest back in my bed after retching until there's nothing left to come up.

"Where's Tina? How did I get here? What happened?"

My barrage of questions makes Mark smile.

"One thing at a time! I've been sitting here with you for about an hour. You were brought from the Infirmary after they bandaged your head and legs, but no one has said anything about what happened, so I can't tell you. Tina's still in the Infirmary. I tried to ask after her when they brought you across on the stretcher, but all they said was that she was very poorly and needed to rest. Don't ask any more, sweetheart."

Memories slowly return. Either Tina or I could have been killed. Thank goodness Dominic arrived. I vaguely recall him coming in to that cell and shouting at Thomas, but that's it. The rest is a blank.

Before he came is all too clear, though. Why has he handed me over to Mark? Is he busy caring for Tina, or is he punishing Thomas?

My skull feels as though I've done a few rounds with Mike Tyson. And my legs are not much better. I lay back against the pillows. A brief survey of the surroundings reveals me to be in my own bed in the dormitory, but looking at anything for more than a few seconds brings back those awful waves of nausea. I shut my eyes for a few moments and allow it to subside.

"Would you be able to try and see Tina later, do you think?"

"I'll try, but I can't promise." Mark is perched on the edge of the bed, his warmth permeating to my battered legs. "You try and have a sleep now."

Obeying seems to be the easiest thing I've ever done.

Somehow, I make it down to dinner, shaky and in pain. Mark sits next to me and whispers, "She's still in the Infirmary and she's being looked after. I didn't see any sign of your friendly doctor, and there are two wardens outside her room, so I couldn't get in. I had to creep round the back and check on her through the window. She seemed to be asleep, and a nurse was sitting with her."

"Thanks Mark. I really appreciate that. I needed to know she's okay, at least physically."

He gives my hand a squeeze under the table. I suppose we're both conscious of the wardens, who now seem intent on scrutinising my every move. I try to catch Dominic's eye over dinner, but he's at the other end of the room, and never looks in my direction.

I still feel sick and dizzy from the bang on my head, and through the bandage I can feel a bump, which is sore to touch. My headache has subsided a bit by the time we leave the table after dinner, but my legs are excruciatingly painful. I'm excused from clearing up. Apart from Mark, most people seem inclined to avoid me, and as I stumble back to my dormitory after the meal I wonder what's been said to my Chapter about my current state. I wish someone could accompany me, but Mark has to help with the clearing up. At least they've let me go back to bed, and when I reach my cubicle, I don't even bother to change before getting between the sheets. The walk from the Chapel has set my head to explosion point again, and it's an intense relief to close my eyes.

Sleep evades me. The traumatic events of the last twenty-four hours rush round my head. There's nothing I can do now to help Tina, but at least she's being looked after, if Mark can be trusted. I'm confident of that at least. Mark's proved to be a real friend.

I can't believe Dominic hasn't been to see me. I thought he would have checked up on me, but he seems to have handed me over to Mark and left it at that. The whole situation is beyond my comprehension.

For the moment, I suppose it's enough that Mark's looking out for me while I recover physically from the day's events. I finally fall in to an uneasy sleep filled with nightmares of Thomas and Geoff taking it in turns to beat me senseless.

Chapter Seventeen

For the next week Mark stays by my side whenever possible, protecting me from the wardens as my headache gradually improves and the dizziness eases. Life begins, on the surface at least, to return to some semblance of normality. Life before The Brotherhood seems distant and unreal, and even the frightening memory of the dummy now returns only rarely, to be dismissed by a laugh or a joke with Jimmy, Brie or Mark. But the scene in the cell with Tina is much harder to dismiss, and I am desperate to find out how she is.

When I go to the Infirmary to get my bandages removed, I look for her, and ask the nurse who attends to me.

"Do you know how Tina is? She came in a week ago. I think she was in a bad way."

"Come on. You know I can't discuss another patient with you."

"I'm not asking for confidential information; I just want to know if she's recovering." I struggle to keep the frustration from my voice.

"She's alive and conscious. I really can't tell you anything else, so stop asking. I don't want to have to report that you've been difficult." The nurse finishes unwrapping the bandage from my head and inspects the wound, giving it a hard prod with her gloved hand. I wince. "That's healing nicely. Does it hurt when I press?"

"Yes." I try not to shriek as her fingers hit a tender spot.

"You gave yourself quite a crack on the ground there. You're lucky it wasn't a lot worse. People have died from lesser injuries than that."

Such a lovely bedside manner. I hope she's not the one looking after Tina.

"Will I be okay?"

"Maybe. We'll have to see." She shrugs and swings me round to face her.

She conducts a few basic tests, making me follow her finger with my eyes, and checking my reflexes. She refuses to tell me if the tests are normal, but gives me two packs of paracetamol before dismissing me. She scowls the whole time I'm there, and although I'm very grateful for the painkillers (and I wouldn't say no to something stronger), I sense a lack of sympathy or care.

Relieved to escape from her, I return to the common room, where I've been spending most of my time since acquiring my injuries.

The wounds on my legs have begun to heal and I can at last sit on the chair in the corner of the room without wincing. I keep my eyes steadfast on my knitting, but wonder why Mark's not at my side. He's been with me almost constantly until today, and I feel bereft. I don't see him again until dinner. He sits by me but is silent, and refuses all my attempts to draw him into the conversation.

Prayers follow, and Dominic nods at me as he passes along the lines inspecting all the members present. My stomach knots. I've had no contact with him since he rescued us from Thomas, and I don't understand why he's been so distant.

Next to me, Mark stands close – not invading my space, but his presence has my skin tingling, as if awaiting his touch. I struggle to breathe evenly. He makes me feel protected though, so I focus on shutting out the sensory signals. After his silence, I'm relieved to have him near again – at least he isn't completely ignoring me. Dominic's gaze settles on Mark for a moment, as if asking a silent question, but he must be satisfied because he nods again and moves on. His weekly inspection continues.

"Angelica, where have you been getting lip gloss? The Almighty One would prefer his chosen children not to hide behind masks of make-up. Please don't use it again."

He moves on.

"Katherine, you're looking pale. Do you have another of your headaches?" He puts his hand against her forehead for a moment. "Can you feel the heat? I'm taking away the pain now." He lowers his hand and rests it on her shoulder. "Better now, child?" he asks.

"The pain's gone. Thank you so much."

He kisses Katherine on her forehead, and jealousy stabs at me. The vivid recollection of him kissing me the same way has me gritting my teeth, and struggling not to give way to tears. Maybe Dominic doesn't like me anymore. He hasn't even smiled at me on the way past, let alone offered to cure my headache or sore legs. Again, I wonder why he needs an Infirmary when he has the ability to heal.

Failing to come to a conclusion, I watch Dominic's progress around the Chapel, as he checks everyone present. But no one else evokes either reprimand or healing, and I calm down a bit.

Finally the inspection finishes.

"Before you all go, I would just like to remind you that my office door is open for the next hour, if anyone needs to speak to me, or wishes for a special blessing or prayer."

Perhaps I should speak up. I could go to him with my fears and worries about Tina, and ask how he's planning to protect her from Thomas. Somehow though, I don't feel Dominic's offer is open to me. Confused, I watch and wait, and pray that he'll keep Tina safe, even if he doesn't like me any more.

***

I spend the next fortnight fighting an internal battle about Tina, and wondering whether to speak to Dominic about her. I've been unable to see or ask after her, but eventually I see her coming into prayers with her old Chapter. She looks thin and pale, and doesn't glance up. I don't see her for long; she gets hidden from view as we all line up in our Chapters.

Thomas mentions at breakfast that she's been moved back to her previous group to 'keep her away from bad influences'. It doesn't take the sideways leer from Thomas for me to realise who the 'bad influence' is meant to be.

Mark sees me trying to spot her in the crowd. He nudges

me and whispers, "Hey, eyes front. The wardens are on the alert and Dominic's coming in. You don't want to be spotted looking around do you?"

As he speaks under his breath, he is to all appearances standing still and straight, just like a good boy trying to impress the headmaster. It works. Dominic glances over, and seeing Mark, gives a nod and a slight smile. He then looks at me. His gaze seems speculative. What's he thinking? Then he announces the name of the first hymn and we began to sing.

At the end of prayers, Dominic gives out a few domestic notices and then says, "Mark and Melissa from the Cistercians, come here."

I look at Mark in surprise, but he flushes, and keeps his eyes on the Leader. We squeeze past all the other people on our row and head over to where Dominic waits for us, frowning and tapping his foot.

"Mark, I believe you have something you would like to say to Melissa?"

Mark nods and turns to me. Then he gets down on one knee on the cold parquet floor and takes my left hand. I gasp.

"Melissa, will you marry me?"

I stare at him. Mark mouths, "Say yes," and there's an urgency in his eyes that belies the romantic position he's in. I risk a quick look at Dominic; his face is impassive, but I figure he wants me to say yes and quickly. Otherwise, why call us up in front of the whole Brotherhood for a public proposal?

I'm so not ready for this.

My eyes return to Mark's face. He's frowning and biting his lower lip. My delayed response is obviously making him anxious. I take a deep breath.

"Yes. Yes okay. Er. Yeah that would be great. I'd love to."

Mark mouths, "That's enough, shh," and then puts his right hand in his pocket and fishes out a delicate white gold ring, which he hastily transfers to the third finger of my left hand. The solitary diamond winks at me as it catches the light, and my heart contracts at its beauty. Then he stands up and, still holding my hand, turns to face the Leader.

Dominic dismisses us back to our places with a wave of his hand, and then turns to the assembled Chapters. As we return, several of our group smile at us and discreetly pat our arms as we pass down the row.

He waits until we're back before speaking again. "Mark and Melissa will be joined in holy matrimony as ordained by the Almighty One after prayers, in exactly one month from now. The ceremony will be followed by a special breakfast, and then the day will return to normal. The happy couple of course will be excused work for the rest of that day." He gives me the first genuine smile for weeks. "That's it for this morning. Off to your chores now everyone. Mark and Melissa, I wish to see you both in my office immediately after lunch."

When we leave the Chapel, we adjourn to the kitchen for washing up. The rest of our Chapter huddle around us as Mark and I don rubber gloves.

"Congratulations," says Brie. "You kept that quiet, dearies. So let's see it then!"

"See what?" I look at her, bemused.

"The ring, love!"

I take my glove off and hold out my hand for her to inspect. I try not to keep looking at it; my feelings are too conflicted for me to deal with just yet.

"Aaahh, that's really pretty. It suits you as well." Brie turns to look at Mark. "How did you get it? It's not like we can just go out shopping."

"I asked Dominic for a catalogue, and chose it – I knew it would suit Melissa. It's almost as beautiful as she is."

I feel myself blushing. Does Mark really think me beautiful? How do I feel about that? A certain wobbliness in my legs suggests I quite like the idea, but it's all so new. I don't know what to make of it all.

Keith grimaces. "Pass the bucket! Come on mate – don't go all soppy on us. Congrats and all that sort of thing."

Jimmy says nothing, but looks surprisingly grim. I try to catch his eye and smile, but he avoids my gaze and concentrates on scrubbing the ovens. Everyone else seems to be taking the proposal at face value. I want to look happy and in love, and maybe my acting passes muster, as the majority of the Chapter members smile and wish us happy before getting on with their own tasks. I can't quite bring myself to look at Mark though. Despite my elation at being called beautiful, I feel betrayed.

Why did he do that? He must know I don't love him. I like him a lot; he's been very sweet to me and he sets off flutters every time he smiles, reminding me that he's eminently fanciable. Except, until today, I thought and hoped we were friends. I have too many other things to worry about to focus on what I've mentally dismissed as a small crush; considerably smaller anyway than my crush on Dominic. Being honest with myself, I'm gutted that Dominic wants me to marry Mark. It must mean that despite his kindness to me that night he rescued me from the cell, he doesn't truly care about me.

Eventually everyone moves away to other areas of the kitchen, and Mark and I are left scrubbing pots and pans at the double sink. I turn the cold tap on hard, and under cover of the rushing water, I say a single word: "Why?"

I look round at him and am shocked to see tears glistening in his eyes.

"Because it's the only way to keep you safe. Dominic gave me the choice of marrying you or giving you to Thomas, who's desperate to get his revenge on you for attacking him. I thought for one horrible moment you were going to say no."

"I didn't want to embarrass you in front of everyone." I concentrate on scrubbing the burnt porridge off the large saucepan in my hand. I can't see the connection between not marrying Mark, and Thomas getting hold of me, but bile rises in my throat as a vivid image of Thomas' cell reappears in my head.

"I'm sorry if you don't like the idea. I know there's not a lot of time to get used to it, but I won't force you to do anything you don't want to do." He looks away from me, his shoulders tense; and I see I've upset him.

Guilt grips me. I don't want to hurt this man. He's done so

much for me. I'd like to reach out and reassure him, but don't know what to say that won't make things worse.

"Turn off that bloody tap and stop wasting water!" A warden has come up behind us and catches us unawares. I turn off the tap, and then carry on scrubbing. "Just 'cos you're getting married, don't mean you can get away with stuff. I been told to keep a special on eye on you two, so don't try nothing."

We stop talking as the warden stands behind us while we complete the washing up. I have no idea what's going on – everyone seems content for Mark and me to be together physically – but for the rest of the morning, any attempts at conversation result in rebuke from the warden, who seems to have become stuck to us like glue.

***

As soon as lunch is cleared away, Mark and I head to Dominic's office. Neither of us has eaten much, and I'm consumed with painful cramps in my stomach. My headache, which has improved dramatically over the last few weeks, threatens to overcome me. Zigzags float in front of my eyes, and a poker begins a vicious assault inside my head, jabbing the area above my left eyebrow.

I stumble in Mark's wake and he takes my hand and half-guides, half-supports me to our destination. Dominic arrives at the same time, and beckons us to follow him in. He indicates two hard wooden chairs and bids us sit down.

"This has to be. The Almighty One spoke to me last week and foretold that the two of you must marry. He said The Brotherhood's survival depended on your compliance."

Mark waits until Dominic finishes his sentence, and then breaks in. "But, you told me—"

"I told you that Melissa would not be safe if you didn't do this. I am now being merciful despite your aggressive attitude, and informing you of the divine purpose of your union. It is not just to keep Melissa safe, but your marriage will serve as the sacrifice necessary to prevent the

Apocalypse. Only this will persuade the Almighty One to protect us all from the impending doom that will obliterate the world outside."

Mark and I remain silent. Thoughts fizz like fireworks round my throbbing head. Is Dominic right? Does our marriage have to happen? Is he really the Messiah, or is he delusional? Either way, it seems we have no choice.

Mark squeezes my hand, and I squeeze back. I don't know what it will mean to be a sacrifice, but I feel better with Mark at my side to help me through it.

"Go," says Dominic. "And remember: you are to be our salvation."

Chapter Eighteen

Numb shock carries me through the rest of the day.

I manage to keep smiling at my friends as they continue with their expressions of delight. Only Mark seems to realise it's a façade; perhaps because away from the others, my demeanour shows fleeting evidence of betrayal and confusion.

I'm relieved when bedtime arrives and I can finally lie down, rest my aching head, and try to work out what's happened. I shut my eyes to block out the dim moonlight shining through the thin curtains and attempt to get my thoughts under control.

Dominic wants me to marry Mark.

Mark wants to marry me.

Do I want to marry Mark? I don't know. I like him; a lot, if I'm being honest. I've never considered marriage though. I didn't even know it was allowed before today. I don't think I've come across any married couples in The Brotherhood. There are certainly no children.

What do I know about Mark? He's kind, caring and sweet. I fancy him. Who wouldn't? He's gorgeous with that black curly hair; and when he smiles at me, those dimples do strange things to my legs – like eliminating all the bones.

But he went behind my back to Dominic. Or maybe Dominic went behind my back to Mark. Either way, Mark should have told me what he was going to do.

"Mel, are you awake?" A soft voice disturbs my reverie. My eyes open wide to see Mark standing in the corner of my cubicle. He looks nervous.

"What are you doing here? You'll wake everyone up." I sit up and swing my feet to the floor.

"Come for a walk with me. I know a place we can talk

103

without being overheard." He puts out his hand and pulls me up.

Slightly off balance, I stumble against his chest. He steadies me, but holds me close for a second. I forget to breathe as he gazes down at me. He's going to kiss me. His lips get to a millimetre away from mine, when he pulls away.

"Not here. Come on." His voice is husky and barely recognisable. He steps back and takes my hand, leading me through the dormitory, where the only sound is snoring, and the occasional murmur from Brie and Keith. Both are known for talking in their sleep.

Once outside the dorm, Mark crouches down to the floor and pulls me down to the same level.

"The cameras are set to pick up anything from waist height and above. As long as we keep below that, we should be out of sight."

He starts to crawl on hands and knees. I follow him, suddenly remembering that he was the one who set up the cameras in the first place, so he should know about details such as angles.

My nightdress is collecting dust from the floor, and I resolve to get a broom out first thing in the morning, to sweep away evidence of our passage. I can't believe how dirty the floor is. One of the groups has been neglecting their chores.

We crawl past the common room, and eventually come to a stop between the kitchen and Dominic's office. Mark pushes at one of the panels in the wall. I haven't noticed them previously, other than to admire the decorative scrollwork and wonder why the monks who originally built the Abbey would go to the expense of all that costly mahogany. Now I discover why.

Mark feels his way around the panel.

"Oh bum. Back up a bit, Mel. I think we've come one too far," he whispers.

I turn and crawl back a few yards to the next panel along, then move aside to give access to my new fiancé.

This time, his fingers on the panel yield results, and it

opens like a door on hinges to reveal a room the size of a broom cupboard. It's empty. Mark stands up after a quick survey of the ceiling.

"We're okay here. Dominic asked me to focus the cameras on the area outside his office, but to leave the kitchen and surrounding corridor clear. This is close enough to the kitchen to be safe. You go first." He gives me a hand to climb in. The entrance is from knee to shoulder height, and it takes me a few seconds to work out how best to get through. His hand is appreciated but unnecessary, and I'm soon standing in the small space.

Mark follows me, with greater ease, despite being several inches taller. He seems to have done this before. He pushes the door shut behind him, and it closes with a click.

"I assume you know how to get out again?" I can't see his face, as it's completely dark inside here. He pauses, and I have no idea if he's just realised we're stuck, or if he's winding me up. He has a way of gently teasing me that normally sets my pulse racing. It's racing now, but out of increasing panic. "Mark?"

"Hey, yes of course I do. Calm down. I'm not a complete idiot."

"Then why didn't you say so?"

"Sorry, love. I was just teasing. I didn't realise you're—"

"Yes, I'm afraid of the dark. One day I'll tell you why, but for now, please can you say what you wanted to, so we can get back to bed?" Even I can hear the irritation in my voice, so I'm not surprised when he puts his hands on my shoulders and pulls me to him for a hug.

His reassuring warmth calms me down. It's difficult to panic for long with Mark holding me like this. After a few seconds, his closeness evokes a different response, and my pulse rate rises again.

"Mark?" My voice is muffled against his chest.

"Yes?"

"Were you going to kiss me back in the dorm?"

"Mmmm. Yes. I could kiss you now if you want?" The teasing note is back, but the tone is husky.

I raise my head, and reach up to find his face in the dark. As my fingers touch his lips, I lift my mouth to meet his. Our first kiss is sweet and filled with promise, and I want so much more. I press against him, and feel a bulge in his trousers. His hand moves to cup my aching breast through the cotton nightie, and he brushes my nipple with his thumb.

I'm about to pull my nightie up around my waist and precipitate our impending vows, when Mark pulls away suddenly, and puts a hand over my mouth. He whispers in my ear very quietly.

"Shh, footsteps."

Feeling slightly disgruntled, I listen, and can hear what made Mark stop so quickly. Heavy footsteps thud in the passage outside. Then a knock. A pause. A muffled voice, becoming clearer.

"... late, Ben. Can't we discuss this in the morning? I've a lot to worry about just now."

"The trial's in the setting-up stage. We need to get them in and ready. I need funds now. And don't call me that. Someone might hear."

"Don't be ridiculous, man. No one's around to hear. And I'll get the money to you in the morning." This sounds like Dominic, but is less formal than I've ever heard him, even when we first met.

"Well, if anyone does hear, it's on your head. You set the whole thing up. I was content where I was."

"That's bull, Ben. You'd bombed out. You'd have nothing if it wasn't for me. Now bugger off. If we keep talking out here, someone might actually hear."

Little does he know...

"If you'd let me into your office, we could talk in private."

I suddenly recognise the sarcastic tones of Dr Harper, and just manage to suppress a gasp.

"I've got company, Ben. Now get out of here. I'll get the money transferred in the morning."

A door slams and the heavy footsteps pass our hiding place again before subsiding. Mark keeps his hand over my mouth until Dr Harper is well past, but it's not necessary. I wouldn't dare say anything.

I'm a bit disappointed at the idea that Dominic has company. At this time of night, it's unlikely to be business. Meanwhile, if Mark was covering my mouth with his own, instead of with his hand, I might be a lot happier. When he finally removes the gentle restraint, I press myself against him, keen to resume our earlier activity. My thoughts are too confused to want to discuss them just yet, but hormones are running wild, and when I find the evidence of Mark's response, I pull him down into another intense kiss. It doesn't entirely help. Slightly intimidated by the conversation outside, I resist the temptation to remove the flimsy barriers between us, but bring on next month. If I can wait that long.

Mark finally breaks off the kiss.

"Bloody hell, Mel, I can't think straight. That's not good just now. We need to be sensible."

"I don't want to be sensible. Not really. I don't want to wait until we're married, Mark. Do you know any places less exposed?"

"No. Or at least, none that are appropriate."

"What do you mean by that?"

"I don't think you want to know. Or at least, you do already know, and it's not the place I want to make love to you."

It dawns on me. He's talking about the cellars, and he's quite right. It's private, but definitely not appropriate. I rest my head against his chest, keeping the rest of my body a safe few inches away.

"Of course, you're right. Shame though. I think we should get out of here though, don't you?"

"Don't you want to talk?" Mark strokes my back as he asks, and I wonder if he has the faintest idea what effect he's having on me.

"No. Not yet. Talking is just not on my agenda just now." Something in my brain seems to break; some strand of sense, probably, as I pull off my nightie, and snuggle against Mark, nuzzling against his neck.

"Oh God, Mel!" He cups both my breasts, and gently

shunts me up against the wall. My hands drop to his pyjama bottom waistband, and wiggle it down over his tight bottom. I can feel his erection against my stomach, and what he's doing to my nipples is driving me insane. I guide him so that he's positioned at the entrance, and then slide on to him. I brace myself against the wall as he thrusts into me. We're kissing frantically now, trying to keep quiet; vaguely conscious of the danger in our situation. Perhaps it adds to the excitement, but as he delivers the final thrust, I come too, and sag against the wall, with my arms wrapped around him.

Mark pulls away slowly, as if reluctant, and moves me gently aside, so he can pull up his pyjama bottoms, and clean up a bit. I scrabble on the floor to find my nightie, and somehow manage to get it on, but it's back to front.

I'm about to wriggle it round the right way, when another voice appears, this time from the opposite direction – as if deeper inside the cupboard, but there's definitely a wall there. The voice is muffled, and I can't work out what's being said, or who the owner is. But this hiding place is suddenly much too vulnerable.

Mark's hand stills when the voice is heard, but as it's obviously not in our escape route, he starts probing the panel, and the door opens inwards towards us. We climb out, Mark first to check for unfriendly company. He reaches in to help me, and I clamber out after him; relieved to be out of the dark confined space, despite the passion within. We're not safe yet though. Once again, he drops to his hands and knees, and I follow suit, before we crawl back to the dormitory.

As soon as we get inside, there's a call from the passage.

"…thought I heard something, Geoff. You see owt on the monitors?"

"No mate. All clear. Maybe have a ganders in the rooms though. See if anyone's up to what ought not to be. I'm itching to punish someone. Getting out of practice."

We don't wait for any further comments, but dash back to our beds. I just manage to get under the covers with my head on the pillow in my bed at the far end of the room, before the door opens, and the heavy tread of my least favourite warden breaks the quiet of the dorm. I take slow deep breaths and keep my eyes shut, hoping he'll think I'm asleep.

I smell his sweat and cheap aftershave as he enters my cubicle. He stands there for several moments, while I try to control my nerves.

"I know you're awake. Lucky for you I can't prove you've been out of your bed, but I'll get you. Trust me for that." He laughs, and then stomps back to the other end of the dorm, before shutting the door loudly behind him.

With the amount of adrenaline pumping round my body, it's many hours before I fall asleep.

Chapter Nineteen

The next morning, I manage to sweep the floor of the passageway, mentioning loudly to Brie how dirty the floor seems to be this week. Whilst deflecting attention to the lack of sweeping ability of the Benedictine Chapter, I slip my soiled nightdress in to the laundry, and get the load into the machine before anyone questions it. On the way, I collect Mark's pyjama bottoms, with their evidence of illicit activity, and the machine is on before anyone thinks to ask why I'm doing the washing and sweeping when Cistercians are on kitchen duty this week.

My tiredness must be obvious, as Brie stops me on the way back from the laundry room.

"Up late last night, love, dreaming of marital bliss?"

"Something like that. Took me a while to get to sleep." I lower my voice. "Just as I was dropping off, that awful warden, Geoff, dropped in."

"I thought I heard someone. Can't stand those bloody wardens." Brie grimaces at me, before patting me on the shoulder. "Anyway, I'd better go, otherwise they'll find some reason to throw us back into that ruddy cell, and I don't want any more floggings, thank you very much."

I give her a sympathetic smile, and watch her go, before heading to the bathroom to wash my hands.

It's hard to keep a delighted grin from my face; but as the events of last night were most definitely illicit, I need to try. The potential for trouble is unthinkable if anyone finds out Mark and I precipitated our vows. The biggest problem, though, is that I want to do it again. I've barely seen Mark today, but the few times our paths have crossed, I've had to clamp down on the urge to drag him into the nearest cupboard. Judging from the sizzling looks he's given me, it's

110

mutual.

Unfortunately, the sudden sexual tension must be palpable. After dinner, we go into the Chapel for prayers, and automatically stand next to each other. Brie is on my other side, and gives me a knowing look.

"I don't know what's happened to you two," she whispers, "but you'd better put a lid on it. There's enough chemistry simmering to take the roof off."

"I guess the timing's bad; I should have waited until we got married to start fancying him."

"Yes, you should." Brie nods towards Dominic, as he comes in fully robed for the evening. He looks very impressive, but for once, I feel nothing for him. My emotions are so keyed in Mark's direction, there's no space for anything else.

Dominic begins an inspection of the ranks. While he's in the rows behind us, Mark takes my hand and squeezes it. He's still holding on when Dominic gets to the Cistercians.

The Messiah glances down at our interlinked hands, and then at each of our faces. I hope mine doesn't look as flushed as it feels.

"I believe it would be wise to separate the two of you until the wedding. Mark, go and stand with the Benedictines for the moment. After prayers, you can move your possessions. They have a vacancy in their dormitory at the moment." His tone is cold and almost contemptuous. Why? He was the one who decided we should marry. Surely he should be pleased to see that we like each other?

Mark gives my hand a final squeeze, which I return, before he lets go, and moves reluctantly to the back row where the Benedictine Chapter stands. I don't know anyone in that group, but I vaguely recall Brie showing me round the whole Abbey in my first week; the Benedictines reside on the first floor, above the Chapel. About as far away from my Chapter as it's possible to get.

***

111

It's now three weeks since Mark was transferred, and the pain of not having him with me every day has not yet eased. That pain was a shock at first. I hadn't realised how much I'd come to care for him. It took me most of the first week to realise I've fallen in love. Since then, I've been grieving. Attempts to see him have been thwarted by the ever-present wardens, who seem to have an extra pair of eyes where I'm concerned. Jimmy and Brie remain my constant and loyal friends, but neither dares to assist a secret meeting.

I see Mark across the dining room at meal times. Occasionally he looks back at the same time, and we exchange longing smiles. It's good to know he's missing me too, but I still don't understand why we can't be together.

Maybe it's one of these smiles, or perhaps Mark has been to Dominic to complain, but when I enter the Chapel for evening prayers, Mark's missing. The rest of the Benedictines are standing in line. A tall fair-haired chap in his thirties, who usually stands to Mark's right, catches my concerned look and shrugs his shoulders, then turns quickly away. I scan the rows of Brotherhood members, desperate to spot my fiancé.

"Mel, are you okay?" Brie asks me in a low voice. Dominic hasn't yet arrived, and as usual there's a quiet hum of chatter around us.

"I can't see Mark anywhere." She must hear the frantic note in my voice, as she puts an arm around my shoulders and gives me a brief hug.

"He'll be fine, love. He's probably…" Her voice dies away. There are a few reasons why Mark might miss prayers, and none of them are great. Either he's ill, or injured, or being punished. Brie and I stare at each other. "There might be an innocent reason, Mel. Just because we can't think of one, doesn't mean he isn't okay."

I nod, but don't reply, because Dominic has arrived, and the room falls silent. I look at him to see if there's any sign he knows where Mark is, but his face is impassive, and prayers begin immediately. There's no inspection this evening.

Prayers seem interminable. I join in the singing because I have to, but I'm feverishly reviewing all possibilities. Not all the wardens are present, but there is often only a handful of them in the Chapel anyway. They aren't members, so they aren't obligated to attend. Only the ones scheduled to be in Chapel are there. Geoff and Dennis are both missing this evening. Are they responsible for this? Do they have Mark secreted somewhere? Or is he ill, and been taken to the Infirmary?

When we're finally released from prayers, it's six-thirty, and we're supposed to go to our common rooms. Rain is hammering against the stained glass windows as we leave the Chapel, so there's no chance of escaping to the gardens, and perhaps from there to the Infirmary. Could I go to the Infirmary anyway?

I look round for Jimmy, but he's disappeared. I didn't see anyone come to get him, but my attention has been focussed elsewhere. Maybe though, if he's gone somewhere, perhaps I can too.

"Brie, will you cover for me please? I need to check if Mark's in the Infirmary. I need to know he's okay."

"Sure. If anyone asks, I'll say you have a headache and are going to ask for painkillers. If you bump into someone on the way, I suggest you give the same excuse."

"Yes, good idea. Thanks. I don't know what I'd do without you."

Brie's face darkens. "Let's hope you don't have to find out. Go. There's not a lot of time."

I force myself to walk at a steady pace to the Infirmary. Someone with a headache wouldn't be running. Meeting no one en route, I arrive in just a few minutes. The reception area is empty, but as I venture down one of the corridors to check on the wards, I spot Emily coming towards me. Her face breaks into a smile.

"Melissa, isn't it? How lovely to see you. Are you settling... Hey, what's the matter? Come in here." Her delight at seeing me, in such contrast to what's been going on, has reduced me to tears. She escorts me into a small empty office, and indicates a plastic chair for me to sit on. Emily pulls a similar chair over and sits right in front of me. "So, tell me, what's up."

"I need to find Mark." I sniff, and Emily hands me a tissue from the box on the desk. In response to her questions, I tell her briefly about our engagement, and about Mark going missing. I don't mention anything about secret assignations, but it seems I don't need to.

"Melissa, strictly in confidence, is there any chance you could be pregnant?"

"I don't know. My breasts feel a bit more swollen than usual, and my period is a bit late, but it can be a bit erratic anyway." I had wondered, but thought it more likely to be stress. If I am pregnant, I must keep it hidden for at least a month after the wedding. "Why do you ask?"

"Because, oh for lots of reasons. Come on, Mel, you're not stupid. No one must find out, and for that, you're going to need some help. But you also need medical care, and I'm going to provide it."

"How can we cover it up? And shouldn't we check if I actually am first?" The shock of hearing my fears voiced had pushed thoughts of Mark to one side for a moment, but they quickly return. "And I need to find Mark."

"Mark's not been brought in here. We'll deal with that in a minute though. Where do you normally get supplies of tampons?"

"They don't give us tampons, only towels, and we have to sign for them when we collect them from the head of the Benedictines. As the only female Chapter head, she's in charge of supplies of all feminine items."

"Towels are even better, because you can actually use them, and there won't be any evidence that you don't have your period. I wouldn't suggest using tampons when you don't have a period. At least you won't need to stockpile the sanitary towels somewhere. If you use three or four a day, that should be sufficient to fool anyone. I don't imagine anyone would be crazy enough to check your personal supplies. Yes, that's good. For the moment, let's get that confirmation." She hands me a small sample pot. "Put that in your pocket. The toilet is second door on your left if you turn right out of this room."

Returning to the room a couple of minutes later with a full pot, my heart is hammering loudly enough to be heard in the Abbey. Emily takes out a pot of test strips and holds one in the sample for a moment. Her expression hovers somewhere between delight and fear, perhaps a reflection of my own. I raise my eyebrows in a question, and she nods.

"We need to look after you, but I totally understand the need for secrecy. You're not married yet. I won't ask how it happened. You're obviously a resourceful couple." She smiles; a mischievous grin that lights up her face. "You said the wedding is next week? That's not too unmanageable. Babies are born a month early often enough. You should get away with it." She nods in the direction of my bust. "It's those that are the problem. They've definitely grown."

I know my dress has felt a bit tighter the last few days, but I haven't wanted to face facts. The idea of having Mark's baby is thrilling, but with not being allowed to even speak to him, the future is worrying, at the very least.

For now, the priority is to find him.

"If Mark's not here, where do you think he might be?" Emily's thoughts are clearly following my own. Maybe my worried expression has given it away.

"The only place I can think of is the cellars, where Thomas took Tina and me. But I was blindfolded. I don't actually know the way in."

"I can't help you with that, but I think you'll need these." She delves in a cupboard in the wall – white and shelved, rather than dark and panelled – and retrieves a cardigan and a small pen torch. "Put this on. It will help to hide the… er… enlargements. The torch fits neatly in the pocket, without really showing. If anyone asks, it just looks like you're carrying a pen."

"Thanks so much, Emily. I really appreciate your help." I give her a hug, which seems to surprise her, but she hugs me back.

"Take care of yourself. And bring Mark to me when you find him. It sounds like he might need some medical attention."

I nod, and head back to the Abbey, armed with a secret, and my gifts from Emily. Now all I need to do is locate, and possibly rescue, Mark.

Chapter Twenty

In case Mark has returned while I've been in the Infirmary, I pop my head into the common room. Brie sees me and springs out of her seat. She ushers me back in to the corridor.

"Any news, Mel?"

Well, there's lots, actually, but not that I can share.

"He's not there. I ran into Emily, one of the nurses – the nicest one – and she said he's not been admitted. We had a chat, which is why I was such a long time. I hoped he'd be back by the time I got here though."

"He can't come here any more. He's not part of our group now. I guess we could check the Benedictine common room?" Brie's hesitant. I know she doesn't want to give the wardens any excuse to punish her.

"You stay here, in case there's any news, or to cover for me if anyone comes asking. I'll go and check." I smile at her. It's hard to convey how much I appreciate her friendship. Everyone has been taken from me now, except for her and Jimmy. I can't afford to risk them too.

There are a few members roaming the corridors, mostly heads and wardens, but I have a legitimate excuse ready if anyone asks. I find my way to the Benedictine common room, and after a few seconds debating with myself if I should knock, turn the handle and go in.

A quick glance round reveals that Mark's not there, but someone – a middle-aged, dark-haired woman with a scowl – looks up at my entrance.

"What do you want? You're not allowed in here. And if you're looking for Mark, don't bother. He's being punished. Stupid bloke swore at a warden this afternoon. If you ask me, they only wanted half an excuse. Mark's been on their hit list for weeks."

A hole forms in my gut. Maybe the contents have found their way to my chest, as a knot is constricting my ability to breathe. I take a deep breath, and remember my excuse. Even though I've found the information I need, I mustn't abandon the plan. I can't give them an excuse to incarcerate me too. Not now, when I have a baby growing inside me.

"Actually, I was looking for Sheila. I've run out of supplies and I've just come on," I say quietly. It's not something I would shout about if it were true, and I have to be convincing.

"She went to the store room to check on stocks. You'll catch her there if you're quick."

"Great, thanks." I manage a grateful smile, but the woman is glaring at me as if she's seen through my excuse. I don't completely care. It will be down in the store records that I collected supplies for this month, and that's what counts more at the moment. When I've got that sorted, I can go and find Mark. I check my watch on the way to the stores. It's nearly eight-thirty. By the time I've sorted this out, it will be bedtime.

The advantages of searching for Mark after everyone's settled for the night are numerous, as I'll need to search the whole Abbey for an entrance to the cellars, and the risks of being found in the wrong place without an excuse are huge. It will be easier in the dark.

Sheila emerges from the store room between the kitchen and the hidden cupboard as I turn into that corridor.

"Sheila? Excuse me, sorry," I call out as she turns to go in the opposite direction. The corridors of the Abbey are laid out in a square, with some rooms on the inside, such as the common rooms, and dining room, and others on the outside, such as the kitchen, store room and Dominic's office. The rooms on the inside look out on a small grass quadrangle, exposed to a dim light most of the year, but very little sunshine, except in the middle of summer.

Sheila looks over her shoulder, and then turns back with a smile. I don't know her very well, but she's always been friendly and approachable – one of the nicer Chapter heads.

"Melissa, are you okay?"

"Please could I have some supplies? I'm on my last one, and could really do with another before bedtime. I didn't realise I was so low until after prayers. I've only just started again." I give her a rueful grin.

"Yes, of course. Come in for a minute. We'll have to be quick."

I follow her into the store room and wait while she unlocks a cupboard. I gaze around the room and notice a door ajar in the corner. It reminds me of a holiday in France with my family, before Jess was taken. We stayed in a big farmhouse, and in the corner of the kitchen there was a door leading to huge cellars. Dad said they were filled with wine, but Jess and I decided there would be rats or spiders (or possibly both) down there, and we never dared to investigate.

Could this be the entrance to the cellars here? Will I be able to find Mark down there? Plans start to form in my mind, and I'm speculating on how I'll locate the right cellar without being caught myself, when Sheila turns to me with a smile and two packets of sanitary towels.

"Here you go. Have you got any period pains? Do you want some paracetamol?" She gives me a conspiratorial grin. "I managed to get one of the wardens to get these for me. I did him a favour. So I have a few packs in reserve for the nicer ladies in my care. You're one of them, so you can have some if you like."

"Thank you." A small glow eases the knot in my chest. That's so kind of her. With recurrent headaches following my fall in the cellar, I accept gratefully, feeling a bit guilty at taking them under false pretences.

The bell rings for bed, and we both leave to head to our respective dormitories. I hide the paracetamol in amongst the pads, knowing no one would search in there for contraband.

Jimmy is in his cubicle, but seems subdued and won't look at me when I give him his injection.

"Are you okay?"

"Aye, lass, just a bit tired. Be fine after a good night's sleep. Thanks."

I squeeze his shoulder on the way out, and go straight to my cubicle, to lie in bed and wait for the dormitory occupants to fall asleep.

***

The sounds of snoring and sleep-talking are all that can be heard. I've been lying in bed for an hour waiting and thinking; hovering between excitement at my pregnancy and fear for Mark. I can't wait here any more. I have to take a chance and hope that everyone is asleep.

I get up and don the cardigan provided by Emily. It's September now, and the evenings are getting chilly. The cellars have been cold whatever the weather. As an afterthought, I slip on socks and shoes. If I tread quietly, I should be able to prevent loud footsteps, but going without is asking for either a bad cold, or to step on something painful on the way.

Tiptoeing past the rest of my group, my ears are alert to any suggestion of anyone being awake, but I've reached the point now when I just want to get on with it. No one stirs, and I turn the door handle carefully, remembering that in the last week or two it's started to squeak. No squeaks escape tonight, though, and in a minute I'm down on my hands and knees, crawling along the corridors to the store room. The group on sweeping duty this week are much more diligent, and there's no dust on the floor.

The store room door is ajar, and I'm able to squeeze through whilst still on my knees. Although it's dark, there's enough moonlight coming through the window for me to see the shapes of boxes stacked on the floor. I make my way to the door in the corner and take a deep breath. Once inside, I stand up. It must be safe from cameras here. I don't suppose Thomas and the wardens would want their activities spied on. I pull the door to behind me, but it's completely black in here.

What the hell am I doing here? I hate the dark and the musty smell. I want to go back to bed. There's a faint noise

120

from below; maybe mice, or it could be a cry for help. Mark might be down there. It could be him shouting. I have to carry on. I wrap the cardigan round me more tightly and something hard in the pocket bumps against my stomach. Emily's torch. Bless her. When I take it out and twist it, I get a gentle beam; bright enough to light my way down the stone stairs, but not so brilliant as to alert everyone to my presence.

There's no handrail, but I make my way slowly down the staircase with the help of the walls on either side. The right-hand wall runs out three-quarters of the way down, but I'm near the bottom now, and further cries in the distance curb my panic.

***

The passageway at the bottom of the stairways forks, leading both straight ahead and right, but the noise is coming from the right, so I follow the sound of thuds and yells, my stomach clenching in fear at what I might find. I move slowly, anxious not to alert anyone to my whereabouts. After a couple of minutes, another passageway branches off to the right. Should I carry on, or take the branch? The noises sound very close now, and I hear a voice I recognise. Thomas.

"Hit the bugger harder. He deserves it. See if he'll scream a bit. These yells are pathetic."

I flash my torch around looking for a door. They must be in the room next to this passage, but I can't see how to get in.

I continue on, looking for a door, but within a few paces I'm at a dead end. I flash the torch around; there's a bend off to the left. I creep along a few steps, but the yells have lost volume. I stop and back-track – first to the corner, and then back to the T-junction. I can hear it all clearly now: the slashes of a belt or whip; each slash accompanied by a cry of pain. The sound brings tears to my ears. How can they do that to Mark? Why are they? But there's no time to worry about that now.

Creeping along the passageway, I try to be silent. I stop when I get to a door. Now I've got so far, what do I do? What if I make it worse? What if they kill Mark? Perhaps they're killing him now.

I can't bear it any longer, and yank the door handle. Opening the door, I run into a small cell. It's in darkness, but a dull light penetrates through a gap near the far corner, where another door is slightly open.

"Hey, stop a minute. Shut up. I thought I heard something," says Thomas, his voice clear. They're definitely in the next room. Just behind that door. And they know I'm here. Or at least that someone is.

I've nothing to lose now. I run to the door between the two cells. Tugging it open, I enter the room like a fired cannon ball – but one that runs out of momentum before hitting its target. I stop dead at the scene in front of me. Mark's wrists are chained above his head to a hook dangling from the ceiling, and his bare back is covered in blood-filled weals. Thomas leans against the far wall, smirking at me, with his arms folded arrogantly across his chest. The other man – I assume it's a man – is nowhere to be seen.

"Mel, what the hell are you doing here?" Mark twists his head around to see me. He looks awful – pale and haggard – probably as a result of the beating he's just received.

"Let him down from there!" I shout at Thomas, trying to sound authoritative, but even I can hear the pleading in a voice not far from tears. Time to change tack. "Please, Thomas? Just let him go."

I glimpse a shadow at the edge of my vision. There's a whack on the back of my head, and then nothing.

Chapter Twenty-One

I open my eyes slowly. Bright light. Everywhere. I shut them again, but can still sense this intense intrusion. It won't go away. My eyelids flicker open – a minuscule crack. The light's too much.

Other senses: where are they? I sniff. Nothing but familiar smells, but that's good. The awful musty stink of the cells has gone. So, what can I smell? Soap. But it doesn't smell like Mark. Another friend? Someone's holding my hand. Rough skin. Callouses. I know that hand. I open my eyes properly, getting a quick look at the owner before the light overwhelms me again, and I drop my eyelids quickly against the agonising brightness. Jimmy strokes the hand he's holding.

"Are you okay, lassie? I found you on the floor in the cells. You were out of it, and you had a wee bump on the back of your head, so I brought you back here." He seems anxious.

"Whassa mata?"

"Sorry, lass. What did you say?"

I take a deep breath and try again. "Wha sa mata?"

"What's the matter? Is that what you said?"

I nod, and a lorryload of bricks rattles around my head. "Sick! Goin' be sick!" Turning on to my side, I instinctively aim at the floor, away from Jimmy and the bed. I retch until there's nothing left, but there wasn't much to come up anyway – I've hardly eaten all day. While I throw up, my big friend holds my hair out of the way, and pats my shoulder.

Finally, I sink back against my pillow, feeling exhausted and ill. I feel fully conscious now though, and the light no longer hurts. I lie on top of the bedclothes, still in my nightdress and cardigan, though it's now speckled with gastric juice.

"Are you done now, lass? I'll go get some stuff and clean up." He's whispering, and I realise that we're in the dorm, and the rest of the occupants appear to have slept through.

"Jimmy, wait. Did you see Mark when you found me?"

He hesitates, then, "Aye, he was in a bad state, beaten up. On the way up here with you, I popped my head in here, and sent Keith down to take Mark to the Infirmary."

"Does everyone but me know how to get to the underground bit?"

"Aye, maybe. Guess you know the way yourself now though." He looks out of the window into the darkness for a moment, then gets up and closes the curtains. "How did you find it?" he asks, returning to his perch on the edge of my bed.

"I remembered finding a door to the cellars in the store room of an old farmhouse in France. I stayed there when I was a child. It seemed to be a good place to start. I could hear Mark's yells from the common room, but they sounded as though they came from underground. I got taken there blindfolded a while back – with Tina." I stop, unable to say any more. It was mostly a lie anyway. I went to the cellars because I couldn't think of anywhere else Mark could be. I hope Tina is still safe. Dominic had promised, but maybe Thomas is out of control. Why else would he attack Mark?

Swallowing the lump in my throat, I reach out and grasp Jimmy's wrist.

"Jimmy, do you have any idea why Thomas would attack Mark?"

He shakes his head slowly. "Nope, I've not got a clue."

"How did you find us? Weren't you supposed to be in bed asleep?"

"Aye, but I couldn't sleep. After ye did my injection this evening, it stung. I went along to the common room to see if I couldn't find myself a book to read, to take my mind off it. When I got there, I could hear yells. I didn't know whose, but I went to investigate. I nearly fell over you in the dark, and then I found your torch next to you. I turned it on to check you were okay, and then I saw Mark. I already told you the rest. I brought you back here past the dorm, and got Keith up on the way."

I release his wrist.

"Thank you for rescuing us. Did you see Thomas while you were there? Or anyone else? I don't think Thomas was beating Mark himself. It sounded as though he had an accomplice, but I didn't see anyone else."

"I only saw you and Mark." Jimmy put his hands on my shoulders. "Are you okay? Have you stopped being sick now?"

"I think so. My head feels horrible though. I think someone's trying to break out of there with a hammer."

"Let's get you over to the Infirmary as well then. I'll come back and clear up this mess."

I try to sit up, but a wave of nausea rises, and I fall back to my pillows.

"Just wait there, lass. I'll carry you in a minute. Do you mind if I fish around in your drawer for nightclothes?"

"No, whatever. My clean nightie and wash bag are in the top drawer."

I don't quite believe his story about how he found me, but I'm not sure why. Thinking makes my head spin. I don't want to think. I want to make sure that Mark's safe, and then go to sleep.

I shut my eyes for a moment while Jimmy bustles around getting my things together. I doze off, and am vaguely aware of being lifted, and carried like a child in a pair of strong, protective arms.

***

Daylight streams in through an Infirmary window. I wince at the brightness. The escape attempt inside my head is still going on. Maybe the hammers are a bit less violent now – it's hard to judge.

I carefully turn my head to look around me. There's only one other occupant of the four-bedded room. Directly opposite me lies my fiancé, also awake, and watching me with a tender expression on his face.

"Hello," I can't stop a huge smile crossing my face. I'm so relieved to see him. "How are you?"

"That's very polite. I thought you'd ask something a bit more specific."

"Like what? And don't evade the question. How are you feeling?"

"First things first. Okay. I'm a bit sore."

I glare at him.

"All right, very sore. Otherwise I'm fine. I thought you'd want to know what happened and why I was there!"

"Well yes, of course. But it's more important to me that you're okay. The whys and wherefores come later."

"Fair point. How are you feeling? The bloke who was walloping me on the back with a belt stopped when you came in, and disappeared. A minute later he came up behind you and hit you on the head."

"Do you have any idea who it was?" I ask.

"No. Maybe one of the wardens, but for some reason, he kept his head and face covered. He didn't speak either. It was a bit weird. He just seemed to be taking instructions from Thomas. And you still haven't said how you're feeling."

"Sick and headachey. You still haven't said why you were there," I add.

"I'm not sure." He frowns and lowers his voice. "I was on the way to the common room when Thomas pounced on me from behind."

"What do you mean by 'pounced on you' exactly?"

"Okay, that was a bit of an exaggeration. He came up behind me and grabbed my arm. Nearly gave me a heart attack. He had a go at me for smiling at you. Bloody ridiculous. We're engaged, for Christ's sake."

I lie back against the profusion of spotless white pillows. Nothing makes sense any more.

Mark comes over and perches on the edge of my bed. His blue hospital pyjamas are a bit small for him, and his wrists and ankles have goosebumps. I shuffle over to the opposite edge of the bed.

"Get in. You're freezing. And it will save us having to shout across the ward."

Mark pulls the curtains round before climbing in beside me. We snuggle down together. The bed is only just big enough for the two of us, but cuddling him, I realise it's been weeks since I've had a chance to speak to him, let alone hold him. I hug him tight, savouring his closeness.

"Finish your story now anyway," I say, although my words come out muffled against his pyjamas.

"Where was I up to?"

"Thomas grabbed you and told you off for smiling."

"Oh yeah. He seemed really angry, and—"

The curtains open, and Dominic's standing there, glowering.

In his immaculate navy suit, he's dressed more like a bank manager than the Messiah, but the aura of power emanating from him as he glares at Mark sends shivers through me. My fiancé keeps his nerve and stays next to me. What should I do? Dominic's fury seems to stem from finding me in bed with Mark – however innocent the situation – but he's no right to be angry. He wanted us to get engaged. I don't understand his change of heart. This man who started out as a friend, and brought me here to the Abbey, is now completely incomprehensible.

The ominous silence continues. Mark's biceps tense against my arm. I steal a quick look at his face. The anger in his expression shocks me. I don't understand it. Why would Mark be angry with Dominic? Then I realise. He must know Dominic is involved in his beating. The Messiah's look of fury would seem to back up that theory. My revelation loosens my tongue.

"Dominic, you know that Mark's injured as well, don't you? He's a patient here too. He was beaten half to death by Thomas and one of the wardens. We were talking and got cold, so we were just warming each other…"

I tail off. This isn't coming out as I hoped.

Dominic strides over and hauls Mark out of the bed.

"Hey. There's no need for that." Mark yanks his arm out of

the Leader's grasp, and stands up straight. "I am allowed to spend time with my fiancée, I trust?"

"Not in the Infirmary. You should be in separate wards. In fact, I don't think you need to be an inpatient at all. You've got a few grazes, that's all."

"Do you want to see?" Without waiting for an answer, Mark pulls up his pyjama top, revealing a mass of red, angry welts. Some of them have been stitched, and are obviously quite deep. I gasp.

"You can't send him back to the Abbey. He needs to rest." A lump lodges itself at the back of my throat. I can't reconcile this furious and unreasonable Leader with the sweet, kind and charismatic man who enticed me here. This man is now terrifying me with the threat of violence in his eyes. I can almost believe he could be responsible for Mark's predicament, but fear for Mark's welfare keeps me talking.

"Please, Dominic, let him stay? He won't come back in to my bed while we're here, I promise."

"He'd better not." Dominic turns to Mark. "I'll get you moved to a men's ward. You'll both recover more quickly apart. You need to rest in bed, and that won't happen if you keep popping over to see Melissa. Exertion and excitement are bad for concussion patients, so she'll get better more quickly too if you're not here. Get back to the bed you were put in last night for now. I'll arrange for you to be moved as soon as there's a bed made in another ward. When I get back, I expect to see you both lying quietly in your own beds."

He leaves without waiting to see if he's obeyed, but neither of us have the energy or confidence to defy him. Mark returns to his own bed and slumps on to the mattress, covering himself over with the sheets and blankets, and shuts his eyes. He looks defeated and miserable.

Maybe I've made things worse by speaking up, but although my feelings about Dominic are confused, I love Mark too much to allow him to be bullied.

"Mark?" I risk a whisper, and he rewards me by opening his eyes, and flashing me a tired smile.

"Shhh. Not worth getting into trouble," he says quietly. "I

love you."

"I love you too," I say, suddenly worried about why he's saying it. What does he expect to happen?

A moment later, our Leader reappears in the doorway, accompanied by Dr Griffiths. Dominic seems to have calmed down. A gentle smile lights up his face, and he now radiates warmth and charm.

"My children, I apologise. I was so anxious about you both, I lost my temper. Like a parent seeing a naughty child run into the road. You didn't seem to be resting as you need to, so the angry parent in me reacted. I hope you accept my apology?"

Relief floods through me at his explanation. Such a rational reason for his anger. He doesn't hate Mark or feel vengeful towards him. I beam.

"Of course," I glance over at Mark. He still looks weary, perhaps drained by the emotions of the morning, and he must be in considerable pain from his wounds. He raises a half-smile at Dominic.

"Yeah, sure. Can I stay here then?"

"Sorry, Mark. Dr Griffiths agrees with me that it would be better for you to be in separate wards, but he will make sure you're wheeled in to see each other for at least an hour a day as soon as you're well enough. Maybe in a couple of days."

Dr Griffiths' resigned expression tells me he had no choice but to agree.

Chapter Twenty-Two

After another long sleep to try to ease my throbbing head, I wake to find myself in darkness. It's obviously night time. All the lights are off in the ward, although there's a dull glow from the corridor showing through the internal window.

The sleep hasn't worked very well, and I lift a hand to rub a spot on the top of my head – probably the bit that received the blow. It's sore to touch. Some painkillers would be nice, but I have to think of the baby growing inside me. I'll have to ask for some paracetamol. The nausea has eased a bit, so I sit up.

"How are you feeling?"

Dominic's voice startles me, and my heart starts thumping. I turn my head. He's sitting on a chair in the shadows by the half-open cubicle curtain.

"Oh. Hello. I didn't see you there. Sorry. Have you been there long?"

"I've been waiting a while for you to wake up. You didn't answer my question: how are you feeling?"

Confused. I'm trying to gauge his mood, but it's becoming harder to do. His tone is friendly and concerned at the moment. I swallow hard.

"Yes, sorry. My head's hurting and I feel a bit queasy. But otherwise I guess I'm okay."

"Do you feel up to a walk to my office?"

"I don't know. I can try." It's the middle of the night. At least I assume it is, from the quietness and the dark. And from the fact that Dominic is here at all. Why does he want me to go to his office? My pulse is racing now. Nerves or excitement? I honestly don't know.

I sit up and dangle my legs over the side of the bed away from Dominic. I'm only wearing a nightdress now – a white cotton article that falls only to mid-thigh and buttons down the front to the waist. Getting out of bed with no knickers isn't something I like to do with the Messiah watching.

He's round at my side in a few seconds though, and I've barely had time to cover myself with the thin, almost see-through garment. He glances down as I stand up, and I hope he didn't see anything inappropriate.

I'm a bit wobbly on my feet at first, and he puts his arm around me for support. His hand rests under my arm, almost touching my breast, but not quite. His attitude seems informal and caring, but somehow impersonal, and I still have no idea what's going on.

We make slow progress to his office, with me shuffling along at his side. I have no slippers or shoes on, and the floor is quite cold, but the heat coming from the person next to me is keeping the rest of me warm – very warm. By the time we get to the office, his hand has moved slightly and is resting on the side of my breast. My breathing is ragged, and I hope he thinks it's just from the exertion. All my old feelings of attraction have returned, and everything else seems unimportant right now.

Once inside his office, he opens another door, and leads me through to a bedroom. I don't have time to notice much more than the mahogany four-poster bed before he pulls me against him and his mouth is on mine. He tastes of whisky, but I don't care. I can't believe Dominic is kissing me. I've wanted this for such a long time now. He pulls up my nightdress, and he's caressing between my thighs, as he lifts me on to the bed.

A second later, and I'm lying naked on the dark red satin quilt. I watch in a daze as he removes his socks, trousers, shirt and tie, and finally his pants. Then he's lying next to me on the bed, kissing me again. His mouth caresses mine; his tongue invading and exploring gently. All other thoughts have disappeared. All I'm aware of is his hands and his mouth. The hands are touching, massaging and investigating every inch of my body, and I'm trying to do the same to him, but I keep getting distracted. As I get close to touching him intimately, he releases my mouth, and lowers his own gently to a breast, taking the nipple inside his mouth and sucking. A tugging between my legs reminds me how much I want him inside me.

"Please, Dominic, I want you so much. Please."

He lifts his mouth from my nipple and looks at me; a strangely gentle and yet insistent gaze.

"Are you sure about this, Melissa? Do you want me to carry on?" Despite his words, his hand is between my thighs, working me to a fever. I'll die if he stops now.

"Yes," I cry out. "I need you now. Please."

He moves on top of me, and slides between my legs. I open at his touch and allow him to slip inside. His hands massage my breasts, almost painfully as he thrusts inside me, but I don't care. I need this so much. The explosion is sudden and huge. He collapses on top of me for a minute before rolling off and handing me a tissue.

"Bathroom's in there if you want to clean up a bit, darling."

Dominic calling me by that name seems surreal. This whole situation seems strange and dreamlike. I get off the bed and go to the bathroom, where I use the toilet, and clean myself up. I'm shaking, and my headache has returned in full force. I stay in there for a few minutes, waiting for the nausea to settle. It doesn't, but throwing up in the toilet sorts me out, and a couple of minutes lying on the bathroom floor enables me to stand up and return to the bedroom.

"I was just wondering where you'd got to, Melissa. Are you all right?" His voice is gentle and kind, allowing me to relax slightly.

"Just the concussion. I was a bit sick. Perhaps a bit too much strenuous activity." I laugh to show him I don't mind. I don't want him to think I'm criticising him. I still can't believe he wants me.

"Come here. I want to talk to you." Once I'm lying on the bed next to him, conscious now of being cold, he continues. "I can't allow you to marry Mark. I've been having second thoughts for a while now. Before I came to you this evening,

I spoke with the Almighty One, and he relented. You don't need to make the sacrifice to save The Brotherhood anymore. You can be mine."

Shock stills my tongue. I want to marry Mark. I love him. That sounds awful, given what I've just done. This must be my punishment for giving in to lust. But what would happen if I say I don't want to belong to Dominic?

"Yes, darling, you're silent now. I've surprised you. Don't worry; I'll be kind to Mark. You won't be allowed to see him again though. It wouldn't be right. I know you're fond of him and it's not his fault I fell in love with you. You obviously love me too. You begged me to make love to you, and I couldn't resist such sweet innocence. As Messiah, I'm not permitted to marry, but you shall be my consort."

Oh my God. I'm having Mark's baby. What would happen to him if Dominic knew? He mustn't find out. It's been four weeks since I conceived, and if I can only spend the next four weeks making Dominic believe I'm not pregnant, I should be able to carry it off. Lots of babies are born a few weeks early, and four weeks isn't unheard of.

I force a smile, and pretend I'm delighted.

"You're still looking pale, darling. Do you want to go back to the Infirmary for a day or two?"

"Yes please." At least when I'm there, there's a chance I might be able to see Mark and explain to him what's happened. Oh God! How can I? I'd have to explain that I betrayed him. I'm going to have to work this out later.

For now, I put my nightdress back on, ignoring the pounding in my head. Dominic wraps a blanket round me, and escorts me back to the Infirmary. He's holding me as close as he did on the way to his office, but thanks to the blanket, he can't touch me so intimately. It's a relief. I need time to think, but already I'm regretting my actions.

Once back at my bedside, I fall onto the bed. Just that short walk has wiped me out. Well, maybe the activity before didn't help, but there's a dagger-thrower practising inside my skull and I feel as if I might be sick again.

"Please could you pass me that top hat thing?" I point to

the papier-mâché sick bowl on the bedside table opposite mine. Dominic obliges, then kisses me on the forehead. A dagger hits the spot a millisecond later. *Shame that wasn't a real dagger hitting him.* How can I think that? I've just slept with this man. I'm not in love with him but he thinks I am. And he thinks he's in love with me. Daggers won't solve my problem regarding Mark. *Won't they? Surely if Dominic wasn't around, I could be with Mark forever?*

"Goodnight, Melissa. I'll come and see you in the morning." He looks at his watch. "Well, in a few hours anyhow. It's nearly five now."

I force myself to smile and wave, but as soon as he's gone, I slump against my pillows. Digging deep into my motives is an old habit – remnants of therapy after Jess went missing. It's not really Dominic I want to kill, it's myself. I'm mortified by what I've done. I'm carrying Mark's child, and yet I've allowed myself to be seduced by Dominic. I'm a slut. I don't deserve Mark. Dominic won't ever let me see Mark again.

Bile rises in my throat, and I grab the bowl on my bed, vomiting the small amounts of fluid left in my stomach. There's nothing left to come up now, but I continue to retch; torn up by guilt, grief, and made physically unwell by concussion. And I need to protect my baby.

What am I going to do?

Chapter Twenty-Three

Dominic doesn't keep his promise to visit me in the morning, but I don't mind. I don't think I could face him yet. I need to learn to love him. Unfortunately, every time I try to conjure his image, Mark's appears before me instead. The actual Mark has returned to the Abbey. I ask Emily about him.

"I'm sorry, Mel. I tried to convince Dr Griffiths to let him stay here for a while." She lowers her voice. "I could have smuggled him in to see you. I think orders were left that he had to return as soon as possible, and Dr Griffiths has to obey orders."

Why does he have to obey orders? Perhaps it's because Dominic's his boss. I don't know why, but somehow it doesn't sound as though that's the reason. It's a worry for another day, and probably none of my business anyway.

"I wish I could tell him my news." I gaze wistfully across the ward in the direction of the Abbey. "I don't suppose...?"

"I can't, hun. I wish I could. I wanted to when he was here, but I didn't have a chance to ask you, then he disappeared back to the Abbey. It's not a good idea to send him a message."

"No, of course not." I burst into tears, and Emily puts her arms round me in a gentle hug. "Dominic doesn't... want me... to marry Mark... any more," I stammer, between sobs.

"I know. When he left last night, he looked kind of smug. He strode past the office, then came back, and said 'Melissa's mine – no one else is to see her without my express permission.' Git! Sorry, I didn't say that. Christ, that could get me sacked."

That shocks me out of my tears, and I lean back. Emily moves away from the bed and starts to wipe the bedside table. I watch her with affection. She's the only person who knows what's at stake.

"You're fine, I won't be telling anyone. And you're right. He is." I pause. I trust her, but it's hard to say. Deep breath. "He seduced me. I didn't mean it to happen. I feel awful." I run a hand through my tangled hair. "I've betrayed Mark and now I can't even see him."

"Dominic is very charismatic. Don't blame yourself. If he intended it to happen, I don't think there would have been much you could have done to stop him. Look, I'll see if I can arrange for Mark to come to the infirmary for tests or something. I don't expect I'll be able to bring him to you, but I might at least be able to tell him about the baby."

"If you can, that would be great. Please could you tell him I love him?"

"Of course I will." Emily gives me a sympathetic smile, and a pat on the shoulder, before leaving me to my thoughts.

I feel better for having spoken with her. She'll try to see Mark if it's at all possible, and she can let me know how he is. At least Dominic promised not to hurt him.

Two weeks pass before I see anyone from the Abbey. Long boring weeks, punctuated by episodes of sickness, throbbing nauseating headaches, and irregular sleep patterns.

Across the corridor is a ward full of men on a clinical trial. They arrived a week after my chat with Emily, and provide sporadic entertainment. I quickly lose interest in the frequency of blood tests and pill taking, but the short bald man is a moody devil, and likes to pick fights with the other men. I persuade Emily to leave my ward door open a crack, and I can hear the raised voices when they start arguing.

The highlight comes after lunch on the sixth day of their stay. As I return from depositing my lunch in the toilet, I flop on to the bed. I shut my eyes, allowing the world to settle down on its axis.

"Oy, Charlie!" someone shouts from the men's ward. I open my eyes a fraction and glance towards the source.

"That's Charles to you, Frank," comes the pompous voice of an older man in blue satin pyjamas.

"Don't your pretty wife work down the Victoria 'otel?"

says Frank.

"My wife is the restaurant manager there, yes. I'm sure she'd be thrilled to discover you find her pretty," Charles replies drily.

"Oh, she knows, mate, she knows!"

"What do you mean?"

"She likes her men bald and cuddly, does Beryl. Not the dried-up old stick she married. She told me she went off you years ago, after you 'ad it off wi' that tart wot worked down your office."

Charles remains still in his bed, apart from his mouth which opens and shuts like a demented fish. His reaction tells me, and probably the other ten men in his ward, that Frank's right – on all counts. Charles apparently didn't know that his wife discovered his infidelity. Silence reigns in the ward for several heartbeats, as the 'dried-up old stick' processes the information.

I feel slightly sorry for Charles. How can I condemn anyone for giving in to lust? And whilst Frank has perhaps been in the same unfortunate dilemma, his crass announcement of Beryl's preferences antagonise me instantly.

Suddenly, the man in satin pyjamas leaps out of bed, grabs his bald offender by the throat, yanks him on to the floor, and starts pummelling him with his fists, adding in the odd kick for good measure. Everyone, me included, stares in shock. Charles gets in several blows before a thin wiry man jumps in and hauls Charles off, before he can beat Frank to a pulp.

Charles fights against him for a moment, before turning and bursting into tears on the thin man's shoulder. I watch, fascinated, as the occupants of the men's ward focus their attention purely on Charles, and ignore the battered man writhing, bruised and bleeding on the floor. Pity wrenches at me. Just because Frank's a stirrer, and wife-stealer, doesn't mean that he should be allowed to bleed to death. He might have internal injuries as well. Both he and Charles look to be well into their fifties, or even older.

I slip out of bed, and run in to the ward opposite. Eleven

men turn to stare at me. The twelfth stops rolling around the floor, and sits up gingerly to see who's invaded their precinct. Charles ceases crying on the thin man's green cotton nightwear, and disappears through a door in the corner – the bathroom, I presume.

"Are you okay?" I ask Frank. He's even less attractive close up, but I'm sure the fast-developing black eye, and blood pouring from the corner of his mouth, doesn't help.

"Do I friggin' look okay?" He grips my wrist and pulls me down so I'm at eye level with him. Maybe rescuing him was a mistake.

"No, but there's no need to be nasty. I didn't need to come in here. I'm a patient just like you. I was trying to be nice, but if you don't want any help, you can let go, and I'll go back to my bed."

Applause hits my ears like a tidal wave, and I look round. The other men are standing in a semi-circle behind me, clapping. I catch the eye of the tall thin man, and he comes over to where I'm crouching on the floor in front of Frank. He gently removes Frank's hand from my wrist, and pulls me away.

"Lee, go and get one of the staff. Someone needs to clean up our little troublemaker there. I'll help this young lady back to her room." A ginger-haired man with what I consider to be a very silly-looking beard leaves the room, and heads in the direction of the exit.

"Excuse me," I call out. "The staff room is that way." I point in the opposite direction. Ginger-bearded Lee grins and turns round.

The thin man puts a hand on my shoulder and guides me out of the door.

"I'm Greg Matthews, at your service. Where's your ward?"

"Just here, thank you. I'm Melissa, or Mel if you prefer."

"Excellent. Mel it is then. I should have guessed you were this close. You must have heard what was going on."

"Yes. I wouldn't have interfered. I wasn't very impressed with Frank, to be honest, but everyone seemed to be more interested in Charles crying than the fact that one of your room-mates was bleeding all over the floor." I don't mean to sound critical. Greg's being very sweet to me.

"No, you were quite right. Frank is a wart – a thoroughly unpleasant, and painful chap – but we should have sorted him out. I expect Lee will be along in a moment with one of your doctors, so perhaps you'd better get back to bed. Thanks for your help, Mel. May I pop in and visit you later, when everything has settled a bit?"

"That would be lovely, thanks. See you later then."

I give him a cheery wave, and slip back into bed – just in time, because seconds later, Dr Harper marches down the corridor and erupts into the men's ward. Greg slips in unnoticed behind the doctor, and after a quick wink through the window, sneaks back to his own bed, which fortunately is out of Harper's line of sight.

***

After yesterday's fiasco on the ward, I've vowed to stay out of trouble, at least for a day. I dread to think what would have happened if Dr Harper caught me out of bed, however good the cause. I'm still watching the activities opposite, but discreetly. I'm trying not to dwell on the situation with Mark and Dominic, or on my pregnancy, so focussing on the men's ward is a good distraction. Regular visits to the bathroom to be sick have become part of my daily pattern. I'm also taking paracetamol four times a day for the appalling headaches. It isn't making a lot of difference, but I daren't use anything stronger, particularly in this first trimester.

It seems as if the men are also trying to behave, as they're gathered in little groups, chatting and playing cards. Everything remains calm until after lunch. A nurse is trotting around the ward giving injections. I assume they're a standard part of the trial, but when she stops at Frank's bed, she hovers over him for a moment, and then screams like a banshee.

I sit up in bed, unsure whether to go and assist. Greg's at

her side in seconds, pulling her away from the bed, and Lee runs, yet again, in the direction of the staff room, although Dr Harper and Dr Griffiths must have heard, as they meet him in the corridor, at the edge of my field of vision. I crane my head to see past the nurse, and notice that Frank's head has swelled to massive proportions, and he's slumped awkwardly back against his pillows. I can't be sure from my vantage point, but his face seems to have a bluish tinge.

Why didn't anyone notice this before? Why didn't I notice? Were the curtains shut? Desperately searching my memory, I realise that he was under the covers before, and appeared to be asleep. Now he's exposed for everyone to see.

A moment later, Dr Griffiths wheels a defibrillator in to Frank's cubicle, and once Dr Harper and the banshee nurse are inside, he pulls the cubicle curtains shut. A tense silence follows, although as my door remains shut, I wouldn't have heard much anyway.

I wonder what Frank has been given, and why it affected him so differently. Have the injections been labelled with the names of the men? Could anyone have tampered with them? It seems so unlikely. The only man with a real grudge against Frank is Charles, and he really doesn't seem the type to tamper with someone's medication, even supposing he had the opportunity. Or the knowledge.

I give myself a shake – how could I think such things? What a stupid theory! It must be an accident. Frank must have some undiagnosed medical condition that's reacted badly with what he's been given.

Just as I reach this conclusion, the cubicle curtains open. Frank's eyes are closed, but he looks grey and his face is swollen. All the men stand up, even Charles, showing polite respect as the doctors wheel the bed past them and out into the corridor. I hastily turn on to my side as if I've not been watching the whole time, but no one looks at me.

It's evening, several hours later, when Greg pops his head around the door.

"Are you all right, Mel? Has anyone been in to see you today?"

"I'm okay thanks, but no, not really. Only to bring meals and take away empty plates. My favourite nurse seems to be off duty, and none of the others bother to chat." I hesitate. My time in the Abbey has made me reluctant to ask questions. Greg sits down in the chair by the end of my bed and gives me a sympathetic smile.

"Did you see what happened?" he asks.

"A bit. I heard screaming and tried to see what was going on. I saw them wheeling someone out. Who was it?" Again, that reluctance to be completely open. I like Greg, and am inclined to trust him, but natural caution prevails.

"It was Frank."

"What happened?"

"As far as I could tell, he had the same injection that three of the other men had received already. It seemed to react badly with Frank, although the others were all fine. His head swelled up like a balloon, and he went blue and stopped breathing. The nurse screamed, and the medical team arrived to resuscitate. They managed to bring him round and he's been taken to one of the big teaching hospitals – I believe he's in Intensive Care now."

"Oh my goodness! What happened to the rest of the injections?"

Greg shoots me a curious glance, as though I've asked a strange question.

"I don't know. I expect they will be sent back to the labs for analysis. One of the doctors said this evening that they'd been filling out forms all afternoon. Needless to say, after Frank's injection went so badly wrong, none of the other injections were given out."

"Good, I should hope not." I smile at him. "Thanks for coming to tell me anyway. It's so nice to see a friendly face, especially when something horrible has happened."

He reaches over and squeezes my hand. "No problem, Mel. I'll come and see you again tomorrow if I can. Try not to worry about anything, okay? Goodnight."

"Thanks, Greg. Goodnight."

***

Greg becomes a regular visitor over the next three days, and keeps me entertained with gossip about the other inmates of the ward. More interestingly, he tells me about himself – although I have to drag it out of him. On the third day after the removal of Frank, Greg pops his head round the cubicle curtains after lunch. I still feel queasy, and the half-eaten remains of beans on toast lurk on the tray nearby.

"Afternoon, Mel." He smiles. "Can I come in?"

"Yes, of course. You can draw back the curtains if you like. I always have them closed while I eat lunch." I decline to add that it's a precaution in case the food makes me throw up. Chatting usually helps though, so I'm fairly safe now that I have company. Greg draws back the curtains and sits on the orange chair next to the bed.

"I have to be back on the ward for tests in half an hour, but we should be okay until then."

"Are you enjoying the trial?" I ask. "It seems strange to choose to spend a couple of weeks in hospital."

"I'm getting paid," he says. "We're only here for a few more days anyway, to observe the effects of the pills they gave us. The injection aspect of the trial was obviously stopped. I think they're just trying to salvage some data if possible."

"You know what I mean. I can't believe the pay is that good. Surely they're not allowed to bribe you to participate?" I'd like to ask if there's been any news about Frank, but I'm not sure I want to know the answer. I guess if he'd died, we'd be swarming with police now anyway.

"Not exactly, but it compensates for missing a couple of weeks at work. I could have gone on holiday instead, but the kids are all grown up now, and my wife has gone on a two-week writing retreat. It's been something she's wanted to do for ages, and this seemed to be a good opportunity. I didn't want to stand in her way."

"What does she write?" I ask.

"Children's books mostly, but I've read both her novels,

and enjoyed them very much from an adult perspective. I may be a bit biased, but I'm an avid reader, and I think she has talent. She's not found an agent yet, and hopefully this retreat will help towards that goal. She should get a chance to do a bit of networking while she's there."

"What do you do?" I manage to slip the question in as though it hasn't been driving me mad with curiosity for days.

"I'm a lawyer," he says. "Do you have an email address?"

"An old one. I've not used it since I've been here though." I give him the address anyway, which is an easy one to remember, and comes back to me automatically as soon as I think about it.

"I'll email my details to you. If the worst comes to the worst, look me up online when you get out of here."

"What makes you think I'll leave?" I frown. I can't think about leaving. Not while Mark's here. And Tina. And Pete's out there, waiting.

"I don't know, Mel. Sorry, I didn't mean to offend you. Sometimes life can move in unexpected directions. I wanted you to know there will always be a friend for you out there. Don't worry about costs or fees or anything. If circumstances change, and you want somewhere to go, give me a call. Do you promise?"

"Yes, of course. Thank you." I'm still confused. Perhaps he doesn't understand my commitment to The Brotherhood, and to my friends, but I appreciate his kindness.

Maybe things will change when I've had the baby. I've never seen a baby in The Brotherhood, so it might be difficult, but I have to trust Dominic to make sure everything works out.

I turn to Greg with a friendly smile, trying to make up for my earlier frown. Standing in the doorway, Dominic glowers. My heart contracts, and my stomach does its own internal belly-flop. I take a deep breath, and strain to keep my smile in place.

"Hi, Dominic. This is one of the men from the trial. Greg's been kind enough to keep me company a couple of times. It can be a bit boring in here otherwise."

I know as soon as I've said it that it's the wrong thing to say. Dominic's face wears the same expression he has when speaking to Mark – a barely-suppressed revulsion. I couldn't understand it then, and I still don't understand why he's looking at Greg the same way now.

"Melissa, get your things together. You've rested here long enough, if you're well enough to get bored."

I cringe at the sarcasm in his voice, and hope Greg won't take offence by the Messiah's malevolent behaviour. I hope I'll get an opportunity to explain, but it doesn't look promising.

"I'll take myself off then. It was nice speaking to you Melissa. Good to meet you, Dominic." Greg doesn't offer to shake hands with the Messiah. He clearly has the sense to realise it wouldn't be welcome.

I flash him an apologetic smile, and with his back to Dominic, Greg gives me a friendly wink. I relax a little. Whether offence has been taken or not, the tall man doesn't seem to hold it against me.

When he's gone back into his ward and shut the door behind him, Dominic turns to me.

"Can't you get through a week without flirting with someone?" he says coldly.

"I wasn't flirting. No one's been to see me for days. Even Jimmy hasn't come in for his injections. I suppose Brie's been doing them."

"He's been taught to do them for himself. It's getting ridiculous. He's a grown man. Children inject themselves with insulin – there was no reason he couldn't do it himself. Anyway, that's not the point. Melissa, my child, you need to return to the Abbey. I want you to move into my quarters so I can keep an eye on you."

"I'm still not feeling well," I argue, hoping to be allowed to stay a bit longer. It's about a week too soon to be able to convince Dominic that I could be pregnant with his child. After seeing his reaction to my mild friendship with Greg, I dread to think what he would do to Mark if he knew I was already pregnant before he'd seduced me. "Can't I stay a bit longer? You can put me in a different ward if you prefer."

"Perhaps you're not ready to be in with me just yet. I can't always control my passion when we're alone, and if you're still suffering from the concussion, it wouldn't be good for you. There's a small bedroom upstairs from me, that's unused. It has an en-suite. I occasionally have visitors who need to stay over, and it's suitable for them. That way, if you need to rest in bed, you can have the peace and quiet you need. I'll ask Dr Griffiths to visit you each day to check up on you."

His eyes have softened, and relieved at the solution, I smile and nod. An en-suite will be adequate concealment for the vomiting, which continues to make my mornings miserable, and maybe later in the day I can join the rest of my group.

"That would work, thank you, Dominic. It's not that I don't want to be with you, but I am still getting these headaches."

"It's fine, my child. I'm here to look after you, not inflict pain." A strange light gleams in his eyes, but maybe I imagined it, as he pats me on the shoulder, and walks back to the door. "Come to see me when you get back to the Abbey. I'll expect you in my office in twenty minutes. That should be long enough for you to get dressed and bring your things across."

Twenty minutes is barely enough time to get showered and dressed, and get across to the Abbey. I have to make do with something my mum used to call 'a lick and a promise', and with a quick wave at Greg, who's having his blood pressure checked in the ward opposite, I carry my bag quickly through the corridors and over to the Abbey.

I still don't know if Emily has had a chance to speak to Mark, but I have to put that out of my mind for a while. It's time to face Dominic in his office. I take a deep breath and knock on the door.

145

Chapter Twenty-Four

My racing pulse and rapid breathing refuse to settle. My feelings towards Dominic are complicated; the attraction that led me to sleep with him is still present, but is tempered by his curtness in the Infirmary and my feelings for Mark.

A silence follows my knock. Was it too quiet? I try again, a bit more firmly.

"Come in." Dominic's voice sounds friendly, and I relax a fraction. I open the door. He waves me to the chair in front of his desk.

I sit in front of him on the hard wood. Sitting back in his black leather swivel chair, he watches me. The smile on his face suddenly reminds me of a spider with a fly caught in its web. Fear catches in my throat, and desire disappears. It seems unlikely ever to return.

"When did you find out you're pregnant?" he asks.

How does he know?

"This morning," I say. "My headache seemed better, but I still felt sick. And I should have come on by now. I don't know for certain though. How did you know?"

"One of the doctors mentioned you're still being sick. I put two and two together. Is it mine?"

"Of course," I lie. In theory there's been no opportunity for me to have relations with Mark, or indeed anyone else. I hope Dominic's not got enough experience of women to do the maths. He comes round the desk and stands right in front of me.

"I've changed my mind about sleeping arrangements. You're definitely going to be staying in here with me. I'll ask Brie to bring your things in from the other room."

"Can't I go and get them myself?" The reason to avoid Dominic's presence in the mornings has just vanished, but I'd like a few minutes space to get my head around the latest development.

"I need to keep an eye on you, Melissa. I can't have you speaking to Mark anymore. I'd banish him from The Brotherhood, but I recognise this isn't entirely his fault, and I prefer to show mercy. I'm not unkind."

As Dominic has already hinted that Mark and I are to be separated, this isn't a shock. It's not kind though. Mark and I love each other, even if I did betray him. My insides do a strange attempt at a somersault, and I suppress the urge to be sick.

"All this change has made me feel a bit funny. Do you mind if I go and lie down? Maybe Brie can bring my things through to your room?"

He grabs my wrist and hauls me up.

"You go lie down on my bed, Melissa," he whispers in my ear. "Brie will bring your clothes through to my office. You won't be seeing her for a while."

His hand brushes against my breast, but now that fear has replaced lust, I pull away.

He glances down at me. "I'll make you want me again. I know you're in shock at the moment, but things have to change. I can't risk you running off with Mark and my baby. This is my baby you're carrying, Melissa. I own you, and you will not leave this suite until I say so." His lips crash down on mine, and his tongue invades my mouth in a cruel imitation of his previous seductions, but it only lasts a moment. He releases my mouth, and yanks me by the wrist into his room.

Hanging from a beam across the four-poster bed, suspended by a pair of tights, is that resuscitation doll. The knife still protrudes from her chest.

The room shimmers in front of me and then fades.

When I come round, I'm tucked up tightly in the four-poster. I have no clothes on under the sheets. Annie's still hanging from the beam, and Dominic stands behind her in the middle of the room. I don't know how long I've been out of it, but he's still wearing his suit. He looks the same as usual, except for the expression on his face. The spider has caught his fly now, and is making it very clear that the fly is trapped, and completely at his mercy.

Once it's obvious that I'm fully conscious, he strolls from the room. A click suggests he's locked the door behind him, and when I get out of bed and tentatively turn the handle, nothing happens, except a mocking voice from the other side of the door,

"Nice try, Melissa. Rest now. I'll see you later."

***

I get back into bed, and try not to look at the dummy. I fail. Gritting my teeth, I slither out from beneath the sheets and look around for some clothes. The room is tidy, and there's nothing lying around for me to dress myself in. I feel vulnerable naked, but I'm alone except for this awful doll suspended from the four poster. I stand on the end of the bed, and reach up. My fingers quickly become numb from being raised up, and the weight has made the knot very small and fiddly. I struggle to untie it, and when I start feeling dizzy, I give up and get back into bed. I can't bear looking at the dummy and turn my face away, shutting my eyes tightly.

It seems like a year ago that I was in the Infirmary chatting away to Greg. Now I'm trapped in a room with a stabbed and strangled doll. I thought it was Pete. All along I've thought it was him that put it in my room to scare me. Now I don't know. Did Dominic see it there and take it away for future use? Or did he plant it in the first place, to induce such fear in me that I had to come here to escape?

I try to face the probable facts. I've been duped. A horrible squirming sensation accompanies this thought – like worms in my gut.

Focus on the good things. I've made some lovely friends here: a new family. Brie, Jimmy, Tina and Mark are more than friends. But I've betrayed Mark! I'm carrying his child. I haven't the guts to admit it to Dominic. However much I rationalise that I'm protecting Mark (and I might well be), if I had enough courage, I would have found him, told him he's going to be a father, and got the pair of us out of this place. We could have sorted out somewhere to live. He might have friends or family around. Or we could have gone to a shelter.

It's too late now. There's no escape from here. I have to keep quiet, or Dominic might kill Mark. I've no doubt now that our Leader is capable of violence. Murder might be a bit extreme, but if pushed, I believe Dominic would go that far.

A vice tightens around my chest, and I find it hard to breathe. I force myself to take a few slow breaths to calm myself down, but it doesn't ease, and I start to panic. I sit up, averting my gaze from Annie, and try again to breathe normally. I fail. I'm hyperventilating.

I'm going to die. Mark will never know I'm carrying his child.

The door opens. Dominic comes in. He rushes over to me, and puts his arms around me, rubbing my back. He mutters soothing nothings in my ear. I struggle, scared, but my breathing is really shallow now, and that's more frightening than the Messiah's closeness. I give in and eventually his treatment works. I begin to relax, my breathing settling down to some semblance of normality.

His gentleness reassures me. Perhaps he's going to relent. Then I catch sight of Annie dangling from the beam still and I stiffen.

He must be able to sense the change as he disentangles himself and stands up.

"Are you going to be a good girl, Melissa?"

"I'll try." I don't know what being good means, but if it will help protect my friends and me, I'll do anything.

He watches me for a long moment from the end of the bed, and finally extracts something small from his trouser pocket. It's a penknife. He cuts the tights and Annie falls, catching a glancing blow on her bare torso from the wood surrounding the mattress, before ending up on the floor with a thud. He leaves her there, but at least I can't see her now.

"Rest now, child. You should try to sleep. I'll be back later with some food for you."

Exhausted and confused, I fall into a deep sleep.

***

I awake to a dim light to find Dominic standing over me with a plate and a glass in his hands. He sets them down on the mahogany bedside table.

"Feeling better now, child?" His voice sounds solicitous.

I feel the grogginess that comes from sleeping heavily during the day, but caution enters my brain quickly, and I give him a polite half-truth.

"Much better, thank you." I can at least breathe properly; a distinct improvement.

"Sit up then, and have some food. It's not very exciting, but then food is for sustenance, not enjoyment." He puts the plate on my knees, and I look down at the dish of nut roast, mashed potatoes and cabbage. I ignore the queasy lurch of my stomach, and take the proffered cutlery.

"Thank you."

He waits in a nearby armchair until I've finished eating, before he speaks again.

"Brie brought over your things from your old room. I had a rootle around, and found your knitting. I thought you might like it to give you something to do. I won't be around much for you to talk to, and there won't be any visitors, so you'll be better to have something to occupy yourself. Would you like me to get you some patterns and appropriate wool, so you can start knitting some baby clothes?"

For the first time since leaving the Infirmary, enthusiasm takes a grip.

"That would be great. I'd love that." I smile, until I realise he's frowning. My smile falters.

"What do you say?"

"Sorry, what do you mean?"

"What's the magic word?" He towers over me, oozing aggression.

I gaze at him, perplexed. A distant memory returns, of a spiteful teacher saying the same thing to me when I'd been a child of about eight. I shiver, and goosebumps rise on my arms.

"Please," I say tentatively. Surely this is not a sensible conversation for two adults.

"*Please could you get some nice wool and baby patterns, Dominic?* is what you must say." He picks up my empty plate and throws it on the floor, where it smashes into tiny fragments. An ugly sneer mars his usually handsome features.

"Please will you get me some wool and baby patterns, Dominic?" Fear constricts my throat, and the words sound hoarse.

He sits down on the bed, and brings his face to inches away from mine. Cold fury gleams in his eyes.

"You didn't repeat it properly, Melissa. Say it again."

"I can't remember the exact words, I'm sorry," I say, even more hoarsely. I want to back away from him but I'm pinned against the headboard.

He takes my knitting needles and wool from the holdall on the floor by the door. He pulls the needles out of the knitting, and yanks at the navy blue wool, unravelling the first inch or so of my ten inches of knitted scarf before giving up and throwing the resultant mess on the covers next to me. He returns to the bed, and pulls away the sheet that I'd wrapped around me before eating. He stares at my bare breast. Something akin to disgust is on his face; I'm not sure why, but I daren't ask.

I hardly dare to breathe. I just sit up in the bed, terrified of what he might do next.

"You'd better make this wool last a long, long time then, Melissa, because you won't be getting any more."

Seconds later, he's gone from the room. I hear the click of the lock, and with a sense of relief, pull the sheet back up.

Chapter Twenty-Five

When Dominic returns later that evening, he finds me sitting up in bed knitting. Red rims round my eyes and a damp handkerchief at my side show I've spent much of the intervening time crying. Although I hope he doesn't notice.

"What am I to do with you, child?" His voice sounds weary and resigned. I sniff and pick up the hankie, blowing my nose loudly. "I can't relent, I'm afraid. You need to learn who's in charge – for the sake of you and our baby. Discipline is paramount in bringing up a child."

"So is love," I summon my courage. Maybe this is my opportunity to reason with him.

"You don't love me just now. You're angry with me for taking you from Mark and your friends. Believe me, it's for the best. You'll learn to love me again. In the meantime, we'll have to make do with discipline. Go and wash your face, Melissa, you look a mess. I don't want to sleep with someone who looks as ugly as you do right now."

My stomach lurches in shock as his words hit me. I don't think I'm vain, but I've got used to thinking of myself as okay-looking. Perhaps my pregnancy has sapped my looks, or maybe it's just the crying I've indulged in for the last couple of hours. I leave the bed, pulling the sheet with me, and rush to the en-suite bathroom in the corner of the room. My washbag is on the shelf, and I open it with relief, extracting toothbrush, paste, soap and flannel. Dominic must have brought it in this afternoon while I was asleep.

I check myself in the mirror. He's right – I look dreadful. A good wash improves matters, but my eyes are still a bit red, and my hair hangs limply around my face. I take a deep breath.

"Dominic," I call out from the bathroom, "would you

mind if I wash my hair? I can do it in cold water."

A second later he's in the doorway of the en-suite, shoulder resting casually against the doorframe.

"What did I tell you about saying please?"

"Sorry, Dominic, please can I wash my hair?"

"Did no one ever teach you the difference between 'can' and 'may'? Yes, you can, but you may not. You should have asked properly to start with." He stands up straight and beckons. "Come with me. You're not sleeping with me tonight."

My heart leaps for a brief moment; maybe he'll allow me to sleep in the dormitory. Perhaps he'll take me back to the Infirmary. Then I look at his face. A cruel smile distorts his features, turning him into an evil stranger. I know now – deep down in the pit of my stomach – that I won't be sleeping somewhere safe and familiar.

He leads me first back into his room, where he opens a wardrobe, and extracts a blanket and pillow from a shelf. I take the opportunity to don my slippers, a nightdress and cardigan.

He shoves the bedding into my arms, and removes a hardback copy of *Oliver Twist* from the bookcase opposite the bed. His hand reaches in, and the bookcase slides to the side to reveal a set of stone steps, similar to those leading from the storeroom. Dominic grabs my shoulder and, turning on a torch collected from the fake bookshelf, propels me down the steps, and along a stone passageway. In the dim light, I see another staircase – presumably the one I descended last time I came in to the cellars.

Marching past the passage on the right where I found Mark, a few metres further on, we turn left, and then right again. Dominic opens the next door we come to, and shoves me in. I just manage not to fall, but I graze my hands on the stone wall as I steady myself. He shines the torch on the floor, and speaks for the first time since we left the bathroom.

"You have one minute to make your bed, then I'm leaving. Such a shame I didn't think to bring another torch. How will I get back if I leave it here?" He pretends to consider the difficulty. "Hmm, oh dear! I'll have to take the torch with me and you'll have to stay in the dark, by yourself. Are you scared of the dark, Melissa? Yes, of course you are. I remember how terrified you were that night Leonard died. I came to get you. You thought it was the first time I'd noticed you, but I'd marked you out a long time ago – as soon as I read of your parents' death, and discovered they'd left a daughter and a house. I engineered our meeting, and made sure you were keen to join here. I watched you round the hospital for a few days before the memorial service, and noticed the dummy in that big meeting room. I sent Thomas to plant the dummy in your room that day. He's quite talented at picking locks. I didn't have time to mess about 'grooming' you for ever. It worked. You ran straight into my arms. Then I waited for you to fall in love with me. It was important that you liked me enough for my plan to work. Mark nearly ruined it, and the Almighty One seemed to be giving me conflicting advice. But I worked it out in the end. He only wanted you to like Mark, to ensure your good behaviour. " He pauses, then adds in a soft voice, "Don't waste time, Melissa. You have about ten seconds left. And be grateful I allowed you some clothes. Next time I won't be so nice."

I hastily lower my bundle to the ground, and start to spread out the blanket, but before I get any further, the torch light disappears and the door slams. I hear the familiar click of a key in a lock, albeit a different lock, and probably a different key. Now I'm left in total darkness. Panic envelops me in its icy grip, and once again I struggle to breathe, as my heart pounds against my ribs. Chilled, I dig my hands deep into my cardigan pockets to wrap it round myself – and find a glimmer of hope.

Nestled in the right-hand pocket is the pen torch Emily had given me. Anxious in case Dominic is still standing outside the door (I forgot in my panic to listen for receding footsteps), I turn the torch away from the door, and shine it towards the blanket on the ground. The pale light calms the panic, and the tight band eases from around my chest. I sit down on the thin bedding, and place the pillow at one end. I wrap the blanket around me, and rest on my side, trying without success to find a comfortable position.

I don't know how long my battery will last, so I ration myself. I'll only turn it on when I can't stand the pitch darkness anymore. When panic creeps in, I'll count to ten. Only then, if I have to, can I turn on the torch.

I spend a long time thinking about how dark it is, and wondering how long I can last without turning on my torch. I turn it on once but then turn it straight off again. Crazy thoughts run around my head. What if he's left me here to starve? Does he want to kill me? How long can I survive in the dark with no food or water? The blackness seems to envelope me, and the panic intensifies.

I fumbled for the *On* button and frantically press it. Nothing happens. A scream rises in my throat, but I manage to suppress it. My fingers shift, and another button comes within their touch. I push it, and the dim light fills the cell.

I draw a deep breath. The walls are no closer than they were at first. My blanket and pillow are still within reach. Nothing has moved, nothing has changed.

I take another long, deep breath and feel myself relaxing. I sit up. It feels better than lying down. I'm more in control. I force myself to turn off the torch again. How will I cope if the battery dies? I realise it's better to keep it off, and have it there in case of an emergency. My panic will be far worse if I've no torch to use.

Somehow, making that decision empowers me. I stand up – the unlit torch still in my hand – and count paces, walking directly forwards to the wall. Keeping my hand on the wall, I measure the paces along each side of the room, returning eventually, with five paces, to the pillow on the ground. I pick it up, and pace my way so that I'm in the corner of the room, along the wall from the door. Not directly opposite the door, as I first thought would be preferable. A new instinct of preservation has kicked in. Now when that door opens, I'll have a split second to get myself together before he sees me.

Settled in my corner, with the pillow resting against the wall, and my eyes closed, I pretend to myself that it isn't really dark – I'm just trying to get to sleep. Thoughts crowd into my head.

When did everything go wrong? And why? From what Dominic said, he's been planning this for months.

I curl up in my corner, hugging my knees, as I think back to recent weeks. Dominic seduced me. I shouldn't have let that happen – I was flattered at being chosen by the Messiah. I've had a crush on him for ages, dating back partly to when he rescued me from the cell the night Leonard was taken away, but probably even further back – to when he was nice to me before I came here. If he lets me behave, I will try to be good, but everything I do or say seems to be wrong at the moment.

A vision of Mark's bloody, scarred back creeps into my mind. I do know what Dominic meant. If I do anything to make him angry – properly angry – he'll take it out on Mark.

Power: the ability to manipulate me by threatening harm to those I care about most. Once Dominic realised the intensity of my feelings for Mark, he knew he'd won.

What horrifies me most is knowing that this is the real Dominic. The charm he's been using on me for all these months has been his way of gaining control. Now he has it. Locked in this cell, or even if he allows me to return to his room, there's no prospect of escape.

I fight back an urge to cry. Tears won't help me. Not now. I wonder what he'll do to me once he realises I understand him. I shudder. It doesn't bear thinking about, but given his recent comments, the more pertinent question is: *What will he do to Mark?*

I can't let Dominic know how I really feel. He has to think I'm shocked and upset by his behaviour (true anyway), but also confused. Maybe I can induce more of the charm with a bit of careful planning. That is, if I ever get out of my current predicament.

While he's manipulating me, I shall have to manipulate him, but the stakes for me are so much higher. I need to be clever. And I need to pretend I didn't understand what he told me at the door.

I don't know if I can get through this. I grit my teeth and ignore the fear tying up my insides.

I shift my bottom, which is getting pins and needles, and against all the odds I fall asleep.

***

Gradually the cold from the stone floor seeps through the blanket and penetrates my consciousness. I awake to stiff, cold limbs, and open my eyes to the pitch darkness.

My heart rate accelerates and it takes several deep breaths to stifle the panic, until I remember the resolutions I decided on earlier.

I rub all the bits of me that have been in contact with the floor. I need the toilet. Shining the torch around quickly I spot a grate in the opposite corner. Not ideal, but it'll have to do. Standing up, I wiggle my legs and arms feebly to eliminate the kinks, but the other sort of elimination is becoming urgent.

I feel my way along the walls to the relevant area, and take my slippers off. I left the torch over by my bedding, so have to sort myself out in the dark. No matter – the dark has been conquered to some extent, and has fewer fears for me now. Feeling with my bare feet, I locate the grate, and squat down for my morning wee. With a bit of careful handling, my cardigan and nightie are kept out of harm's way, but I daren't remove my nightie completely – Dominic could return any moment. I hated him pulling away the sheet yesterday. I don't want him looking at me anymore. Rising from my squat, I rearrange my clothing, don my slippers (which have been left neatly in the corner, three paces from the grate), and feel my way back to the bedding. I lie down again for a moment. Morning sickness has failed to take account of my situation, and I wonder how long I can control it before having to return to the grate.

As I struggle for control over my stomach, the sound of footsteps intrudes. I prepare myself mentally for the door to open. The footsteps get louder for a moment, then pause – the owner can't be far from the door. I hold my breath. The sound resumes, then subsides. Whoever it is must have decided to go away. I breathe again, but then start to panic once more. What if Dominic has left me here to die?

Another wave of nausea hits me. I feel my way hurriedly round the room, hoping to get to the grate before vomiting. The smell of sick won't improve the facilities. I make it – just! Even so, by the light of the torch, which I flash round for a second, I see some of the part-digested contents of last night's dinner splattered around the edge – and I've nothing to clean it with.

Feeling weak and drained, I use the torch again to help me back to the bedding. I'm about to turn it off once I reach the bedding, when some instinct makes me shine it round once more, this time at shoulder level. I put my head in my hands and groan. Adjacent to the door, cemented in against the stone work, is a light switch. It mocks me.

I turn off the torch. I can't believe how stupid I've been. All that panic of the preceding hours – totally unnecessary.

Summoning a final scrap of energy, I stand up again, and with the torch on, I stagger over to the switch. I flick it.

Chapter Twenty-Six

Nothing happens.

My momentary euphoria vanishes as fast as it arrived. I sink to the floor, and hug my knees as I sob – the shock of losing the light source has overwhelmed me totally; even though I only knew of it for less than a minute.

I cry for several minutes, then I realise nothing has actually changed. I still have my torch, my blanket and pillow, my meagre clothing, and a vomit-covered grate. A few deep breaths later, and the sobbing subsides. Morning sickness is a symbol and a sign of my pregnancy. While Dominic believes the baby might be his, he won't kill me – or so I hope. This is a warning. I have to behave – to do exactly as he wants. Every time he speaks, I'll have to study the exact words, in case I'm called on to repeat them. I must be completely obedient, and ask for no concessions; no items that could help beguile the tedium of days with nothing to do except miss my ex-fiancé and my friends.

Assuming Dominic really does believe the baby could be his, he'll make sure I get fed and watered. He has no reason to believe it could be anyone else's. As far as he knows, I've had no opportunity to sleep with Mark.

Hopefully he'll include a proper bed and lighting in the package, but I'm not feeling very hopeful just now. What will happen after the baby arrives? Well, that's a problem to be solved when I've had some rest and water. I crawl back to my bedding, realising that I've begun to develop a sense of space within the room – an awareness of the layout. Also, as I lie back on the blanket, I wonder if perhaps my eyes have begun to adjust a little. The door seems to stand proud of its frame – the thinnest sliver of dim light surrounds it. This throws faint shadows around the room.

Reassured, I shut my eyes and sleep again. There's nothing else to do.

***

I get woken by a torch shining in my face.

"Let's get you out of here, Melissa. This room stinks. You stink."

I blink at the bright light and then look in to the shadowy face of Dominic. I can't see his expression, but decide to play it safe.

"Thank you." I clamber to my feet and reach down to collect the blanket and pillow.

"Leave it," he says. "The wardens will sort it out when I send them down to clean the room. I've had my eye on one of them – fat, lazy imbecile called Fred. It would do him good to scrub your vomit and urine from the floor."

Poor Fred...

Grabbing my shoulder briefly, Dominic propels me to the now open door. Light trickles into the passage through a grate in the ceiling, and I can see well enough to avoid collision with doors and walls, but I'm disorientated and turn the wrong way.

"Are you stupid, or were you planning to explore?"

I ignore the sarcasm, and turn to face the other way. I throw him what I hope is a disarming smile. "Sorry, Dominic. I've a dreadful sense of direction."

He tuts, and grips my arm, escorting me roughly through the passage. Relief sweeps through me. He hasn't let me starve to death, and has rescued me before anything too awful happened. I hope that will be the last I see of the cellars. My sense of direction being less appalling than I claimed, I reckon we're heading back towards the stairs, and hopefully returning to the main part of the Abbey.

The light from the grate doesn't reach the staircase, and the stairwell is in darkness. I wait for Dominic to turn on his torch. Mine rests in my pocket, but I've no desire for him to learn of its existence. We stand at the bottom of the stairs in

160

silence for a moment.

"I have excellent night vision, Melissa. I don't need the torch to get back. Shall I leave you here to find your way back to my office?"

The cruelty in his voice no longer shocks me. A night in a cellar with no light, food, drink or toilet facilities has shown me his true nature only too clearly.

"Please turn on your torch," I beg. He seems to like being pleaded with, and I must stay on his good side – if he has one.

"You've learnt to say the P word – well done, Melissa! A night in my cellar has obviously done you some good. I'll remember that next time I need to teach you something." He turns on the torch, and leads the way up the narrow stone stairs. I follow, clinging nervously to the rope at the side to prevent me falling. The stairs are open to one side, and one false step would have me cracking my head open as I fall to the ground below. I breathe a sigh of relief once we get through the door at the top of the stairs, and I find myself back in Dominic's room, on the safe side of the bookshelf.

Glancing around the room, I see a camp bed set up in a corner. A sheet and blanket lie folded at one end, and a thin pillow at the other. Dominic seems to be watching me.

"Yes, that's your bed from now on – as long as you behave yourself. I don't want you sharing my bed anymore, but we must protect my baby, so this bed seems the best solution. During the days, you can occupy yourself by keeping my room clean. I won't be allowing anyone else in here for now, so it will be your job to make sure everything is spotless. Now get in the shower. You really do stink."

Wordlessly, I creep into the bathroom, and remove my cardigan and admittedly disgusting nightdress. The cardigan I fold neatly, encompassing the torch pocket within the folds. The nightie gets left on the floor for the moment. I'll rinse it out, when I've had my shower.

It feels lovely to stand in the bath and get clean, even with the cold water cascading from the shower-head. I don't dare to use any hot – we're not allowed it usually except first thing in the morning, and I don't want to stretch my luck. Once showered, and with my hair shampooed and rinsed, I grab a towel from the pile, and wrap it round myself. Dominic's towels are white and fluffy, unlike the threadbare, greying articles the rest of us get to use. Wrapping the bath sheet around me, and tucking it in, I start work on the soiled clothing I removed. I use a drop of liquid soap, and scrub the nightie clean in the bath. I'm standing up, wringing it out, when Dominic flings open the door and strides in.

"What the hell are you...?" he starts, but then must realise the answer, as he continues with, "Oh good. You're cleaning it yourself." He grasps the towel that's wrapped around me, and yanks it away, leaving me naked and shivering. "You'll have to make do with your cardigan until this is dry. You're getting no other clothes from me, and I won't have you using my lovely towels."

He looks round. "Where is your cardigan?"

I retrieve it from its spot out of the way behind the toilet, and carefully unfold it. Slipping it on, I do up the buttons, thankful it reaches down to my thighs. I'm very self-conscious, knowing that it's the only thing concealing my nakedness.

He watches me for a moment, and then leaves the bathroom.

Once I'm finished washing the nightdress, I hang it carefully over the towel rail to dry out, and return to the bedroom.

I find him sitting on the bed. He's wearing just his underpants.

"Come here, Melissa. It's time for us to kiss and make up, don't you think?"

I'm too scared and confused to argue, so I nod and walk over to him. He pulls me on to his lap, and slips his hand inside my cardigan to my breasts. He's a little rough, and far more intent on his own pleasure than mine, not caring that I'm not ready when he thrusts into me. His own lust finally satiated, he collapses on top of me, withdrawing a moment later to leave me sore and aching.

After getting dressed a short while later, he throws me another nightdress that I recognise as one of my own.

"You'd better wear this. I can't afford to be turned on every time I walk into my own bedroom. I'm supposed to be the one in control here. I'll bring some food with me after lunch. You must be hungry."

"Thank you," I say. Though I don't know if I'm thanking him for the clothes or the anticipated food. I feel a strange sense of power. The sex, though not enjoyable in any way, seems to have had the effect of reducing his level of control. Maybe it's something I should encourage whenever possible. I can always lie back and dream of Mark.

A searing pain burns in my chest at the thought of Mark, and I fight back tears. Will I ever see him again?

Chapter Twenty-Seven

It's now five days since my release from the cellar. The bell goes at 5am as usual. I sit up, and dive for the bathroom, to vomit noisily.

"Go back to bed, Melissa. You need to save your strength for the baby. I'll wake you at eight," Dominic says as I stagger woozily from the en-suite. Happy to comply, I return to the camp bed and go back to sleep.

I'm woken as promised by the sound of the kettle and the smell of toast. My stomach churns, and another hurried visit to the bathroom ensues. I use the opportunity to wash and clean my teeth, as soon as I feel well enough to stand up, and that makes me a feel a bit better. Back in the room, I manage to force down the tea Dominic's made for me, but can't face the toast.

"Sorry, Dominic. The thought of food at the moment…"

"That's fine. I brought in the toaster and kettle so you could make yourself a snack whenever you're feeling up to it." He smirks. "You've been most generous the last few days, so I felt you deserved a treat."

I force a smile, hoping it doesn't look like a grimace. My 'generosity' has appalled me. Each afternoon, Dominic has returned to the bedroom with a plate of lunch. He watches me eat, then invites me to his bed. I don't dare refuse. The memory of the cellar has been too fresh in my mind, and although my captor has lost his bullying tone, he's still keeping me a prisoner. I can't even begin to trust him. His sexual appetite has developed since he first seduced me, and the teasing charmer has given way to a dominating, hateful creep. Two days ago, he forced me to take him into my mouth. My innocence amused him at first, and then when I accidentally bit him, he punched me in the eye. When I stopped howling with pain (about thirty seconds, because he threatened to smother me with his pillow), he instructed me, in graphic detail, on the correct technique. Suffice to say, he made me swallow, and I had to run, once again, to the bathroom to throw up. That time it had nothing to do with morning sickness.

So Dominic's reference to my 'generosity' brings bile to my throat, making my eyes water. He leaves me, as he has to lead prayers, instructing me to pray alone.

I pray. I pray for escape; for Mark to rescue me without repercussions; and even for Dominic to be struck down my some mysterious killer disease. I don't feel hopeful of any of those things happening, but I keep sending out the thoughts anyway, desperate that something will soon happen to improve my situation.

After I've been sitting with my thoughts and prayers for a while, I notice the room is untidy, so set about tidying up. I still only have a nightdress and cardigan to wear. Frustrated and feeling dirty, I root through drawers and cupboards to find my clothes. A strange elation shoots through me when I find them, and particularly when I manage to locate another identical cardigan. I immediately transfer my torch to the replacement cardigan, and wash the now grubby one that accompanied me to the cellar. Searching around for somewhere discreet to hang the washed item, I find a piece of cord in the bathroom. In the cupboard where I found my bag, there's enough space, and I fasten the cord between two hooks and place the soap-smelling garment over the cord to dry. I close the cupboard and pray again that Dominic doesn't open it and discover my secret washing.

When he arrives with my lunch, he finds me cleaning the bathroom.

"Good girl," he says. "Now, come and sit down and eat."

I make my way to the small occasional table that's been set next to my camp bed, and sit down to wade through the cheese pie, boiled potatoes and cabbage. Lacking in flavour as always, but cooked well. I eat everything quickly, my stomach in a less queasy state than earlier this morning.

"Cistercians cooking today?" I ask.

"Yes, how can you tell?"

"We're the only group that doesn't overcook cabbage," I say with a tentative smile. Dominic starts to smile back, and a sense of relief sweeps through me. Perhaps we can have some level of a normal relationship.

My relief is short-lived. His expression clouds over, and he picks up the empty plate and smashes it on the floor at my feet.

"You should be grateful for the food you're given. I'm going to leave you now to pray for forgiveness. When I come back, I expect a very different attitude."

Ignoring the broken plate, he strides out of the room. I listen as usual for the click of the lock – I hope one day he'll forget, and don't want to miss any opportunities for escape.

Slowly, I gather together the bigger pieces of crockery and place them in the bin. I remember from my morning activity the location of a dustpan and brush – in a cupboard in the bathroom – and I go to seek it out. I open the closet door, and hear a knocking sound.

"Hello?"

Is this a trap?

"Melissa?" comes a muffled whisper.

"Mark! Where are you?"

"In the secret cupboard – you remember, don't you?" The location of our first kiss, and more. The memory sets my heart racing; or more likely the knowledge that Mark is only inches away, the other side of a closet wall, seriously accelerates my pulse and breathing.

"Of course I remember. Mark, you know I love you, don't you?"

"Yeah of course. Look Mel, I know this isn't your fault. I messed up, and Dominic's punishing us both."

"But…"

"Don't argue. I love you too. I wanted you to know that, whatever happens. If I can do anything to get you out, I will, but we'll need somewhere to go if I do. If I just rescue you from him, he'll punish us both even more. Oh Christ, someone's coming." He lowers his voice even further. "Got to go. Be brave," he whispers.

I know this might be the last time I speak to him for a long time, maybe forever, and I stagger back to my bed, still holding the dustpan and brush, before my knees give way and I collapse, trembling.

Five minutes later, Dominic returns, and finds me curled up on my camp bed shaking.

"You're not still upset about me breaking the plate are you? Christ, woman, you've not even cleaned it up yet." He grabs my arm and yanks me off the bed. "You've clearly found the tools. Do you know how to use them?"

I nod, and sniff.

"Get on with it then."

I kneel at his feet and sweep up the broken crockery, but when I stand up to put it in the bin, he crashes his hand down on my wrist in karate-chop-style. My fingers automatically loosen their grip and the full dustpan falls from my hand. Oh my God – the pain! I want to scream, but I don't dare. The remains of the plate smash into even more pieces around me, but I cradle my throbbing wrist. Dominic pulls it towards him and examines it.

"Shame, I don't think it's broken. I'll have to try harder next time. Clear up this mess, and then you can come to bed and we can make friends again, yes?"

I nod mutely. He and I have very different ideas on how to make friends.

Chapter Twenty-Eight

Dominic lied – my wrist is broken. I've been struggling with daily activities for the last few weeks, as he didn't allow me to splint it, or rest at all. In fact, he plied me with chores: cleaning and tidying his apartment, massaging his back, and other – more intimate – tasks for which supple wrists are a necessity. After receiving a number of bruises in various locations, I've managed to develop some strength and coordination in my left wrist, but I've been crying myself silently to sleep on a regular basis. I daren't make a noise. Retribution falls more quickly than rain in Cheshire – and with similar frequency.

The throbbing in my wrist is finally subsiding. In the time taken for my wrist to knit together, my abdomen has grown larger. I'm nearly four months pregnant, and I'm definitely showing, although my loose nightdress has concealed my bump until now.

I've learned when to keep my mouth shut, when to speak, how to speak, what to do and when to do it. It took several weeks. I've prayed again and again – for help, for Mark to find a way of escape, or even just to hear his voice again – but there's been nothing. No further whispers at the bathroom cupboard, and no more hope.

Days pass. Dominic brings me food and water. If I behave well, he allows me to eat and drink before he knocks the plate to the floor. I dream of successions of smashed plates in front of me: I start to clear the crockery, then another plate smashes. In reality, he only smashes one plate at a time. I'm numb to it, but I've learned to eat and drink quickly, despite my fractured wrist. Feeding myself and my unborn baby in time has become a challenge.

This morning, I wake at five as usual to find Dominic

standing over me holding a green cardigan. I rub my eyes, and glance at the chair next to the bed. A similar garment is neatly folded on the chair. Oh hell!

"And why have you been hiding clothes from me, Melissa?"

"I'm s-s-s-sorry," I cower in the bed. He lowers the cardigan to my face, and holds it over my mouth and nose. I'm gasping for breath. Grey blurry splodges fill my vision, and a sudden image of Mark hearing about the death of me and the baby pops into my head. It gives me strength, and I throw off my blankets and kick Dominic where it hurts.

He instantly lets go of the cardigan, and dropping it on the floor, hops around the room howling.

"You fucking bitch – I'll make you pay for this." He must be livid. He hardly ever swears – even in front of me, he tries to preserve the image of the Messiah, albeit a violent one.

I take huge gulps of air into my lungs, re-saturating my blood with life-giving oxygen. After a minute, Dominic sits on his bed, and takes a few deep breaths of his own. His hand still protectively covers his genitals.

"Take your nightdress off," he says calmly.

I stare at him; surely he can't want sex after what I've just done to him. He begins to rise from the bed, and I hastily remove my nightie. I sit naked on the camp bed, not daring to cover myself in any way. He picks up the nightie and both the green cardigans, and takes them to the bathroom. "Come with me," he says.

Following him in to the bathroom, I see him throw my clothing into the empty bath, pick up a box of matches, and light one. He flings the lit match on top of the pile, and the acrid smell of burning wool fills my nostrils. I gag from the smell. He waits until the room is full of smoke, and my clothes are completely destroyed, before he turns on the shower and puts out the fire. I cough and splutter, trying not to breathe the smoke. Dominic also seems to be suffering from smoke inhalation, because, as soon as the shower is doing its job, he grabs my injured wrist and yanks me out of the bathroom.

I follow him out, willingly for once, shutting the bathroom door behind us.

"Be grateful I didn't put you in the bath to burn too. If you hadn't been expecting my child, I would have done. It is my child you've got in there isn't it, Melissa?"

I nod, between coughing.

"Good, because if there's any possibility you got pregnant with that ugly bastard out there, I'll burn all three of you."

How can he think that? He doesn't know about the cupboard. He has no idea what I've done.

I huddle naked against the wall near my camp bed. Tears sting my eyes, but I don't let them fall. Any sign that I still love Mark could be fatal – for him or me. Fear is the only emotion allowed, and often that too evokes a terrible response.

Dominic watches me, a strange light in his eyes. Recent weeks have shown me that same expression on three occasions – each when he was planning some terrible punishment: the oral sex, confinement in the cellar, and this morning's burning of my clothes.

I stop coughing, but terror paralyses my breathing. How much more can he inflict on me in one day?

"Are you cold, child?" he says, a suddenly concerned expression on his face. I've seen that one before too, on numerous occasions. I don't trust him anymore. And, yes – I'm naked in a badly-heated room in December, in an Abbey with cold stone walls. Even my bones are cold. The only help I have in that direction is my pregnancy – my internal central heating system – possibly as much use as a candle in an igloo.

"Yes." Lying will get me nowhere.

The concerned expression disappears to be replaced by a cruel grin. What a surprise!

"Aww, what a shame. I'm sure the Almighty One will keep you warm. You're not getting any more clothes. You've shown you can't be trusted with them. Anyway, I don't need you to wear anything now. You're too fat and ugly to turn me on."

He watches me – presumably to see if this would upset me – but I no longer value his good opinion. I stopped caring about him a long time ago. I just pray to be spared any further sexual favours.

The cruel grin remains in place for a few moments, then he shrugs, puts on his tie and suit jacket, and leaves the room. I wait until I hear the lock click, and then grab the sheets and blankets from my bed, wrap myself up in them and curl up on the thin mattress.

Still the tears don't fall. They never do when I'm alone and safe. The room continues to reek of smoke, and I can't risk using the bathroom yet. My bladder screams in fury at my decision, and I squeeze to prevent an accident. I look round the room for inspiration. The cupboard containing the mop and bucket is in the bathroom. A half-empty glass of water stands on Dominic's bedside table. The consequences of using it would be horrific, but then I don't want to wee on the floor either.

It's going to have to be the bathroom, and if I can get in, I can turn on the extractor fan as well. I use the water in the glass to dampen the shirt I've found in Dominic's laundry basket. I leave my bedding on the bed as I don't have enough hands free to hold the blankets around me. I try to ignore the goosebumps and shivers, and focus on the job. I wrap the damp shirt over my mouth and nose, making sure I'm able to breathe through it, and tie the sleeves at the back of my head.

Taking a deep breath, I open the bathroom door slowly, reach in and grab the cord that turns on the light and extractor. The electric light suffuses the smoke, giving the room a strange, foggy glow. The thick smoke fills the room, and even with my makeshift mask, it's difficult to breathe. I keep my breathing shallow, and feel along the wall for the cistern and toilet bowl. Unhampered by clothes, I use the toilet quickly, and hurry to the door, which I can now see outlined dimly as the smoke thins.

Once back in the bedroom, I tear the shirt from my face, and throw it back in the laundry basket. Thank goodness Dominic keeps it in a corner of his bedroom, rather than in the bathroom, like most people. I wrap myself back up in the bedclothes, and lie on my camp bed once more.

When I hear the lock click again, I check the clock on the wall. Half past one. With the stresses of the morning, and feeling nauseous from the smoke, I don't feel hungry at all, but I need food for the baby. When Dominic comes in empty-handed, disappointment and fear hit me in the gut.

He comes over and jerks the covers from me.

"Why haven't you been cleaning up? Just because I've burned your clothes doesn't mean you can lie there day in, day out. Get up and start work. The smoke has made the skirting boards dirty. Get a cloth and start scrubbing, woman."

I stand up, acutely conscious of my nakedness, and his appraising look at my chest, where my nipples are peaking in the cold air. I slink over to the bathroom door, and open it tentatively. The smoke has dissipated to leave grime all around the room, and an ashy mess in the bath. The smell of burning still lingers, stinging my eyes and the back of my throat.

Retrieving the cleaning materials from the cupboard, I return to the room, to find Dominic undressed on his bed.

"Get here," he commands. "You might be fat and ugly, but you're all I can get for the moment."

Shaking but resigned, I put the cloths and bleach on the floor by the bathroom door, and trundle over to him. I get a brief vision of pouring bleach all over him, but suppress it. I don't think I could get away with it, and the repercussions would be too awful to contemplate.

***

I grow accustomed to the cold. Heating in the Abbey is sporadic, and the stone walls radiate no warmth. On the chilliest days, I do everything possible to make Dominic relent and allow me to wrap myself in the sheets and blankets from my bed. I hate myself for it, but sometimes survival trumps everything else.

A few weeks after the burning, I wake to see my breath misting in front of me; the room is so cold. Dominic puts a t-shirt on under his shirt, and a grey v-neck pullover between his shirt and jacket.

"It's snowing," he says, looking out of the slit of window, which is at eye-level for him but too high for me to see out.

"It looks lighter out than usual for the time of day," I say, nervously making conversation. Sometimes this can placate Dominic and put him in a good mood for the day, but he has been known to put his hands over his ears and start singing when I speak. But then, that's preferable to the times he's come over and clapped a hand over my mouth, threatening to slit my throat if I 'carry on yattering'.

"It does. It's coming down really heavily. A regular blizzard. You'll be wanting to scrub the walls today. It might warm you up a bit."

I get out of bed and go to use the bathroom. If possible, it feels even colder in there. Goosebumps rise on the goosebumps I already have. After three weeks of nakedness, I've lost much of my embarrassment at being undressed, but every pore screams at me this morning. I hurry through washing and cleaning my teeth. A glance in the toilet bowl before using it reveals a few icicles, although it's not completely frozen over. I send up a quick prayer to the Almighty One, not to let the pipes freeze.

I return to the bedroom to find Dominic gone. I listen at the door, in case he's about to come back in, but can hear nothing. I breathe a sigh of relief, and don the blanket from my bed. I've learned to wrap it round me like a toga, but can get it off in seconds, so that as soon as I hear the lock click, it's off and back on the bed neatly before Dominic is through the door.

Scrubbing walls does warm me up a bit, but the air is still clouding as I breathe out. I'm on my knees between his bed and wardrobe, when I feel a strange fluttering below my ribcage. I stop and sit back on my heels for a moment. There it goes again. More than a flutter. Is it a kick? Perhaps a gentle one – more a ballet dancer than a footballer. A big grin spreads across my face. I imagine the joy of holding my little dancer in my arms for the first time. I rock my arms as if holding her (although I've no problems with a little boy either). Lost in my own happy world for the first time in months, I nearly miss the sound of the lock clicking in the door. I leap to my feet unwrapping the toga. There's no time to get it back on the bed, so I slip it to the floor in a folded heap, as though I've been kneeling on it.

Dominic barges in to the room. His eyes flickers over to the bed, and then seeing me, with a cloth in one hand, his shoulders relax forwards, and he nods approvingly.

"Where's your blanket, Melissa?"

"I was kneeling on it. Sorry. My knees got sore." I pick it up and start to walk over to the camp bed with it, my daydream forgotten.

He grabs my arm. "I'll make more than your knees sore if you do that again. The blanket stays on the bed. Or would you like me to burn that as well?" In the three weeks since he burned my clothes, the smell has never quite left the bathroom – a constant reminder of the perils of disobedience. Only the extreme cold of the Abbey in December persuaded me to turn my blanket into a toga. He extracts a box of matches from his jacket pocket and waves them in front of me. I back away instinctively. "Perhaps I should burn you instead? Get you out of my life?"

He lets go of me, and I run to the other side of the room and crouch behind his bed, as he lights a match and holds it up for me to see. He lets it burn itself out, then takes out another.

"Ready for a bath, Melissa?"

No, please no! I feel the colour drain from my cheeks, and my heart's thudding in my chest. I cling to the mahogany post of Dominic's bed, as though it can protect me.

He laughs – a manic sound. He's lost it. He's gone crazy. No sane person would threaten to burn someone to death.

I must fight the urge to pass out. To lose consciousness now would be fatal.

"It's as well you're expecting my baby. You're safe for the

moment." He puts the second match back in the box.

The room spins for a moment, as relief makes me dizzy. The immediate danger may be over. He picks up my blanket and leaves the room, locking the door behind him once again.

Not daring to take the covers from Dominic's bed, I crawl, trembling, around the room to get to my own. He's left me the sheets, so I climb in and curl up, bile rising in my throat. Despite all odds, I fall asleep.

I wake feeling sick, in pitch darkness, with my wrists and ankles bound, lying on a cold stone floor.

Chapter Twenty-Nine

I have no clothes on, no sheets, pillows or blankets, and no torch neatly hiding in a cardigan pocket. Is this Dominic's idea of safe? On the plus side, there doesn't seem to be anyone in the room with me. I strain my ears for the sound of breathing, but can only hear my own. I cough. No response. My brain feels foggy, as though I've been drugged. Thoughts ground round my head slowly as though in a thick vat of treacle.

"Hello," I call softly into the emptiness. Again no response. Unlike last time, when the dark terrified me, my main concerns now are practical. Or they would be, if I could think straight.

If my hands and feet are bound, how do I get to the toilet? Is there a toilet? Or a grate? A bucket? Anything? How will I get food? Dominic supposedly values the life of the baby he believes to be his. Surely he'll provide food and drink to enable the baby to survive. In order to do that, he has to keep me alive long enough for me to give birth. Thinking about my baby helps to lift the fog.

I'm almost five months pregnant. He believes me to be four months or thereabouts. Another four months from his perspective should be enough to expect a viable birth. Three and a half months could be chancy. Either way, he has to feed me.

I stay on the floor shivering for several moments. Despite the cold, the hunger and the thirst, I'm not scared. Perhaps it's reaction from being threatened with death by burning, but my chief emotion is relief at being alone. Admittedly, the practical issues are worrying, but maybe I can do something about that.

The rope is cutting into my wrists, I'm extremely

uncomfortable, and the cold has seeped into my bones. God knows if I'll ever be warm again. Baby is kicking me again. I don't think she (or he) likes being cold, and has started doing warm up exercises at the barre of my abdomen. I can't help smiling at the thought, then grimace, as I roll over onto my back, with my bound wrists underneath me, and then onto my other side. The whole process takes several minutes, and a few mild and silent swear words. I still don't fully believe that no one can hear me. My head is getting clearer with each passing moment.

I run my tongue over my dry, chapped lips, and try to generate some saliva, but I haven't had anything to eat or drink all day, and dehydration threatens. If someone doesn't come soon, I'll die anyway. A slower death than burning, and perhaps less painful – but not a route I plan to explore.

I lied. I am scared.

I shut my dry eyes and pray for food, water, warmth, freedom of movement, and a toilet.

A short while later, a door opens and a light shines in. I take a deep breath, and wince at the sudden brightness. Blinded for a moment, I can't see my visitor.

"Oy, Melissa. Not seen you around for a while. You've got fat, bitch!"

I blink and peer up at Thomas. I'm not sure yet if he's a welcome change from Dominic. The light dims a little as I become accustomed to it.

He leaves the room for a moment, and returns with a two-tiered trolley. The top contains a wind-up lamp, a plate of bread, a tub of margarine, a plastic knife, a cup and a jug of water. On the bottom shelf, through the dim light, I can see a blanket and a pillow. I could kiss Thomas, and given how much I dislike him, that's a huge sign of how relieved I am.

He kneels down behind me. "I'll cut your ropes, so you can move around, and I'll show you round the room. You'll be living here a while. But I want payment, and I don't want to have to fight for it."

I nod, resigned. Thomas is strong enough to rape me anyway if I don't give him what he wants. At least if I keep

177

him happy, he might be kinder to me than Dominic has been.

He fiddles behind me, releasing the ropes on my wrists, reaching round every now and again and squeezing the breast nearest to him. I don't like it much, but it's bearable. When he's cut the ropes around my ankles, he turns me on my back, and lies on top of me. I open my legs and let him in. I don't really care anymore, and as things stand I would open my legs to all the wardens in the Abbey in return for blankets, food and water. Anyway, this is preferable to giving Dominic blow jobs and being forced to swallow. Thomas is rough but quick, and once sated, he gets off me quickly, and throws me a paper towel to wipe myself with.

"Thank you," I say.

"Bloody hell. I ain't used to being thanked. What the fuck's Dominic been doing to you?"

I shrug. I don't want to give Thomas any ideas.

"Get up, I'll show you round. Just don't try to escape."

"Where would I go?" I ask.

He ignores the question, but shines the light on a door in the corner of the room.

"That one's unlocked. You can go in and 'ave a look." I struggle to my feet, and waddle over to where he pointed. Opening the door, I shine the torch he passed me, and see another stone room – also unlit – containing a flushable toilet and a washbasin. "During the day, there'll be a bit of light in here. There's a grate in the top. Not big enough to get out, and no one'll hear you if you yell, so it ain't worth trying, but if you get fed up with the dark you can come in here for a bit. On the other 'and, it's bloody cold in 'ere, so you might want to stay in the other room."

I shiver and nod. My breath is even more misty in here than it was in Dominic's room. We return to the outer cell and shut the bathroom door.

"I'm kind, see, and if you keep giving me what I want, I'll keep bringing you food and water. I'll also leave you with light and a blanket. Any trouble and… well… you don't want to find out what would happen."

"No, of course not. Thanks, Thomas." He gives me

another surprised look, and a lecherous gleam appears in his eyes as his gaze falls to my bare breasts.

"Once more for now then," he says, grabbing my chest and kneading as though making bread.

I let him do what he wants. I'm ridiculously grateful to him.

After he's gone, I wrap the blanket round me and wind up the lantern. It's not very bright, but it gives out enough light, and at least I can be sure it won't run out of batteries. I walk round the room. It doesn't take long – the room must be about three metres in each direction. Like all the other cells I've been in, this one has stone walls, a stone ceiling and a small grate in the floor. Unlike the others, the room boasts an en-suite bathroom, with a toilet and sink, and a skylight. I'm honoured. It seems I've been given the best room in the Abbey dungeons!

I suspect this means I'll be here a long time – perhaps until the baby's born. A sense of relief floods through me. I'm completely exhausted by the constant emotional turmoil of living with Dominic. The prospect of peace and quiet, even punctuated by demands of sex from Thomas, seems very appealing.

On the downside, I have no clothes, no heating, and minimal food. My gaze falls on the trolley that Thomas left. I set upon the contents of the top shelf. The first priority is water, and I drink thirstily – three glasses full from the jug provided, before I feel ready to eat anything. I have to use the small plastic knife to spread the margarine; they obviously don't trust me with a proper knife, but it does the job. Thomas brought six slices of bread, so I ration it. Two slices are enough for now – particularly after all the water.

The sink in the bathroom provides a refill for the jug, and I feel privileged to have an endless supply of water on tap. Something soft falls on my arm. Glancing up at the skylight, as I'm calling the small hole in the ceiling, I see it's snowing again. This could be a pain. The en-suite bathroom really is open to the elements. On the other hand, there's nothing on the floor, so perhaps most of the snow has got caught in the grate.

Even after all that's happened, cautious optimism reasserts itself. Behind the snow, the sky is still dark. So it could be anything from five in the evening to seven in the morning. I'd slept earlier in the day, but I've no idea how long for. I still don't know how Dominic brought me here without waking me up, but perhaps he used some chloroform from the Infirmary. It would have had to be that or an injection, and I don't think he'd risk harming the baby. Although he clearly doesn't care if I freeze to death.

Emptying the bottom shelf of the trolley, I find two sheets – to supplement the blanket I'm already wearing – and a pillow. Dominic (or Thomas) has aimed for survival rather than comfort. I spread the sheets and the pillow as far from the bathroom door as possible and behind the main door leading to the corridor. Cocooning myself my tightly in the blanket, I lie down on the sheets, and tuck the blanket around my feet. With eyes shut tightly, I pray for sleep to come, but the Almighty One isn't listening this time.

It doesn't take long for the relief at being alone to disappear. Trying to find a comfortable spot on the floor seems futile. The cold stone remains solid and inflexible – a hard barrier against my sore, aching body. Baby doesn't like it either, and kicks hard throughout the night, as if telling me to find a proper bed to sleep in.

I must have dozed off eventually. The sound of muffled screams mixes in with my dreams at first, then seeps into my consciousness. Opening gritty eyes to the pitch darkness, I reach out and grab the lantern, fumbling until I locate the switch. A dim light suffuses the immediate area, but the screaming continues.

There are no words, only the distressing sound of someone in pain. I concentrate for a moment, and think I make out the swish of a belt or whip. I shudder, and put my hands over my ears. It might be Mark getting beaten again. Why would I want to listen? There's nothing I can do to help, except behave myself as well as possible, and cause no trouble.

A trip to the bathroom to use the toilet, wash my hands

and face, and scrub my teeth in cold water with my finger blots out the noise for a few minutes. I wrap the blanket tight around me, to keep out the freezing air, but the small pile of snow under the grate is surrounded by ice. It must have melted at some point in the night only to freeze again.

Shivering, I return to the main cell and sit down. The screams keep coming. I shut my eyes and pray – again.

"Please, Almighty One, don't let them be hurting Mark or Tina or Brie or Jimmy. Please stop them from hurting anyone. And if it's not too much trouble, please could you stop the snow and warm it up a bit. Amen."

The screams sound female, so it's unlikely to be Mark or Jimmy, but that doesn't mean they're safe. I shut my eyes and repeat the prayer over and over again. After a while, I realise the screaming has stopped, and I cease to pray, excepting a quick thank you. I strain my ears again for voices. Nothing. The silence envelopes me, until I hear nothing but my own breathing. The baby kicks, and I rest a hand on my abdomen, and stroke. A tiny flame of excitement burns. One day I'll be holding this little bundle in my arms – my baby and Mark's.

A cloud descends and the dream bursts. I look around the dingy cell with the dim light and no heat. Assuming I survive the cold – which might be a stretch in current conditions – I can't imagine Dominic allowing Mark and me to raise this child together. My heart is suddenly as cold as the bathroom, and I struggle to swallow past the lump in my throat.

When the door opens some time later, Thomas strides in to find me huddled in a corner, sniffing and with tears dry on my cheeks. He holds a white plastic bag in his right hand and a small camping heater in his left. I stop sniffing and look hopefully at him.

"Is that for me?" I say.

"No, it's for the fucking pope. Course it's for you, you silly tart."

"Thank you." I stand up uncertainly as he sets up the camping heater and turns it on.

"There are spare cylinders here for you, but I can't get loads. If you limit it to about an hour a day, it should take the

181

worst of the chill off, and keep you going for a couple of months. I'll try and get more if I can, and if you're nice to me, but I can't promise, so be sensible."

"I will do, thank you." I move nearer to the heater, which is now giving out a warm glow, and allow myself to thaw out. Glancing over at Thomas, I see him lining up six spare cylinders in a corner of the room. He also extracts a loaf of bread and a packet of cheese slices from the carrier bag.

"I raided the kitchen on my way down. Dominic don't know about this," he says, holding up the cheese. I don't like Thomas much, but he's being kinder to me than anyone has been since I've left the Infirmary. What does he expect in return?

"Is Dominic going to come down here?"

"Not while it's this blinkin' cold. Maybe in a few weeks. He said he wanted a bit o' time to calm down, else he might throttle you, and he don't want to do that 'cos of the babe. What did you do to get him so angry?"

I think back – he's done so many awful things to me, but how much have I retaliated? Then it comes to me…

"I kicked him in the groin. To be fair to me, he was trying to strangle me at the time, and I just kicked out. I can't think of anything else, but he's been angry with me for ages, and I never really did find out why."

"Yeah, well. He's the Messiah. I expect he's under a lot of pressure."

I don't miss the dry note in Thomas' voice, but I prefer not to ask. Thomas has been Dominic's henchman, so my trust in Thomas is limited. For all I know, the heater and food might be a trap.

Chapter Thirty

That heater's saving my life. The weather has got even colder. A sheet of ice grows on the bathroom floor as snow is dripping in through the grate and then re-freezing. I've developed a technique of waddling into the bathroom with the corners of the blanket under my feet. Thomas catches me coming out of there, and laughs so hard he has to run into the bathroom himself. There's a yell. A moment later, he emerges.

"Fucking, shitting hell, Melissa. That sodding ice nearly killed me."

I hide a smile. "Are you okay?" I try to sound concerned, but he gives me a disgusted look.

"Slipped over and banged my sodding elbow on the sink. And don't you dare fucking laugh."

"Sorry," I say. "Come over to the heater. I'll turn it on for a bit. It's horrible at the moment."

"It's worse outside – there's a foot and a half of snow out there. And half the fucking pipes have frozen. There ain't no heat in the whole place, except these things." Thomas points at the heater. "Dominic ordered about a hundred of 'em off the internet."

My face clouds – the constriction in my chest surprises me. Just hearing his name has sent chills through me – an impressive feat in a freezing cellar.

We stand for a few minutes in silence, thawing out in front of the heater. Then Thomas grabs my arm and pushes me to the edge of the room. He undoes his trousers, and pulls the edges of my blanket apart, exposing my breasts and increasingly rounded abdomen. I say nothing. I know he wants payment for the food and heat, and this is a small price to pay. A million times better than being with Dominic.

Afterwards, I sit on the floor and swaddle myself in the blanket again as Thomas rearranges his clothing.

"Cheers. By the way, Tina said thanks."

My head jerks up as I stare at him in shock. "Is she okay?"

"Yeah. I ditched her and said I'd left her for a fatter model. I've not had her for a while anyway. Dominic told me to leave her alone for a bit, then once he brought you down here, I couldn't be arsed taking up with her again. Not when I had you all grateful to me and everything."

I try to breathe normally. I've felt guilty for abandoning her, but at least there's something I can do to prevent Thomas hassling her any more. Please God, she doesn't know exactly what's going on.

"Does she know that you're helping me?" I ask.

He leers, but it doesn't bother me like it used to. His lechery has diminished to a minor irritation and a benefit – a trait I can use for my own survival.

"I didn't say much. She still scuttles away like a frightened rabbit every time I look in her direction, but I grabbed her arm and whispered in her ear yesterday as she left the Chapter house after prayers. Made me laugh she did – she just stared at me with those fucking big eyes and said, 'Is she safe then? Can I go and see her?' What do you reckon, Melissa, should I bring her to see you?"

I sit gaping at him, open mouthed. I'd love to see her, but…

"Wouldn't it get her into trouble? What if Dominic found out?"

"Yeah." He sighs. "I reckon you're right. Better not risk it, eh? Shame – it's been a while since I had you both down here together." I think he sees my look of horror. "Sorry, just joking. Calm down. I've stopped all that stuff – don't need to force anyone these days do I?"

He's right. In exchange for food, heating, extra blankets and pillows that he sneaks down to me occasionally, I'm selling my body to him daily.

***

184

Two weeks later, the door opens and Dominic strides in. He's carrying a book.

"Made yourself quite at home here, haven't you, Melissa?" he says.

I swallow hard, my breathing suddenly erratic.

"Take that blanket off. The snow's gone. It's March already."

I let the blanket slide to the floor, and try not to feel self-conscious as his critical gaze surveys me from head to foot.

"Quite big now, aren't you? When are you due?"

I hesitate. It's vital I get the maths right. Dominic first seduced me in August, even though I knew by then I'd been pregnant for a couple of weeks, as the symptoms had just begun to appear. My actual due date is mid-April.

"Sometime in May I think – I can't be exact though." I pray the baby will be a couple of weeks late and show up in May. *Please don't be early.*

"I would have left you to Thomas, but he's been looking smug recently, so I've assigned him to other duties. I get the unpleasant duty of making sure you're fed until the baby turns up." He looks around the room, lit by the trusty wind-up lamp. His stare rests at the pile of bedding I've accumulated thanks to my lecherous benefactor. "You don't need those anymore. Don't pregnant women have some internal heating? I heard that somewhere. It must be true, you're not shivering, and you're standing there starkers like an idiot."

I wince. I'm 'starkers' because he told me to take off my blanket, and has deprived me of clothes. Even Thomas didn't dare bring me any. But Dominic's right about the internal heating system. Even in a cellar in March with no clothes on, I feel reasonably warm. The blanket has stayed on for reasons of modesty and habit more than for warmth in the last few days. I stay quiet though; I don't want to irritate him.

"Have you been saying your prayers, Melissa?"

I nod.

He gives a mirthless laugh. "Obviously you've not been praying hard enough, as you've got me back now. And I owe you. I was in pain for weeks after you kicked me. And sex hurt for ages." He must see my look of shock. "You didn't think I'd been celibate while you've been down here, did you?"

"Hadn't thought about it," I mumble.

"There are always plenty of *willing* volunteers. I've started playing them off against each other. Most entertaining. I've learnt what works best by talking to you. You've been so generous, Melissa, advising me on how to make women scared, how to make them beg, and then how to get them to forgive me. Should I get you to forgive me?" Perhaps he sees the faint glimmer of hope in my eyes. He slaps his thigh and lets out a huge roar of laughter. "Got you going, didn't I? No, child, I don't want your forgiveness. I've not forgiven you – why should I do anything to make you forgive me?"

He swoops down and picks up all my bedding, including the pillow. He appears to ponder the heater for a moment.

"Might as well leave you with that. You're not cold anyway. It's just something else for you to trip over in the dark. Oh, and that reminds me. You won't be needing this, will you?" He collects my wind-up lamp. "I'll bring you down some food later – if I remember. Oh, and in case you were wondering what I brought you this for…" He sets *Oliver Twist* down in front of me. It was the book he removed to open the entrance to the cellars. "Did you ever wonder which book you needed to remove in order to escape? Or did you not work it all out? I'll leave this here for you – just to see if it triggers any regret. Bye."

He exits though the door, leaving me alone with the heater and the one blanket which was around my ankles so somehow escaped his notice when he grabbed my bedding. I send up a prayer of thanks, and realise I need to stow the blanket in the bathroom under the sink. The bathroom dried out after the snow and ice, but not properly until Thomas brought down a few towels last week and gave them to me to dry the floor. He took the sodden ones away the next day, except for a single towel, which I've dried out and shoved behind the cistern in case of a rainy day. I can't risk my only blanket getting wet. I fold it and squeeze it beneath the towel. It should stay dry there.

I notice that the light inside the bathroom is bright enough for me to be able to see reasonably well. I keep the door open as I retreat into the main room, and discover that the daylight coming through the bathroom grate endows the outer room with a dull greyness; enough to be able to make out shapes, but little else. As there's nothing to do, and no objects to trip over, except for the heater stowed at the edge, the dim reprieve from blackness is all the light I need.

I've overcome my fear of the dark. He can't get to me like that anymore.

Oliver Twist is a puzzle. Dominic has obviously brought it down here to torment me. If I don't think about it, he's failed in his attempt. For now, anyway.

Chapter Thirty-One

I wait for Dominic to return – too scared to sit on the blanket in case he comes back and takes it from me. Hunger creeps up, and baby kicks remind me constantly of the importance of food. I know the baby will take what she needs though.

I've got in to the habit of thinking 'she' and 'her' but I know I might be wrong. Days of having no one to talk to, except a brief interlude with Thomas, has strengthened the bond with my baby, who in my head I've named Emma. As the kicks grow stronger, I stroke my swollen belly.

"It's all right, Emma darling. We'll get some food soon. Dominic won't let us starve – he might just let things get a bit uncomfortable." I drop my voice to a whisper. "He's not a nice man, I'm afraid."

The kicks pause when I speak, then resume more strongly. I've heard of unborn babies responding to music being played, but I have no music, and my singing voice – well, relaxing isn't a word often used to describe it. In teenage years, my mum used to shout upstairs, 'Stop that awful caterwauling please, darling,' as I sang along to the latest pop songs in my room. That had been before we lost Jess. I didn't sing afterwards – the family was torn apart by her disappearance, and music brought back too many painful recollections.

Maybe Emma likes listening to me talk, though. Most of the conversations I've had with her before have been silent – telepathic or imaginary chats inside my head. Maybe, now it's time to progress.

"Okay then, Emma. Time for us to have proper chats then. If you don't mind listening, I'll tell you my life story so far. That might take a while and keep us amused until… well, until it's time for you to see the world. If it gets boring, give me a kick and I'll shut up." But as I talk she seems to listen. There are no hard kicks, just the occasional gentle nudge as I pause to think of the next part of the story.

I forget my discomfort and fear as I speak to her, getting lost in the stories of my childhood. I go into intense detail – determined to make the stories last as long as possible, so as not to run out before the birth.

Dominic doesn't turn up that night, and I think I fall asleep mid-sentence, telling Emma about my first day at school – or as much as I remember. I make up bits to fill the gaps in my memory, but when I get exhausted, I just tail off, and drift in to a deep sleep.

I wake naked and cold despite the internal heating. March nights frequently herald temperatures of near freezing, and with the bathroom door open to let in as much light as possible, and no covering or clothing, the cold seeps into my joints. I move stiffly, trying to get going, and have to wrap myself in the blanket for a few minutes and risk the consequences.

I remember that Dominic left me the heater, and fumble in the dim grey from the morning light to turn it on. I stand in front of it, warming through gradually, and after a while, stow the blanket back in its hiding place. A few gentle stretches help to work out the kinks, but nothing can stem the hunger pangs, and Emma begins her leg exercises too!

I resume the story-telling. Half way through a tale about a bully boy at infant school, the door opens. Dominic strides in carrying a loaf of bread, a knife, plate and some cheese triangles. A bag of apples rests in the crook of his arm.

"Talking to yourself, Melissa?" he asks.

I don't reply. Maybe if he thinks me mad, he might give me more things to make me comfortable – maybe. Or maybe not.

"Anyway, this should last you a few days. I'm too busy to come down every day, so you'd better make it last. I'll pop down when I get a minute, but my admirers are taking a lot of my time these days." He looks me up and down. "Just as well – your body holds no appeal for me at all now – fat, ugly bitch, aren't you?" As I stand in front of him, exposed and vulnerable, the words cut deeper than they should.

There have been no opportunities to wash my hair since I've been in the cellar, and it's gone rat-tailed and hydrophobic. I've cleaned myself as well as I could each day (the sliver of soap Thomas provided in return for 'services rendered' has enabled me to stay relatively clean-smelling), but the cellar's dusty, and within hours, without my blanket, I've become covered in a film of grime. So, yes, I probably look awful. But that's his fault, not mine. I've done my best.

I fight back unexpected tears. He's threatened me with fire, starvation and drowning over the last few months; but I want to cry because he called me ugly. How stupid am I? I swallow hard to get rid of the lump in my throat, and watch as he turns away from me without another word and leaves the cellar, locking the door behind him.

When he's gone, another kick from Emma reminds me of the priorities, and I grab some bread and cheese and swallow it down quickly. Still hungry, I force myself to slow down, and carefully munch through one of the green apples. They're Granny Smiths, so a bit tart, but I don't care. A drink of water from the tap in the bathroom helps to wash everything down.

A sense of relief runs through me – if Dominic stays away for a few days, Emma and I can make ourselves at home here. Or at least, as at home as possible in a cellar with no light, limited heat, no bedding and very basic rations.

On the plus side, I have my baby with me. I can tell her stories, sing to her (if I feel very brave), and we won't get shouted at, threatened, or abused.

I lay out the blanket, curl up on it and carry on with my story. The sound of rain falling through the grate intrudes every so often, but Emma doesn't seem to mind if I pause to listen to the tap-tap of the raindrops on the stone floor in the bathroom. The room has gone very dark. Unsure if it's due to the weather, or if time has passed more quickly than usual, I stagger to my feet. Even though I've been on strict rations for weeks, extra weight has distributed in front of me, shifting my centre of gravity. Standing up with nothing but the floor for support is quite a challenge. I steady myself against the wall, and waddle to the bathroom.

On the verge of going in, wrapped in my blanket, I'm startled by the noise of the key in the lock. My breath catches in my throat, and I throw the blanket hastily into the corner of the bathroom, praying it won't get too wet. As the door opens, I emerge into the cellar. Dominic stands there, immaculately dressed in his suit and tie, carrying a box of matches and a lit candle. Unable to speak, I stare at him.

"I thought I'd better check on you, Melissa. I wondered what you'd do if you didn't think I'd be visiting for a while."

Thank you, Almighty One, for sending the rain. If it hadn't been for that, I would have been out here sitting on my blanket. I send up a brief prayer, but remain outwardly silent.

He stares at me for a moment; with his shoulders back and head up, he looks briefly like the handsome Messiah who inspired such a huge crush. Then he smiles – showing his joy at my discomfiture – and turns and leaves the room. I wait for the click in the lock, and head over to the corner where I usually sleep. I huddle on the stone floor hugging my knees, protecting Emma inside me.

Anger surges through me. Dominic cheated: he said he wouldn't be back for a few days.

I knew I'm being ridiculous. Dominic can and does do what he wants, and what he seems to want at the moment is to set me off balance. Why should he succeed? He can only win if I let him. The blanket will have to stay in the bathroom. Having it with me is too risky.

On the other hand, if I don't use it, I might as well not have it. I struggle back to my feet and return to where I've hidden it. The rain is still pouring in, and the edges of the blanket are sodden. I wrap it around me, carefully keeping the wet parts out of the way.

Returning to my corner, I resume my stories, talking to Emma as if she's sitting in front of me listening and able to understand. I keep an ear open for the sound of him coming back, but he doesn't return, so I eat another slice of bread and settle down to go to sleep.

For the last few weeks, I've been blessed with a mattress of sorts – three blankets beneath me – as well as a pillow, and three more blankets wrapped around me. Tonight I'm reduced to one blanket (still damp around the edges), no pillows or mattresses – just a cold stone floor and no light. Perhaps because of the rain, the cellar smells even more musty than usual.

As I try to sleep, muffled yells disturb my rest, setting my heart racing and forcing my eyes wide open. Oh my God. What's Dominic doing now?

"Please, Lord," I pray, "keep Mark, Tina, Brie and Jimmy safe. Don't let it be them." But if it's not them, it has to be someone else. "Please Lord," I start again," make the beatings, or torture, or whatever it is, stop."

The Almighty One ignores me and the yells get louder. I put my hands over my ears but can't block out the pain inherent in those cries. Then... a pause... footsteps outside my door... the key in the lock... the door opens.

Chapter Thirty-Two

Dominic marches in, immaculate in his suit and tie except for a few blood spatters on his otherwise pristine white shirt. A spiked ball lodges itself in my chest as I stand up.

"You won't be seeing anyone for a while, Melissa," he says. He raises his voice. "Roger, bring it in now."

A man in warden's uniform wheels in the kind of trolley used to shift large appliances. On it is a fridge-freezer.

"How are you going to plug it in?" I ask.

Roger smiles across, and then flushes and looks away. Sometimes I forget other people might be embarrassed by my nakedness. It's been such a long time since anyone saw me, other than Dominic and Thomas.

"Oh, sorry, miss. I didn't... er... anyway... yeah... I'm just going to install a socket now. Shouldn't take long." He delves into a satchel at his waist, and extracts various tools and a socket panel.

Sometime later, the new hole in the stone wall has been covered with the socket panel. Roger has also managed to rig up some lighting, which he claims is necessary to be able to install the fridge. It sounds spurious to me, and I wonder who put him up to it, but I'm not arguing. Light and a fridge freezer are luxuries to me now. Dominic watches the whole time, his expression grim.

The spiked ball remains in my chest, eased only slightly by the additions to my cell. Who has been tortured? Whose blood is Dominic wearing on his shirt? For a brief moment I consider asking, but the presence of Roger combined with Dominic's dour look prevent me.

As Roger works, he avoids looking at me much. I've been permitted, by a glance and a wave from the Messiah, to sit down, and I curl up on the floor, hiding as much of my body from view as possible.

Finally the workman finishes and looks cautiously in my direction. Seeing me less exposed, he risks a friendly smile.

"All done now. The freezer's stocked with stuff you can take out and eat once it's defrosted. There's enough butter and jam in the fridge to keep you going for a few months. You'll be fine." He hesitates and casts a nervous glance at his boss. "Erm, I set up a buzzer. In case, like, well, in case baby starts coming, early, like. You can press this, and one of us'll get the doctor and come and find—"

"And if you do that before the baby's on its way, Melissa, you'll regret it. Don't even think about it. Thomas has been very cooperative today, so I've allowed him to wring some concessions for you; hence the light, and sufficient stocks of food to last you until the birth." Dominic turns to Roger. "You can bring in that other bag now."

The bag turns out to contain a sweatshirt, t-shirt and jogging bottoms, three pairs of knickers and one of my old bras. It will be a bit tight on me now, but I really don't care. The joy of being able to wear clothes again, despite not understanding why, makes my heart lift, and the tension eases for a moment.

"Buzz when you go into labour, Melissa. I'll see you then," says Dominic. He and Roger leave together, although the warden throws me a quick apologetic grin as he gets to the door.

As soon as I hear the door lock, I put on the clothes. Such bliss to have the feel of cotton against my skin. The spare knickers go into the corner where I sleep.

Then I turn to the new appliance. In the fridge is a tub of margarine, two packets of cheese slices, and a jar of cheap strawberry jam. There's also a plastic plate, knife and spoon. The freezer contains twelve loaves of granary bread (supplemented with folic acid – probably too late now, but better than nothing), forty-eight packs of cheese slices, and six further tubs of margarine. In the bottom compartment (the opaque one) I find a sleeping bag and an inflatable pillow.

"Thank you, God, and Thomas too, if this is your doing. I

will always remember this. Thank you so much," I mutter under my breath – just on the off-chance anyone's listening, or that Roger had rigged up anything other than the buzzer, light and fridge freezer.

***

Strangely, the addition of such basic necessities as food, water, clothing and somewhere relatively comfortable to sleep, only exacerbates my acute loneliness. A vague recollection of psychology lessons during my nurse training conjures up a triangle, with the basic necessities of life at the bottom, and as each need is met, the person begins to crave the things higher up until the apex is reached. Perhaps, there's always something missing from part of the triangle – after all, nobody has everything.

For now, though, my most urgent needs are met. The only person I can talk to is Emma. The next weeks are filled with my stories to her. When I finish my life story, I start on nursery rhymes, fairy tales, and then classic stories – or at least the bits I remember – and definitely not word for word: *Pride and Prejudice*, *Emma* (of course), *Persuasion* (my three favourite Jane Austen novels), and then *Jane Eyre*, *Wuthering Heights*, and then on to *Harry Potter*. Finally, despite avoiding it as long as possible, I pick up *Oliver Twist*.

I don't know why, but the meeting with the Artful Dodger prompts the sudden realisation of why Dominic left it here. It was sitting on the book shelf except when he removed it that first time he brought me down to the cellar. All those times he was out of the room, I could have removed it again, and found the way down to the cellars. Once there, I could easily have found the stairs up to the store room, and from there to escape.

I bang my head against my knees – I don't want to give myself concussion.

Holy bloody sodding hell! All this time, and I could have escaped.

Furious with myself, I get up and pace the floor, as well as one can pace while waddling. But gradually, logic reasserts itself. Dominic knows all the ways out – he's obviously very familiar with the underground passages in the Abbey. He would have made sure the door from the cellars to the store room was kept locked, except when he needed it; and he possibly made sure I was asleep at those times anyway.

Meanwhile, he left this book down here to annoy me. He knew I'd work it out in the end, and he wants me to be angry with myself. It's another facet of abuse. The inner tap, dripping regret that I didn't get out when I had the chance. But of course, I never had the chance. I still don't fully understand what he wants with me, but he's not going to let me get out and go to the police; or even to re-join his adoring followers and tell them the truth. It's not going to happen.

Once I've worked this out, I carry on telling Emma the story of *Oliver Twist*. Better that than dwelling on what will happen when she's born.

By eating the same amount each day, I've created a calendar of sorts. Dominic told me when he first came in that it was the beginning of March. There were only two days between him removing all my comforts that Thomas brought me and Dominic's visit with Roger. I wonder what Thomas did to get me these things back. Obviously Dominic doesn't know about all the new assets; otherwise, why would the sleeping bag and pillow be hidden?

But then again, he's the king of deviousness – perhaps he does know, and wants me to think he doesn't. I shut my eyes for a moment. Thoughts like this make me dizzy. I'll never be able to get my head round what Dominic's thinking – my brain won't work that way.

One loaf of bread per week is my allocation. As a worst case scenario, Dominic will come back halfway through and count the loaves. If I operate on the principle I'll be out by the end of April or early May, he'll wonder why. I daren't risk it, so I've divided the twelve loaves mentally across the twelve weeks until the end of May – by which time even Dominic would reasonably expect me to have given birth.

There are now four loaves left, which suggests it must now

be around the end of April.

Getting up from the floor has become increasingly difficult. I waddle from one corner of the room to the other, keeping up a never-ending narrative to Emma. By that point, I'm three-quarters through *Oliver Twist*.

Feeling uncomfortable, I shuffle to the fridge, and extract a cheese slice – my second of three allowed for the day. I don't get as far as eating it. A sudden gush of liquid streams down my legs, soaking my knickers and jogging bottoms. Almost immediately, a tightening pain crosses my abdomen.

This is it.

Panic mingles with excitement. After all these weeks of telling stories to my darling baby, I'll finally get to hold her (or him – although I've been thinking of the baby as Emma, I am partly prepared that I might give birth to a boy.)

I don't bother to change. It needs to be obvious my waters have broken. Dangling from a string above the fridge, the alarm cord is right next to me. I give it a tug. Enhanced by adrenaline, as I yank the cord, it becomes detached from the alarm system.

My heart races. Will anyone hear it? There's no sound coming from the cellars.

I pray. "Dear Lord Almighty, please let the wardens hear me, and come and help."

Within minutes of my prayer, and just as another contraction has me squatting in pain, footsteps echo in the corridor. With short breaths and sweat beginning to bead on my forehead, I hear the key in the lock. The door opens, and three men in surgical scrubs came in. None of them are known to me.

A short, tubby, bald one comes across holding a syringe.

"What's that for?" I ask.

He plunges it into my arm, and the room fades.

Chapter Thirty-Three

My belly is on fire!

An intense burning pain consumes my torso. I force my eyes open and raise my head to look at the source of the agony. A dressing covers my lower abdomen, and a drip protrudes from my arm.

Dr Griffiths is standing next to me, looking shocked and distressed.

"Melissa, my dear, how are you feeling?" he asks gently.

"My tummy's burning up," I relapse into baby language.

"The surgeons found a tumour in your uterus. They had to remove the uterus as well as the tumour. I'm so sorry."

What?

"But I was pregnant. What's happened to my baby?"

"There was no baby, my dear. I'm so sorry."

"Where's Emily?"

"Emily left a while ago. Unfortunately she had a disagreement with Dr Harper, and he asked her to leave immediately. She didn't leave a forwarding address I'm afraid." Dr Griffiths looks apologetic, almost distraught.

The shock on top of the surgery is too much for me. The world darkens again.

I open my eyes and find myself on the ward where I endured those early weeks of morning sickness. How ironic. I don't know how much time has passed.

The fire still rages in my abdomen, and heaviness seems to have invaded all my limbs. A poker stabs inside my temple. I shut my eyes but the poker won't stop its assault. I reopen them a fraction. The fluorescent lights scream at me and the assault increases in tempo and ferocity. My head falls back on the pillows as I try to make sense of what I've been told.

A jumble of words and phrases reels around inside my

brain: *never pregnant*, *uterus removed*, *tumour*; all nonsensical. I've felt my baby kicking. I've been talking to her for months. Even Dominic knew I was pregnant. How could this have happened?

"Melissa, how are you feeling?" A nurse speaks from the corner of the room. I haven't spotted her previously, but I suppose, as I've been unconscious, they couldn't leave me alone.

"Where's my baby?" The words slip out. I know beyond doubt that I was pregnant and they've done something to Emma. Is she alive? Panic grips me. My heart pounds and bile rises in my throat. Sweat pours into my eyes mingling with tears.

The nurse calls for assistance, but I'm too busy drowning in my fear and loss to care. Memories of my baby kicking my ribs – such a common occurrence over the last few months – swamp me. I must have been pregnant. Why are they lying?

A swarm of men and women in green scrubs and nurses' uniforms appear at my side.

I scream, "Where's my baby?" over and over again.

They all seem to be bustling about over something. Unable to distinguish any coherent speech, I just hear a jumble of meaningless words. Eventually a tall man with an intimidating glare approaches me with a needle. Oh no. I try to pull back, but a pin pricks my arm and the world fades – yet again.

I come round, and this time the lights are dim. Some of the pain in my gut has eased, now more like dying embers than a raging fire. The poker in my temple has been replaced by a tennis ball – soft and blunt, but still banging against the inside of my head. All concept of time and space has disappeared. My stomach heaves and I call out. Someone shoves a sick bowl in front of me and I vomit into it. The violence of the action tears at my gut, and it feels as though it's ripping apart. I feel warm liquid seeping through the dressings, but can't focus on that until I stop throwing up. Eventually I slump back on my pillows. I cry out in agony and clasp at my abdomen. The dressing is damp and sticky. I withdraw my hand; it's red and bloody. I must have torn my stitches. The nurse rings a bell, and several doctors come running. Another pin-prick.

As I wake, I begin to understand the difference between coming round from an anaesthetic and recovering from a faint. Fainting leaves less of a sensation of grogginess. The anaesthetic both times has left me feeling sick. There's also significantly more pain each time I awake from anaesthetic. The surgery makes the discomfort of months in the cellar seem like a fall in the playground compared with a major car crash. I can't even compare the mental trauma of the surgery in a favourable manner, as I've lost my baby and apparently any evidence of its existence. I can't absorb the information properly yet. The numerous lapses into unconsciousness have only exacerbated the sense of unreality about the whole situation.

The recovery from the second operation occurs under the watchful eye of Dr Griffiths. When a searing pain below my navel drags me into wakefulness, I open my eyes to see him frowning down at me. I try to speak but my dry mouth seems to be stuck together, and the nausea hits me in a wave. As memory returns of the last time I was sick, I force myself to suppress the impulse.

"Good girl," says Dr Griffiths, watching me carefully. "I'm going to give you an injection now to stop the sickness. We can't risk you tearing your stitches and having to fix them yet again. Two operations is enough to be going on with."

He turns me gently and sticks a needle into my bottom. It makes a refreshing change to have an injection that doesn't knock me out. When I return to the most comfortable position of lying with head, shoulders and knees propped on pillows, I grasp the doctor's wrist.

"Please tell me what happened? Why did you say I wasn't pregnant? Were you there during the operation, when they removed what they said was a tumour?"

"All right, my dear, calm down. It's not good for you to get so worked up. I wasn't there, but Dr Harper told me what they'd found. There's no reason for him to lie. He said the

200

tumour would have mimicked a pregnancy in some ways because of the hormones it produced. It was benign though; you don't have cancer, thank the Lord."

Harper has no reason to lie, has he? Why don't I believe that? I've long since associated him as being closely allied to Dominic. If the Messiah asks Harper to do him a favour, the doctor would do it without question. Clearly Dr Griffiths trusts his boss though, so there's no point arguing.

Balls of steam build up inside my head like a pressure cooker. For the moment, I can't remove the lid, and the explosion grows more dangerous as the pressure increases. Forcing myself to focus on dealing with the pain, I take some deep breaths before thanking the kind doctor at my side.

When he leaves the room, and the nurse returns to her chair in the corner, my thoughts drift down dark alleyways. Dominic has kidnapped my baby in the most hideous way imaginable. The bond between me and Emma grew so strong in the cellar. I have absolutely no doubt she exists and has been taken from me. The lies suggest Dominic doesn't intend to return her to me.

The nurse shifts in her chair, and I glance across. She's absorbed in some work she has with her – counting vials and writing on the pre-filled pad which she has perched on a chair at her side. A curious look at the vials fails to discern the contents.

"Excuse me," I say. "Sorry to interrupt. I just wondered what you were doing? I'm trying to take my mind off everything – it's been a bit of a shock."

She glances up and gives me a sympathetic smile. "Of course it has, love. They're trial drugs – silly name they've got – ZXL358."

"What do they do?"

"We've got a new trial starting tomorrow. Ten men coming in for it. All healthy volunteers. I need to count these, and check the labels. Some of the men have been given a pretend drug, and some are getting the real thing. When I've checked them all, I'll be drawing them up into syringes, and then they get labelled and put in the fridge."

A sudden idea crosses my mind.

"Do you want me to get the doctor back, love? You've gone ever so pale."

"Just a stab of pain. To be expected, I'd have thought. It'll get better eventually," I say. "I think I'll try to have a sleep though now. Thanks for chatting to me – it helps." I throw her a wan smile before shutting my eyes and allowing my thoughts to return to the appalling notion that invaded my brain a moment ago.

The room I'm in has only one other bed. An empty bed. I know from my previous experiences in the Infirmary that it will remain empty while I'm here. That should allow me to explore.

The burning in my gut intrudes into my thoughts. I won't be going anywhere until that subsides. Where's my baby? That's the most important question in the whole world right now. Dominic has shown himself to be cruel and evil. He could have had the doctors remove Emma by C-section, and then take away my uterus. He would no doubt have given them a good reason, and why shouldn't they believe him? The swine has not only taken away my baby, he's deprived me of any chance of ever having another.

He's inflicted enough physical pain to incapacitate an elephant; the fiercely burning abdomen, extreme nausea (despite the anti-sickness injection), and the general sensation of having been anaesthetised twice during a short space of time all make me feel seriously grotty.

But none of this even comes close to the agony of loss. Trying to describe the indescribable – I can only pinpoint a large hole in the region of my chest – as though the doctors have reached in and yanked out my heart. While they were at it, they filched my lungs too, as breathing seems to be a struggle.

Emma's gone. How can I carry on? What's the point in staying alive? What will happen if I give in to the pain?

Numbness sweeps over me – a strange kind of numbness – it fails to squash the physical hurt, but prevents the tears that should flow freely. The last time I was unable to cry was

202

when Jess was abducted – a long time ago. The agony then was exacerbated by guilt. I wasn't there for Jess. I'd gone out and left the back door unlocked.

Perhaps I left the back door unlocked for them to take Emma as well. I realise now, Dominic laid a trap, and I fell right in. The alarm buzzer – it wasn't rigged to protect me or Emma. They installed it so I would warn them when I went into labour, and they were able to implement their evil plans to take her from me.

Looking back to when my waters broke, I should have taken the risk, and given birth to her on the floor – alone. But supposing something had gone wrong? How could I have forgiven myself?

I don't know which is worse – what could have happened or what did happen. Eventually the grogginess of two anaesthetics wins out, and I doze off.

The ward is dimly lit when I wake. A different nurse sits in the corner reading a paperback. A quiet intermittent beep alerts me to the blood pressure monitor at my right side, and in addition to the pressure cuff on my arm, my fingertip of my right forefinger is enclosed by a device which measures oxygen saturation. Someone appears to be concerned about my welfare.

My left hand moves to my abdomen and I touch it gently. The dressings seem secure and dry. On the sheet near my right hand lies a button. I explore it, turning it over in my free fingers. It feels like the kind of device they use in hospitals to allow patients to self-administer morphine. Am I in sufficient pain for the opioid? Perhaps – maybe in a short while. My brain feels disassociated from the rest of me at the moment. A peculiar sense of detachment from the mental, physical and emotional pain washes through me.

Morphine. The knowledge of its existence in the Infirmary. Syringes in the trials ward. Probably also in the nurses' station, but the trials ward might be a safer bet.

Revenge, they say, is best served cold. By the time my wounds heal enough for me to walk down the corridor, the age-old emotion will have had ample time to chill. There'll be time enough for me to lay my plans carefully.

The button remains unpressed. Pain or no pain, I need a clear head.

Chapter Thirty-Four

When I wake up, the original nurse has returned to her seat in the corner of my ward. I try to sit up without dislodging anything, and she rushes to help.

"Thanks," I say, after a few minutes of shuffling, shifting wires and tubes, and trying not to extract the needle from the back of my hand. Finally, I'm propped upright in a relatively comfortable position. "That's better. I hadn't realised I had quite so many attachments."

"You were quite poorly yesterday. It seemed best to get you hooked up and monitored. We fixed up some morphine for the pain as well. You just need to press this button if it gets too much."

All the wriggling has re-lit the fires, but they don't seem quite so intense as yesterday, and I'm determined to stick to my resolution. No more drugs if I can avoid them. Or at least, nothing that will affect my ability to think.

"I'd rather not have morphine if I can help it. Please could I have some paracetamol instead?"

"That won't touch it, love. You do realise that, don't you? I could get you some co-codamol?"

Another drug that'll knock me out. I'll have to suffer in silence.

I pretend to concede. It might be useful to have a supply of hard-core painkillers anyway. My plans haven't fully solidified yet. Perhaps back-up supplies will be handy.

The nurse leaves me for a few minutes, but I can't do anything useful, as a stream of men stride down the corridor. I gaze through the glass, vaguely curious, but then see a familiar profile. Charles, he of the unfaithful wife – the attacker of Frank. He had seemed unrepentant of the attack, even when Frank had been whisked to hospital the next day after a bad reaction from the trial drug. Perhaps he had an overdose, or maybe his injuries rendered him less able to cope with the medication. Either way, any sympathy I might have felt for Charles has waned. I don't know why he's decided to return for further research studies. Even back then, he didn't seem the type.

I'm fighting to not dwell on the loss of Emma. I'm convinced she has to be somewhere; I just have to implement my plans, and then I can find her. I keep telling myself this. *I will find her* is the mantra in my head. It keeps me going, and halts the incapacitating grief that threatens me at frequent intervals.

All the other men passing in the corridor are complete strangers. Suppressing a flutter of disappointment – it would be nice to see Greg again – I return my attention to planning.

***

Over the next three days, I become adept at pretending to swallow painkillers. Unfortunately they'll have my germs on, but in the grander scheme, that doesn't seem to matter. The day after the trial subjects arrived, the nurse began to leave me alone for increasing periods. The number of attachments has decreased. They took the morphine away first, then one by one the others disappeared, until the final tube – the catheter – was removed this morning. I'm now allowed to use the toilet.

The trip to the loo – my first escape from bed in about four days – feels like an excursion to the Himalayas. The pain in my abdomen, which subsided to a dull ache, flares like a beacon and screams at me. The effort of merely getting out of bed has me dripping with sweat and struggling for breath. The trip takes thirty minutes each way – an hour of torture and agony, just to do a wee. I collapse back in bed when I've finished, and cry with relief that the ordeal's over.

The second trip to the loo takes fifteen minutes in total; a significant improvement. The recovery also takes less time, and I begin to be hopeful about putting my plans into action.

There are a number of challenges to overcome. If I'm thrown back in to the cellar as soon as I've recovered sufficiently, all the planning will have been a waste of time.

Next time the nurse comes in, I ask her if I can speak to Dr Griffiths. She obliges, and five minutes later, the kind doctor stands at the edge of my bed.

"How are you, my dear?"

"Getting better, thank you. It still hurts a lot to get out of bed though."

"Of course it does. You'll need to be taking it easy for about six weeks. Not lifting anything, being careful, that sort of thing."

"Will I be able to stay here?"

Dr Griffiths scratches his nose and looks away.

"So sorry, my dear. Dominic has told us that you're to go to his rooms to recover as soon as you're well enough to spend more than a few minutes out of bed. I did mention that it might be wiser to have you here where we can keep an eye on you, but he stressed his ability to take care of you himself, and said Dr Harper could go and check up on you each day."

I look round to make sure we're alone, then lower my voice anyway.

"You know he kept me locked up in the cellars for weeks? And before that I was locked in his rooms. He's evil." I reach out and touch the doctor's arm. "Please help me. I don't want to see him again."

Although it's not part of my scheme to stay in the Infirmary forever, I need to be a lot stronger than I am now before going back to Dominic. I can't risk being locked in there and vulnerable without some form of back-up.

It's a risk sharing my fears and horror – it gives me a motive for what I'm planning – but there's already enough evidence of motive to send me away for life. I have to pray that other evidence will predominate.

Dr Griffiths sits heavily on the chair beside my bed, and shakes his head. He's several shades paler than when he came in.

"I'd heard rumours that you disappeared. I hoped they

weren't true. When you turned up in the hospital the other day, I assumed Dominic had been looking after you, but perhaps the circumstances suggest otherwise, my dear. I'm so sorry. I wish I could help. I will keep asking Dr Harper for evidence that you're recovering. Perhaps you could write to me?"

"Please could we use a code word? If I mention 'miracles', it's a sign I need help. Please, Dr Griffiths, if I write that word in a letter to you, please send help – Mark or Jimmy. Please don't rely on Dr Harper to help me. I think he's too closely aligned to Dominic."

He nods, a grave expression on his usually smiling face. Standing up again, he touches my arm.

"Of course. If I see that word on a letter from you, or hear it in a message, in any way – I'll get you some help. I promise. Also if I don't hear from you." He manages a smile. "Meanwhile, I should be able to keep you here for a few more days. Is there anything else I can help you with?"

I think for a moment.

"I'd like to build up my strength before I leave. A few gentle walks would help. Do you have a frame or something I could lean on when I get tired? And perhaps warn the staff I'll be wandering around a bit?"

"Absolutely. But build up slowly, my dear. Stick with walking to the toilet and back for today. Perhaps tomorrow you can wander a little further. I'll see what I can dredge up in the way of walking frames." He glances at his watch. "I'd better be off. You take care now."

"Yes. Thank you," I give him a grateful smile.

Exhausted by my efforts of the day, I fall asleep early that evening, and sleep through. I awake to bright daylight streaming in through the small window and the smell of tea and toast. The nurse who's been with me most days since I arrived here has remained anonymous, but people who bring buttered toast deserve better. I beam at her gratefully.

"Good morning. I'm sorry, I still don't know your name."

"I'm Jane, and don't apologise. It's my fault; should have introduced myself when you were in a fit state to listen. How

208

are you this morning?"

I shuffle myself into an upright position before answering. "Getting a bit better, I think. A couple of days ago, doing that set off volcanoes inside. Now, it's just grumbling. I still feel weak though."

"That'll pass," says Jane, plumping up pillows behind me. "Dr Griffiths mentioned you'd like to walk around a bit. Found a Zimmer frame in the store cupboard. No idea where it came from, but you may as well borrow it until you get a bit stronger. After you've finished your breakfast, I'll walk down the corridor with you, and help you get your bearings a bit. That should be more than enough exercise for this morning."

"Thanks. That's very kind of you. You don't need to come with me every time though." I try to keep any anxiety out of my voice. They mustn't get into the habit of following me everywhere.

"Don't worry. Not planning on it. Far too much to do to hold your hand every moment of the day. I'll just make sure you're okay for the first trip out, then you're on your own, pet. Only be a bit sensible, okay? Don't want to have to pick you up off the floor and rush you back to theatre."

"Thanks." I flash her another grateful smile. She isn't Emily, but she still seems kind.

I hope she won't get into trouble for leaving me, given what I'm about to do.

Chapter Thirty-Five

My first trip takes me past the men's trial ward and the ward where I spent part of my early pregnancy. (At the memory, a sharp pain presents itself in my chest. I clamp down on it quickly.) With a bit of subtle prompting, Jane shows me round the whole Infirmary.

"Said you wanted to see the Pharmacy as well, didn't you? We don't have much of a Pharmacy really, pet. Just in there," she points to a store room, behind a door controlled by a key pad, "we keep all the drugs. Some are in fridges, depending on what they are. What goes in and out gets written in big A4 notebooks. So old-fashioned. In my last job, they used to keep everything logged on computer, but not here. Even the trials stuff is just in one of those note books, but a red one for trials – all the others are black."

My interested expression keeps her chattering on. I mentioned at the start of the walk that I'd trained to be a nurse, so she treats me as a fellow professional. I swallow down the vague feelings of guilt. This has to be done.

"When I was a nurse, they always used to have really silly numbers on the key pad, like their birthdays or the day the matron got her cat."

Jane blushes. "Yeah. Got to have a number you can remember, that's all." She lowers her voice. "I always use the Battle of Hastings. Ten-sixty-six. It's the only date in history I can remember." She shakes her head, laughing, and another surge of guilt runs through me. She's so lovely.

She presses the keys and the door opens. I lean heavily on my walking frame for a moment. Even that short walk has tired me out. I badly need to build up my stamina.

"You tired, pet? Can show you this another time if you like?"

"No, you might be too busy another time. I've not seen a Pharmacy where trials are done. It's really interesting."

"Suppose it is, the first time you see it. Trust me, pet, the novelty soon wears off."

She laughs and leads the way into the small room. It's about three metres square, but the clutter of cupboards, boxes, shelves and the big fridge leaves barely any floor space. I bring my frame in sideways to avoid knocking anything over.

"Bit cramped, I know. Does the job though." She picks up a large red book from the shelf next to the fridge. "All the trial drug entries are in here. Everything's coded, but the codes are in the back. Makes it easier. Did you not do any trials when you were nursing?"

"They didn't let us students anywhere near, but if I'd worked for longer after my training finished, I think I might have liked research. I've really enjoyed watching all the goings-on with the men who've been in for trials. It's fascinating."

With this small encouragement, Jane proceeds to show me where all the drugs are kept, even the morphine. By the time she's finished, I can only just stand up. Necessity and the Zimmer frame keep me on my feet. I won't get another chance.

"Was that someone shouting your name?" I interrupt her as she begins to shut the fridge door.

"Ooh, don't know. You must have sharp ears. You all right here for a moment whilst I go look? You look shattered, pet. I won't be long, and then I can get you back to bed."

She exits, shutting the door behind her. She's left the fridge open, and I reach in and quickly grab two vials of morphine and a couple of vials of trial stuff. A bit of shuffling around of the boxes, and it looks at first glance as though nothing's missing. Then I see the potassium chloride. That would work much more quickly and reliably than the other two drugs. I don't have time to put the others back now though. I grab two ampoules of the potassium chloride, and pray no one will delve too much too soon. I put the loot in my dressing-gown pocket, wrapping the vials quickly in my hankie to reduce clinking. There's a box of tissues on the side, so I take a handful and stuff those in my pocket as well.

I'm shutting the door when Jane comes back in.

"Sorry, I thought I should shut the fridge door in case it got too warm in there."

"Sensible girl. Thanks, pet. Should have done it myself before I went out. Let's get you back to bed – looking downright shattered, you are."

I think about asking who had been calling for her, but decide against drawing attention to my tactic to get her out of the room. Far better for it to seem natural, and let it be forgotten. With any luck, she'll forget she's even taken me in there.

***

Finally back in bed, I get Jane to draw the curtains round, pleading a need to sleep after the excursion. When she's gone, I delve into my dressing-gown pocket and retrieve the vials. The two morphine bottles have instructions on how to administer, and big warning letters. On closer inspection, the label states *5mg/ml – total morphine 60mg*. That sounds like more than enough. Better still, it can be injected into the veins, muscles or skin. It's a possibility, but may be too slow to act.

I have a quick look at the trial drug vials I've collected. They're labelled with a string of letters and numbers, and the only dosing information states *Inject 5ml IV once daily*. I give up any idea of using them.

Then I look at the potassium chloride. I know this has to be diluted in clinical practice, but if it were injected into the muscle, particularly with a quick injection, it would stop the heart very quickly, possibly within a minute for the right dose. This seems a much better option. I wrap the vials of choice back in my hankie and tissues, and return them to my pocket. I put the trial drug and morphine vials loose in my other pocket and settle down to rest.

Sleep evades me, despite the tiredness that envelops every cell in my body. My stitches burn, and my arms and legs are full of hot lead. Yet as soon as I lie down and close my eyes, my brain comes alive; thoughts whirling round it like soup in a blender.

I can't quite believe I'm thinking of doing this. It's only because the alternative – years locked in a cellar and never seeing Emma, or Mark, again – is unthinkable.

***

I must finally doze off, because next thing I know, there's a kiss on my cheek. I open my eyes. A sheepish-looking Mark hovers at my bedside.

Thank you, God.

"Oh Mark, it's so good to see you." I fight past the lump in my throat. "How can you be here? Does Dominic know? How long can you stay?" I grab his hand and grip. I don't want to ever let go.

"Hey, one question at a time. I get to ask first anyway. How are you? That's the most important question of the lot."

"I'm getting better – physically anyway." I lower my voice. "They've taken away our baby. Did they tell you the same stupid story they told me?"

"Dr Griffiths extracted me discreetly after lunch today and brought me over here. He told me that you'd had an operation, and the official records state that you had a tumour removed from your uterus. But now he's beginning to believe your version, and he wants to help us."

That simple word 'us' helps more than anything I've heard all week.

"Before that, I'd heard nothing. You just disappeared, Mel. I've been searching for you for months. The only thing I'd heard was from Thomas, who assured me you were alive and well, but that if he told me anything else, he wouldn't be able to continue helping you. That was about two months ago. Nothing since."

"Has Dominic hurt you at all?"

"The occasional beating in the cellars when he or the wardens caught me roaming at night looking for you. Nothing too major. Did he hurt you? Where have you been?"

"I was in Dominic's rooms at first, then down in the cellars. Thomas did look after me for a while, then Dominic took over. I preferred Thomas."

My eyes must show some of my hatred of the Messiah. Mark covers my hand with his own and leans in close.

"What did Dominic do to you? If he's hurt you, I'll kill him," he whispers. As he sits up, I see the fury in his eyes. I can't let Mark take control of this – it could all go wrong.

"He didn't actually hurt me, he just threatened to. I was frightened of him, that's all." The anger doesn't recede, so I try again. "Mark, you mustn't do anything. I'm not afraid any more. It's fine. Keep your head down, and we'll get through this. I promise. I love you."

At that moment, Dr Griffiths opens the curtains around the bed.

"Mark, you need to go. Come to my office for a moment until it's safe. Melissa, my dear, don't worry, I'll make sure he gets back safely."

I nod, and release Mark's hand with great reluctance. He plants a quick kiss on my lips and follows Dr Griffiths out of the ward.

A sense of urgency fills me. If I don't act soon, Mark will try something. He doesn't have the same resources at his disposal, or the same excuse if everything goes wrong. I could still end up in prison, but with a sympathetic judge and jury I might get away with a short sentence, or even none at all. I pray it won't come to trial. Judges are not famed for their sympathy in domestic abuse cases, and although things may have changed while I've been here, I wouldn't fancy my chances in a criminal court.

The key to success relies, unfortunately, on a lot of luck. Detailed planning is great, but certain things have to happen at the right time, in the right place and in the right order – and I have little control over any of those aspects. I close my eyes. I have to focus on the things I can control.

214

The potassium chloride rests in my pocket. What do I still need? A syringe, some wipes to remove fingerprints, some energy, and a distraction.

Chapter Thirty-Six

The syringe, wipes and energy are my focus today. Many hours of the night, I alternated between dreaming of a happy life with Mark and Emma, panic at the prospect of spending the rest of my life behind bars, and terror at the thought that everything might go completely wrong, and I could end up subjected to Dominic's whims and furies for eternity. Every now and again, I added another possibility to the mixture – the one where Mark beat me to it, and got sent to prison for the rest of his days.

A restless sleep finally overtook me, and when I wake to the smell of toast and coffee, Jane looks horrified.

"Not looking good, pet. Bad night?"

"I didn't sleep well. I had some bad dreams." I could see her about to ask for details, and quickly added, "They're gone now. I never remember my dreams for long." After all the lies I've told already, this one was quite innocent.

With the help of my frame, I hobble to the bathroom, and one look in the mirror assures me that Jane's expression was justified. Lank red curls plaster themselves to my forehead and frame a face that looks pale and thin. Bags under my eyes are large enough to carry the Abbey laundry for a week, and my eyes themselves – well, I hope no one else can see the fear and angst within. Perhaps I only see it because I know it's there.

After washing, I return to bed. A shower and cleaning my teeth after breakfast make further improvements, and a further examination in the mirror reveals only a pale, tired young woman, rather than the horror from first thing this morning.

Clothed in a clean nightdress and my trusty dressing-gown, which hasn't left me since I acquired the drugs yesterday, I prepare to go for another walk. This stroll takes me to the nurses' station, which is unmanned for the moment. An array of coloured boxes on the shelves behind the desk hold such essentials as needles, cotton wool, swabs, tourniquets, and syringes of various sizes.

I check both directions of the corridor, but there's no one in sight. The CCTV on the ceiling faces the opposite direction – away from the station – towards the door between the Abbey and the Infirmary. A hobble towards the boxes takes me within stealing distance, and with a quick sleight of hand, several syringes are in my pocket, nestled against a few sheathed needles and a handful of swabs. I look round again. Dr Harper is walking towards me, the usual cross expression on his face.

"Sorry, doctor, I was just looking. I once trained as a nurse. I was curious."

He gives me a suspicious look, but it holds an element of surprise. I must have withheld that information from our past dealings.

"Well, get back to bed now. You should be resting. Dominic wants you in his rooms tomorrow. If I were you, I would be making the most of my chances to sleep. Once he has you back there, you'll be at his beck and call."

I nod and turn the Zimmer frame back towards my ward. Harper surprised me; unless I imagined it, there was a gleam of pity in his eyes.

Now I have the tools I need, I can afford to rest. I pull the curtains around my bed, and dig into my pocket for the syringes. I'd taken a selection, and have two-, five- and ten-millilitre sizes. Following a quick peek at the potassium chloride vial, I discard the 2ml syringe. The ampoules are each 10ml and contain 1.5 grams of active drug. If I push it in fast, hopefully I'll deliver enough to be lethal before Dominic realises what's happening.

I have two vials of potassium chloride, so can afford to prepare a 5ml and a 10ml syringe. Listening carefully for footsteps, I draw up almost all the contents of one vial, and just under half the contents of the other, into separate syringes, and re-sheath the needles. I have to leave them loose in my pocket, but they'll be safe enough there.

My next challenge is to distract Dominic. I worry about this for a long time. I finally decide to go for a walk to get some inspiration. As I approach the nurses' station, I shut my eyes, and mouth a quick prayer:

Please, Lord. If you really care about me and want to help, give me guidance. Show me how to distract Dominic. I promise if you help me with this, I'll never doubt you again.

Opening my eyes, I see a newspaper, open on the desk. The headline on the page states:

ASTEROID HEADING TOWARDS EARTH

My heart pounds, and I move round the desk to read the rest of the article. It becomes clear, halfway down the page, that there is no danger, and the asteroid will not get closer than a few million miles (mere inches in stellar terms, I suppose). But more importantly, here is my distraction. I breathe a quick but heartfelt prayer of thanks, and fold the paper carefully, with the article showing as the front page. Tucking it under my arm, I hurry, as fast as I can with my Zimmer frame, back to bed.

***

It's late morning the next day when I receive the summons. Dr Griffiths hurries in to the ward, a worried expression on his face.

"My dear, I'm so sorry. It's time. He just phoned." He helps me out of bed and into a wheelchair, before putting slippers on my feet, and a small holdall on my lap. "I'm going to take you down the corridor and leave you with the warden who's waiting for you just inside the Abbey."

I smile gratefully and I reach inside the pocket of my dressing-gown. My hand grasps the contents tightly.

Dr Griffiths hands me a stick in place of the Zimmer frame, and wheels me out of the ward and along the passage towards the Abbey.

I don't recognise the warden who meets us at the entrance. It doesn't matter. Perhaps it's better that way.

"I'll take her from here, Doc."

Dr Griffiths pats me on the shoulder – a much-appreciated gesture of affection.

The warden takes over control of the wheelchair. He knocks on the door when we reach Dominic's office, and waits a moment. A moment that seems to last forever. I try to keep my breathing steady, but my heart is racing, and I felt certain the warden can hear it.

Eventually he speaks. "I'm going to have to leave you here. I've got a key, so I'd better let you in myself and then you can wait inside until he comes along. He said he was going to be here. I don't know where he is, honest."

"It's fine. Don't worry. Please can you just wheel me into the office, then I'll sort myself out? Thanks."

He tries the office door. It opens without the key. This is strange. It's usually locked. My heart races. He wheels me inside, and then leaves, shutting the door behind him.

I remove the newspaper from my holdall and stand up, using the stick for leverage and support. Stitches still bother me, but now is not the time to be worrying. I'm still wearing my nightdress and dressing-gown, now with just the two filled syringes, and the alcohol swabs nestling in the pocket. The door to Dominic's bedroom is ajar, and I push it gently. My heart's really hammering now, probably loud enough to be heard back in the Infirmary, but I creep into the bedroom, uncertain of what to expect.

Shock holds me spellbound for a moment. Dominic's sitting on the bed; his short-sleeved shirt in disarray, his tie askew and his hair standing on end. In front of him, in full view, lies the newspaper – the exact same one I'm holding. I send up a quick prayer of thanks for the short sleeves. They solve so many issues.

"It's happening, Melissa. Sooner than foretold. I'm being punished for my arrogance. The Almighty One neglected to warn me that it starts now. Oh Lord, what have I done to

219

deserve this?" His voice cracks and trembles.

"Oh Dominic, I saw it too. What will happen to us?" I ask, moving carefully behind him and to his left side, as if to look at the headline. I must not mess this up. Dominic is right-handed. Extracting the larger syringe from my pocket, I plunge it into his left upper arm, aiming for the muscles at the side, just below the level of his sleeve; then empty the entire contents.

Dominic doesn't react. It's as though the news of the asteroid has unhinged him. He continues to stare into space for about a minute, before collapsing backwards on the bed.

Wiping my fingerprints away with the sterile swabs, I wrap Dominic's right hand around the syringe, and leave it in his slackened grasp. Looking around, there's nothing else I need to do. I listen to the Messiah's breathing labour, and then one gasp and it stops. My stolen copy of the newspaper goes back in my holdall. It wasn't needed after all. The used swabs are returned to my pocket to be disposed of when convenient. An artistic arrangement of the furniture is my final task.

I hobble to the door, take a deep breath, and scream.

Chapter Thirty-Seven

I retreat to the office, but keep screaming until the door bursts open. Mark, Jimmy, and (even more surprisingly) Greg Matthews storm in. Mark comes straight to me, and puts his arms around my shaking shoulders.

"What's the matter? What happened? Are you okay?" The barrage of questions from Mark only succeeds in reducing me to tears. The relief overwhelms me for a moment. I hope my reaction seems natural under the circumstances.

"Dominic," I point to the bedroom. "He's in there. I think he might be... d...dead." I don't need to fake the sobs that shake my body. No one needs know the real reason for them.

Jimmy and Greg give me sympathetic looks then rush into the bedroom. Mark sits me down on the chair in the office, so I miss their initial reactions, but they come out a moment later.

Greg perches on the desk in front of me.

"Mel, this will possibly be less of a shock to you than to these two. Remember I told you back on the ward that I'm a lawyer?"

I nod.

"That's not strictly true, although I do have a law degree. I'm a detective – undercover variety – and I've been working here. I ostensibly joined The Brotherhood shortly after we met. There were a few concerns here that warranted investigation. No need to go into those now. Suffice to say, I'll be able to take charge of the situation here."

"So what'll happen now?" says Jimmy.

"On first appearances, it would appear that your Leader has committed suicide, but at this stage, we can't rule out the possibility that a crime has been committed. I've seen enough of this place to know he was not... well, he wasn't a nice person."

I almost laugh. Greg has uttered the biggest understatement I've ever heard. The problem now is that I don't know where I stand with him. Trusting him might be dangerous.

As I sort out my thoughts, and struggle to get my emotions under control (complicated by Mark's continued embrace), Greg turns to the phone on Dominic's desk, and dials.

"DI Matthews here... Yes, I'm at Coulson Abbey... Possible homicide, could be suicide... Yep, I'll need SOCO... I'll meet them at the entrance in twenty minutes. For the moment, any chance of a few officers down here? I need to keep everyone out of the immediate area. Thanks, Dean. See you soon."

He puts the phone down and turns back towards us.

"Okay, I've got support on the way. Mel, I think the best place for you is back in the Infirmary, where you can be looked after properly. Hang on, is there a phone number for them?"

"I don't know," I say weakly. The tears have dried up, but exhaustion has crept in, leaving me numb.

"Hello. Greg Matthews here. Is that Dr Griffiths? ... Great. I'm sending Melissa back to you. Can you arrange for Mark to stay on the ward with her until she's fully recovered? She's in shock ... Well, sir, you'd find out soon enough, so I may as well tell you myself. Melissa found Dominic dead in his room. We don't know the details yet, but obviously she's in a bit of a state, and I'd prefer it if her boyfriend could look after her for the time being ... Great. Thanks ... Yes, there's a chair outside. I'll send them along now. Bye." He replaces the receiver on the cradle, and turns to Mark. "You're best placed to look after Mel while we get to the bottom of this. I don't want you to leave her alone until I say so. Just in case there's some madman around. Let's play it safe." He transfers his attention to me. "Sorry, Mel. I know this has been a shock, and I don't want to worry you further, but just until we rule out the possibility that someone hated Dominic enough to murder him, let's keep you and Mark safe together, shall

222

we?"

"And what am I supposed to do?" says Jimmy.

"For the moment, my friend, you can help me keep everyone else away from the area. When I get some reinforcements, you may be able to help me in other ways, but we'll come on to that later."

Mark brings the wheelchair in, and helps me to transfer into it. "Jimmy, can you get some nightclothes and stuff sent over to the Infirmary for me, mate?"

"Aye, of course. If our resident copper'll let me, I'll bob round later with them." He raises his eyebrows at Greg, who nods genially.

With that assurance, Mark wheels me out of the room and back along the corridor, where we're welcomed by a sombre-looking Dr Griffiths.

"Melissa, my dear, I'm so sorry that you had to go through that. Do you know any details?" he asks, as he takes the chair handles from Mark, and pushes me himself.

"I had to virtually break into the room. There was a chair wedged behind the door. I just saw him lying on the bed. His face was kind of blue." I shudder. "It was horrible. He wasn't breathing. I got out of the room as quickly as I could and screamed for help."

Mark, walking at my side, gives me a curious look, but I can't confide in him. I don't know if I'll ever be able to tell him the truth.

When we reach the ward, Dr Griffiths wheels me up to the same bed I left this morning – less than two hours ago – and closes the curtains around us.

"I'll leave you here and make sure you're not disturbed for a while. You've got about an hour until lunch. Just bear in mind you've very recently had an operation, my dear," he says, with a smile, and what looks suspiciously like a wink. Quite what he thinks we'll be doing in the circumstances, I dread to think.

When he's gone, Mark helps me into bed, then puts his arms round me in a comforting hug. I cling to him, scared that we'll be separated again. We've been apart so long. As he strokes my hair, I rest my head on his shoulder.

"Do you think we'll be able to find our baby? Now that Dominic's gone?"

"I don't know, Mel." Mark draws back to look at me. "Perhaps today isn't the best time to start asking. What if they think it's a motive for... well, you know?"

"What if it was?" I whisper nervously.

"Mel, seriously?"

"Would it make a difference to us? I'm not saying it was, but just supposing?"

Mark stands up and walks away from the bed to the corner where the curtains meet. He stares out for an eternity. When he finally turns back to me with a grave expression on his face, my heart falls to somewhere near the earth's core.

"We'll deal with it, somehow." He comes back to perch on the bed and lowers his voice. "I'm pleased he's dead. It means we have a chance at a life together. Let's just pray that there's enough evidence for them to bring in a verdict of suicide. Whatever you've done, or even only thought about doing, is understandable to me, but I don't think a jury would agree. We need to hold off asking questions about our baby for now. I'm sorry."

"I know. I suppose you're right – it would look suspicious." Tears fill my eyes. "I want her back so badly, though. I don't know what they've done with her. What if no one but Dominic knows where she is?"

Sobs overtake me, and Mark wraps his arms round me again. The thought I might have forever destroyed my chances of finding Emma blows me apart. My whole world explodes, and the only things holding me together are Mark's arms.

"You're going to make yourself ill if you carry on like this. I'm going to see if I can find Dr Griffiths and ask if he can give you something. It will help. People suspect Dominic of having imprisoned you in some way, so they wouldn't expect you to be this upset – only shocked. Distraught will seem weird, and..."

"Don't people know I was pregnant? They do, I know they

do! Surely there'll be speculation about what happened? Most people will understand I want my baby back."

"You need some sleep. I'll be back in a minute."

I'm cold with Mark gone. He's withdrawn from me, and doesn't seem to understand my agony of loss. In a strange way, this is worse than when I was told the pregnancy was false. I knew then Dominic would never let me have her back. Now he's gone, I ought to be able get her now. I want her this minute. Not tomorrow, not next week, now!

Mark returns with two tablets and a glass of water. Exhausted beyond fighting, I swallow the tablets quickly and turn on to my side, to face away from Mark and anyone else who might come in. I wait impatiently for sleep to come and smother the pain inside.

Chapter Thirty-Eight

"I've got your stuff. I couldnae find your toothpaste though." Jimmy's strident voice shakes me into consciousness. "Oh Christ! Sorry, lass, did I wake you?"

I sit up and rub my eyes. "It doesn't matter. What time is it? How long have I been asleep?"

"It's nearly five. They'll be bringing dinner soon," says Mark, unpacking the small bag that Jimmy's brought, and stacking everything in neat piles in a bedside cupboard.

"Settling yourself in? You're both well out of it. I'd get over here myself if I could."

"Why, what's happening?" I say.

"Your pal, Greg! He's asking questions, and more questions, and then some more. Honest lass, you're better off here." He pauses, frowning. "The police arrived, and all the forensics lot. They're worried because they can't find the bottle of stuff that was used. Mel, lass, you didn't just pick it up off the floor, not thinking, and put it in your pocket, did you?"

I feel in my dressing gown pockets, and extract a vial.

"I must have seen it on the bed, and picked it up without thinking. It's not something you'd want to leave lying around." I look at the vial, examining it. I picked up the emptier one, fortunately; the one that tallies with the amount Dominic was given, and with the syringe I left in his hand. I give it to Jimmy, who takes it in his bare hand and wraps his fingers carefully around it.

"I don't suppose we need to make it easy for those lads. The more fingerprints the better." He shifts the bottle from one hand to the other, fingering it at different angles, and having a good read of the label. "Fancy a look, Mark?"

"Yeah, let's have it then." Mark takes the vial as well, and

226

examines it, carefully, making sure to handle it thoroughly."

"I assume Dominic's fingerprints are there as well," says Mark.

My throat constricts. Of course they aren't.

"M-maybe they wouldn't find them underneath ours?"

Mark rolls it around his hand a bit more.

"Not now they won't. Anyway, they've not taken our fingerprints yet. We'll have to see."

"Why would you do this for me?" My voice comes out croaky.

"You're his fiancée; or at least you were, and I guess you will be again; and you're my best pal. Why wouldn't we?" says Jimmy.

"Supposing they decided you were guilty of conspiracy, or worse still, of killing him yourself?"

"Listen. That bastard tortured and abused you for months. And he made me do stuff I didn't ever want to do." Jimmy sits heavily on the chair and puts his head in his hands. When he raises his head again, his eyes are glistening. "D'you remember Leonard?"

"Yes, of course." I turn to Mark. "I think it was before you arrived. Leonard just disappeared. He was a sweetie. It was awful. Dominic said he'd died of a heart attack."

"Aye, well. His heart stopped. I was there, Mel. I did it. Dominic gave me this stuff, and sent me across here. It was already in the syringe. I don't know what was in it, I just had to stick it in. My punishment for killing the wasp! He called me his disciple. God, what a shit! If ever anyone deserved to die like that, it was him. And you know what? I'd have done it myself if I'd had the knowledge, or access to the stuff." Tears are streaming down his cheeks now.

Mark puts his hand on Jimmy's shoulder. "Don't worry, mate. We'll get through this. I think we all have things we'd rather the police don't know about."

I look curiously at Mark. What does he have to hide?

He continues, "It's in all our interests for them to believe it's suicide. We just need to stick together."

I glance up at the ceiling. "Is the CCTV active? Doesn't it

look like we're plotting?" I ask Mark.

He grins for the first time since we've been reunited. "While you were asleep, I did a bit of messing about with the electrics. CCTV and bugs are all dead in here. I thought about doing the sort of shenanigans where it looks as though something else is happening, but I reckoned the only person who would care if all the devices were working is no longer with us."

"Some of the wardens have done a bunk already. I heard they gave contact details to Greg, then disappeared," says Jimmy. "From what I know of them, the less contact they have with the police, the better, if you know what I mean."

"Oh yes!" says Mark. "Anyway, that's fewer people to be looking at CCTV anyway. It's going to be interesting to see what happens to The Brotherhood now."

"Aye, well, some have asked Greg if he can help them contact families. He said he'd get people in to help when he's interviewed everyone. Poor lad, he'll have a crap job of that – there's, what, two hundred members?"

I nod. "How's Tina? I've not seen her for months."

"She went back into her shell when you disappeared, lass. She'd speak a bit to Mark and Brie, but she mostly kept to her own group, and even then, I don't think she spoke much. I can ask if she can come over and see you; she'll like that."

"Has Thomas been hassling her?"

"No' really, maybe just a bit at first, then he started leaving her be. She started to fill out a wee bit after that."

We're interrupted by the arrival of Greg. He's carrying something I've not seen in over a year – huge pizza boxes. He puts them on the bedside table and fully opens the curtains round the bed.

"Hungry?" he says with a broad grin.

"Blimey, mate – is that out of the police budget?"

"No, Mark, we can't quite run to that. I do however get paid once in a while, and Inspectors can afford to buy the occasional fourteen-inch pizza in a good cause. I didn't know what you like, but I've got cheese and tomato, and veggie. We'll get you used to normal food before we introduce meat.

228

It might be a bit of a shock to the system at first."

"Greg, you're wonderful, thank you." I beg a slice of cheese and tomato, and the others choose their favourites, and nothing's said for a few minutes, as the mouth-wateringly scrumptious pizza disappears into hungry stomachs. After one slice, though, I begin to worry if the Inspector's trying to soften us up, and if this is a bribe to tell him everything. Cramps prevent me eating any more, and I lie back against the pillows wincing.

"Are you all right? Sorry, I maybe should have bought something a bit easier to digest."

"It's okay. Been a long time since I ate pizza, and all that cheese has probably upset me a bit. It'll settle down. When I was in the cellars, I had rations of two cheese slices and two slices of bread a day, so in some ways, not that different really – just a bit more bland."

I hadn't meant to mention the cellars, but the pain distracted me and it slipped out. I watch Greg's reaction closely. I know Mark is horrified by what I've been through, and also that it's made him furious. I don't need to look. Jimmy's earlier revelation about Leonard alerted me that he's been through a lot too. A quick glance suggests that Greg knows some of this already, and I wonder how. It's a question for later.

There's a tightening around Greg's mouth and eyes – a hint of grim determination – but I don't know what it means. Then he relaxes into the kind, avuncular man who came to see me in the ward months ago.

"You've had a tough time, Mel. I'd expect you to be relieved that Dominic's dead. I've heard from Thomas some of the things you were subjected to. He got scared when he realised that some of his activities could land him a long gaol sentence, and decided to talk."

"What's he said?" asks Mark.

"He admitted to raping Tina, and to carrying out acts of torture under the instructions of Dominic. But he said Dominic had rescued him from a life of poverty and given him a home. There was certainly a sense that Thomas was grateful to Dominic." Greg hesitates and looks at me for a long moment, but there's kindness in his eyes. "I know Thomas helped you to some extent while you were imprisoned, and that will certainly count in his favour. Mel, there's a lot of evidence which is confusing. I need to sort everything out, and work out what's happened."

He stands up and paces the ward.

The cramps in my stomach are replaced by vampire bats. I swallow, and visions of real prison cells creep into my mind – a lifetime surrounded by tough women who might make life with Dominic look easy.

Greg stops pacing and pauses by the bed. He looks down at me gravely.

"If I can find some more evidence to suggest suicide, I'll be only too happy to discuss this with the coroner. It's obviously not my decision, but I'd much prefer it not to end up in court with a charge of murder, or even manslaughter. If you can think of anything to help towards that end, then let me know."

Mark holds out the empty vial.

"Mel was in such a state, she accidentally pocketed this. You'll probably struggle to find any prints on it though. We've all had a good look at it. Sorry."

Greg takes a plastic bag from his pocket and holds it out for Mark to put the vial in.

"Okay, thanks. Too late to worry about it now, but I'll get the lab to have a look anyway. We might be able to pick up something. One of my PCs will be round later to take your prints, to eliminate them. Can you think of anything else that might help?"

His question is met with silence from all of us. We have plenty we could tell him, but nothing that would point towards suicide.

"I'll leave you with the rest of the pizza then. By the way, have any of you seen anything of Dr Harper this afternoon? I tried to see him earlier, and he seems to have disappeared."

"I've been asleep," I say. "Sorry."

"He's not been down this way. I believe there are some

trial patients in though. Maybe they'll have seen him," says Greg.

"Oh yes. That reminds me, Greg. I bet you can't guess who's back in for another trial?" My attempt to lighten the mood works for the moment, and Greg smiles, shaking his head.

"Not got a clue, literally."

"Charles! I saw him the other day. He looked just as miserable as when he was last here. I don't really know why he does it."

Greg laughs. "No, me neither – he was definitely not the life and soul of the party last time. Strange chap. Anyway, I'll leave you to rest. Jimmy, rules seem to be in abeyance, so wander back to the Abbey whenever you like, but don't keep my friends here up too late."

"Aye, of course not. Thanks."

***

After Greg has gone, I dwell again on the possibility of a trial and conviction for murder. It isn't until Mark speaks that I realise we've been sitting in silence for a long time.

"At least he likes you, Mel."

"Who? Oh, Greg. Yes. It won't do any good if the coroner decides on murder though. Do you know what, I don't want to talk about it any more. I've missed my knitting."

"There's some in the common room cupboard. Wool and needles – hasnae been started yet. Do you want me to bring it over for you?"

"Yes please, Jimmy. If you don't mind. Thanks."

Once he's gone, I take the opportunity to go to the bathroom. Once there, I remove the swabs and empty wrappers, and put them in the bin. Next to the sink is a circular yellow bin for the disposal of sharps – needles that are to be sent for incineration. I wipe the remaining syringe and other empty vial with toilet paper and throw them into the yellow container. It has a red lid on it, and once something has been put in, it's hard to extract it.

For good measure, I remove the morphine and trial drug vials from my other pocket, and throw them in too. I grab some more toilet roll to prevent fingerprints, flush the toilet, and under cover of the noise, give the yellow bin a good shake. I see the ex-contents of my pocket disappear into the general melée of needles, syringes and vials by the time the flush is complete.

I wash my hands and go back to join Mark in the ward.

When Jimmy returns about twenty minutes later, he finds Mark and me in exactly the same positions as when he left us.

"Have you two not missed each other? I'd have thought you'd have been in each other's arms." He glances at each of us – tears and a scowl are clearly visible. He refrains from further questions. "Anyhow, I've got your knitting stuff, lass, but better still, one of the coppers on guard outside Dominic's office offered me a pack of cards. Do you fancy a game?"

"I've not played cards in years. You'll have to teach me some games – all I can remember is snap." I try not to focus on Mark, but in truth, my whole body tingles with awareness of him.

It was strange after Jimmy left. Neither of us knew what to say. The axe that hangs over our heads, or at least my head, prevented any trivial conversation between us, but I was scared to reach out and ask for the hug that I need so much. Perhaps after Jimmy has gone to bed – maybe then. Part of my fear, with him returning so soon, was not wanting to reduce us both to quivering jellyfish. It won't matter so much later. We can draw the curtains round.

"I can play rummy and poker. Do you want to teach Mel?" says Mark, directing his gaze at Jimmy.

A strange game ensues, with Jimmy partnering and assisting me, as we play against Mark. The rules eventually come back to me. I'd played with my family before Jess disappeared.

Once I catch Mark watching me when he thinks I'm engrossed in the cards. He flushes and looks away, missing the beseeching look I cast him. We play for about two hours, until Dr Griffiths comes in and turfs Jimmy out.

"My patients need their sleep. Good night, young man."

Jimmy gathers up the cards, and leaves them in a pile on the bedside table.

"Night, night. Talk to each other, okay? Even a blithering idiot could see you need to have a chat. I only stayed to give you both a chance to think it through first. See you tomorrow."

Dr Griffiths remains long enough to dish out tablets. I swallow them quickly, as I did with the previous set.

"Some paracetamol for you too, Mark. You look as though you've got a headache."

"It's been a difficult day. Thanks."

The doctor leaves after a quick goodnight, and Mark and I stay where we are, neither of us speaking for quite some time.

"Mark, will you come here please?" I fight to keep my voice from cracking, but it definitely wobbles. He's sitting facing me on the bed within seconds, and has his arms round me in time for my control to snap completely. He strokes my back in rhythmic circular motions as I sob into his shoulder. "I don't want to go to prison and leave you forever."

"Oh God, Mel, my love, I don't want you to either." He sniffs, and now we're crying together.

Which is exactly how Greg finds us when he returns five minutes later.

Chapter Thirty-Nine

"Sorry to disturb you both, but we've found a letter."

Mark and I break apart, but he stays sitting on the bed, and holds my hand as we face Greg. I swallow hard.

"Who from?" I ask. My voice sounds several notes higher than usual. What if it's from Dominic, with some weird warning of what I might do?

"Well, we were quite surprised to receive this, as although I was searching for him earlier, I didn't realise he'd actually left the premises. I'd sent one of my men to search his quarters, and he came back with this. My PC handled it with gloves of course, but we've fingerprinted it, and the only prints are from… Well, it's a long story, but we've read the letter of course (although it's actually addressed to you, Mel, sorry)."

I wave away his apologies. He still hasn't told us who the letter's from, and fear is clenching its teeth into my stomach.

Greg opens the letter in his hand.

"The easiest way to explain is to read you the letter.

"Melissa,

"Apologies for not telling you this in person. As you will see when you read on, there is too much at stake here for me to stay around, awaiting arrest.

"Perhaps you already know of some of my crimes. I believe your friend Greg, who was kind enough to identify himself to me in the days leading up to Dominic's death, had been on my tail for some time, suspecting (correctly) that I was passing myself off as a renowned Consultant by the name of Len Harper.

"I was born Benedict Bishop, Dominic's older half-brother. I trained as a doctor, but was struck off several years ago for medical negligence. The authorities failed to realise

the full scale of my crimes, so although charged initially, I escaped the prison sentence that could so easily have resulted. On the arrival in my brother's community of a grieving Leonard Harper, Dominic contacted me and suggested I could borrow the man's identity to enable me to resume my medical practices. I had long been interested in research, and Dr Harper's activities as a trial investigator and key opinion leader were well documented. I quickly availed myself of the opportunity.

"Unfortunately, as you know, Leonard became disillusioned with certain aspects of community life and decided he would like to resume a more normal lifestyle. This couldn't be permitted, and Leonard had to be disposed of. Thomas was eager to perform the task, but Dominic was reluctant to allow this, given Thomas' lack of stealth. Dominic had a certain influence over some of the inmates, enhanced by his belief that he was the Messiah. He used this to entice the Scot to the Infirmary in the middle of the night. Jimmy injected Leonard as per Dominic's instructions, and the lethal dose did its work, peacefully and with a minimum of fuss.

"For many years, Dominic suffered from Schizophrenia. Rather than having him spend his life in and out of institutions, it seemed expedient to allow him to indulge his beliefs in a safe environment away from the main population. Any idiots stupid enough to believe he was the Messiah deserved all they got. Dominic used many tricks to convince his followers that he could perform miracles. Most of these relied on sleight of hand, or inducing an adrenaline-heightened state to mask pain. His most convincing trick, though, was his pretence that he could cure blindness. His subject for this was only partially blind, and clever use of lighting was sufficient to persuade the patient – and the witnesses – that a cure had been effected.

"However, Dominic's tendencies towards manipulation and violence were a personal characteristic, and not linked to his condition.

"I am aware of the disappearance of several vials from

235

our clinical supplies. Although these were kept locked up, it would have been an easy matter for Dominic to have borrowed the key and accessed the fridge. His mental stability over recent weeks, and indeed months, has deteriorated; and in the last few days of his life, he was frankly a wreck. It would have been a matter of indifference to him which drugs he used to end his life. He would have selected randomly, and disposed of the remaining drugs correctly, his obsession with tidiness over-riding his condition momentarily. His Messianic beliefs were complicated by the hope and belief in his impending fatherhood, and he struggled to come to terms with the possibility that the child may succeed him as Messiah.

"I didn't disabuse my brother of this ridiculous notion. Nor did I point out to him that you were already pregnant when he seduced you."

Mark releases my hand for a moment, and gives me a confused, hurt look. The agony and desperation that must show in my face seems to affect him, though, and he resumes his grip, painfully tight.

"When your baby was born, I could see instantly that the child was a product of Mark. I've always found it fascinating the way a first-born child so often has the father stamped in its features. I had orders to spirit the child away, and to tell you the ridiculous lies, which you sensibly refused to believe.

"Your child is safe in the custody of Emily, with whom you got on so well. She has been told you required a C-section, and were not well enough afterwards to care for your daughter."

My heart almost stops. I was right. Are we on the brink of getting Emma back?

"Emily's contact details are in my safe; the combination is 251265 – my brother's date of birth. I have no doubt she will be pleased to reunite you with the child.

"You will need to sort out the baby's birth certificate. Obviously you are now free to marry Mark if you would like. I wish you both well.

"I also feel obliged (from guilt, as I knew what my brother

*was doing to you, and did nothing to prevent him) to advise
you of his illegal activities regarding the property belonging
to you, and indeed many of the members.*

"*On arrival in the Abbey, you may recall signing
numerous documents. These effectively signed over all your
assets for the use of Dominic and The Brotherhood. They
were not legally binding, and your property still exists, and
continues to belong to you. Dominic informed me you were a
wealthy woman in your own right, and I know he had plans
to commit that property more firmly into his own possession.
I believe Mark also owns a sizeable property in
Hertfordshire. I have no doubt a good lawyer would help you
resolve any issues, although this should not be too
complicated to achieve. As far as I am aware, my brother was
unable to change the title on any of the deeds he held.*

"*By the time you find this, I hope to be out of the country,
and away from the long reach of the law. No doubt it would
have me convicted as an accessory to abuse, and to the
impersonation and murder of Leonard, in addition to my
earlier crimes. I have no intention of serving time in prison,
so you will not see me again.*

"*I apologise to you for my part in your sufferings. For
those, I do have some remorse. Your only crime was that of
infatuation with a man of tremendous charisma and
insufferable good looks who believed himself to be the
Messiah. Certainly not worthy of the punishment you've
received.*

"*Yours sincerely,*

"*Benedict Bishop – alias Len Harper.*

"So, that solves some of the mysteries. We've already
contacted Emily. She'll be bringing the baby here first thing
tomorrow. She would have come this evening, but had some
transport difficulties."

"Couldn't you have sent a car?"

"Mel, it's gone ten o'clock. You've had a traumatic day,
and let's be realistic. Your baby is a week old. All your time
and energy will be needed for looking after her. Get some
sleep tonight if you can. As I was saying, we'll get the

documentation sorted. Obviously you need to get the birth certificate issued. You've got forty-two days. If you want to have both your married names on the certificate, you could register your plans to marry tomorrow, and get married twenty-eight days later. You would then have about five days left to register the birth in your married names. What do you think?"

"It's all a bit much to take in right now," say Mark. "Harper, or whatever we're supposed to call him, said Dominic had become less stable with his condition, and that he had access to the drugs. Would that affect any coroner decisions?"

Greg gives Mark a sharp look. "It might do. Look, there's no point getting stressed about it for the moment. The pathologist has to do a post-mortem. We need to find medical records to corroborate the evidence in that letter, and we need to... Well, I'll put my cards on the table for you. I think you already know – I've certainly implied – that my strong hope is that the coroner will bring in a verdict of suicide. If not, well, Benedict Bishop has fled the country (apparently), doing his best to suggest that's what happened. I'm sure a motive could be established. He would have had the opportunity, and I'm sure he'd have had the sense to use gloves, so there'd be no fingerprints to find. There's a strong case against him. I don't want to have to look too far for other alternatives. And that's not something I should be saying. As a police officer, I'm sworn to get at the truth. Sometimes the truth is that justice is best served by leaving well alone. Good night."

He nods at us, and leaves the ward.

Dumbfounded, Mark and I sit on the bed holding hands and staring at each other. Finally, I break the silence.

"We're going to see Emma tomorrow. Isn't that wonderful?"

"Emma? Is that short for Emily? I know she's nice, and she'll be bringing our baby, which is fantastic. Now that I am excited about!"

"Sorry Mark. While I was in the cellar, I had no one else to talk to, so I've been telling stories to our daughter for weeks. I had to give her a name. I've always liked the name Emma, so I used it. We can change it if you really want, but I've been thinking of her as Emma for such a long time." I giggle. "Goodness knows what I'd have done if she'd turned out to be a boy."

Mark gives me a quick hug and turns so he's sitting next to me on the bed. It's a bit of a tight squeeze, but I don't care.

"I like the name Emma too. It's simple, pretty and traditional. Mel, I've been so scared of everything for such a long time. I want to believe it will all be okay now, and that Greg will sort everything out. But the fear is so deep-rooted, it's going to take a long time to get rid of it."

"I know. Believe me, I know. What I don't know is how we're going to work it all out. The practical bits will be so easy by comparison – little niggles to get everything sorted out. I feel I've got enough baggage to flatten Everest. There are so many things I want to tell you, but have no idea how to begin. And there are lots of things I don't think I could ever tell, because they're awful, and they're my fault. But you do know I love you, don't you?" I turn to give him a pleading look, and receive a confused one in return.

"Okay," he says, after a long pause during which my breath struggles to escape my lungs. "I love you too. But this is going to be difficult. We have a child together. That's incredibly exciting, and scary. We have to deal with a lot of hang ups, of which... bloody hell, Melissa, you betrayed me! You were pregnant with our child, and you slept with that... scumbag. How could you? How can I trust you not to be unfaithful if we get married?"

"I'm sorry. I made a mistake. He dazzled me, and I was stupid and naïve. And that's how you know you can trust me in future. Has anyone ever been so punished for having an affair? To have endured torment, imprisonment and degradation? For the crime of being charmed into bed? I will never trust charm again. I don't ever want to be alone with a man other than you. The thought of any other men makes feel physically sick. I know it's an overused cliché, but in my case it's true. So many of the things he did to me, and made me do, were so repulsive, I can't think of… sex without wanting to throw up. And that's another fear. I don't know if I'll be able to enjoy it, ever again. There's more chance with you than with anyone else, but it might not happen. Supposing it doesn't? You might start to look elsewhere."

"We've got a lot to deal with. I'm going to go to bed now, and think about things. We'll sort this out though. Together. I promise."

"Thank you."

"One more thing. Mel, will you marry me? Let's get past this ridiculous engagement, okay?"

I shake my head, and Mark draws back, startled.

"Sorry, I didn't mean no. It was just that after all you said, it seems weird to get a proposal. Yes, please. Whatever we have to sort out, we can hopefully face it better together. I'll try not to let you down."

"That's good enough to be going on with. Night, Mel." He gives me a lingering, but closed-mouth kiss, and somewhere, in the depths of my damaged soul, there's a tingle.

Chapter Forty

Next morning, as we're finishing breakfast, Dr Griffiths arrives, followed by a young woman carrying a baby. I give a shriek and dive out of bed.

"Careful, my dear. Not so violently please. You've only just had an operation."

I don't reply, but put my arms round both Emily and my baby daughter a bit more carefully than I first intended.

"Are you okay, Mel?" asks Emily. "I'm so sorry, I didn't realise they'd taken her away from you and hadn't even asked, let alone tell you where she was."

"I'm fine now. Thank you for bringing her to me."

"She's very sweet, and she sleeps occasionally as well."

Mark rushes over in his pyjamas to inspect.

"She's a ginge – like her mum," he says with a huge grin. I suspect the grin has little to do with her hair colour. Mark seems as thrilled as I am with our baby.

I take the small bundle from Emily, and hold my daughter in my arms for the first time. She nuzzles against me, and turns her head towards my breast. My heart does a triple somersault.

"Could I still feed her, do you think?" I whisper. My milk came in three days ago, swelling my breasts to the size of prize watermelons, but they began to ease off the day before I left the ward.

"You could give it a try," says Emily. "Obviously I've been giving her formula, but if you want to breastfeed it would definitely be better. I'll hold her for a moment while you get back into bed, and get yourself comfortable."

A complicated few minutes ensue, during which pillows are arranged, then rearranged, then half of them are discarded. Everyone changes position at least three times, and I quickly realise that privacy is out of the question. Once settled comfortably, I then have to teach Emma how to latch on – tricky, as neither she nor I have read the books. Fortunately, Emily's nurse training included some midwifery, and she helps with the technical details. Now it's up to us.

Suddenly, within half an hour of their arrival, I have my baby suckling at my breast. Tears flow down my cheeks unchecked. I killed a man to achieve this moment. How can I be proud? And yet pride is one of the dominant emotions as I watch Emma feed. Mark and I produced this beautiful baby. She was born despite so many obstacles. Cold, lack of food, and the strain my body and mind have undergone, could have adversely affected her development, and yet she's beautiful. As she feeds, I count ten fingers, and ten toes; eyes, nose and mouth all in the right place.

"Is she completely healthy, Emily?" I ask.

"Yes, she seems to be. She'll need to have a heel-prick test in a few days, but we'll get that sorted. There's no reason to suspect there's anything wrong."

No reason, apart from her history *in utero* and that her mother is a murderer. I feel guilty only for feeling no remorse. Because the alternative is to have remained a slave to Dominic's whims for ever, and never to have seen or held my child. Now she'll have a future. Hopefully one with her mother not in prison.

I need to discuss the immediate future with Mark, but I suspect there's a lot to be done in the Abbey. Not everyone will have instant access to their families, or to money, or be able to find jobs.

I've spent a lot of the night thinking, and plan to stay at the Abbey for a while, sustaining all those who still need a home. Perhaps the peaceful harmony for which I once joined could be the reality. All sorts of ideas floated around my head as I lay there, and the concepts develop further while I feed Emma. I'm the happiest I've been in many months.

I send up intermittent prayers that the coroner will reach a verdict of suicide.

***

We've stayed on at the Abbey, although many changes have been made. Emma is now four weeks old. Mark presides over a committee – an elected form of government for the forty remaining members. The departure of the wardens, and of many of the original members (including Thomas, who disappeared after initial questioning) left a lot of space, and we've been able to alter sleeping arrangements to suit everyone much better. I gather Greg is furious with himself for not taking Thomas into custody immediately.

Mark, Jimmy and Brie have been exploring sections of the Abbey that were prohibited under Dominic's rule, and discovered, amongst other things, a room full of suitcases and bags containing members' valuable possessions. We've all now been reunited with our pre-Brotherhood clothes, and the uniforms have been binned, with great relief all round.

Further improvements are planned to enable single or double en-suite bedrooms. There are still rotas to ensure everyone helps with cooking and cleaning, but anyone who wants to can go out to work. Part of the Abbey may also be opened up as a tourist attraction, although we're still working out the details.

Family and friends are encouraged to visit, and all members have been issued with a mobile phone. Televisions and books have been brought in, and we're all growing accustomed to re-engaging with the outside world.

The coroner dithered. For over two weeks. The post-mortem was inconclusive, other than to confirm Dominic had died of a cardiac arrest. Fingerprints on the vial were also inconclusive. Even mine were barely visible beneath Mark's and Jimmy's; they'd handled it so thoroughly. The pathologist refused to provide an opinion on whether the cardiac arrest was due to the potassium chloride, and whether or not this had been self-administered.

"Might have been," I overheard him say to Greg, who commandeered Dominic's office for the investigation. "Who knows? If you've got enough evidence to suggest suicide, it'd save the taxpayer a costly trial. Sounds like the man was a total git anyway."

Greg saw me pacing the corridor with Emma, and shut the door, so I never heard his response. But a week later, he comes to tell us the case is closed.

He sits in the armchair in the bedroom Mark and I now share. I sit on the bed feeding Emma, although discreetly. I've discovered the knack of covering the essentials with a baggy t-shirt.

"We had a choice. Either bring in a verdict of suicide, or pursue enquiries regarding other people who had the opportunity. My personal favourite was Benedict Bishop – or Dr Harper, as you knew him. In practice, though, it would have been hard to make it stick, even if we'd been able to find him (and we're still looking – he has other crimes to answer to). He's certainly answerable for the murder of Leonard."

"Won't Jimmy be charged for that? Not that I want him to be, but…" I bite my lip. "He wasn't really responsible. He might have been told it would make Leonard better?"

"Jimmy won't be charged. We only have the word of a criminal to suggest Jimmy had anything to do with Leonard's murder. Regarding Dominic's death, the alternatives to suicide don't really bear thinking about. Having said that, I spent many long nights thinking about them. Does an ordinary man, police detective or otherwise, have the right to make a decision on behalf of a judge and jury?"

"And? What's the answer?" asks Mark, from the chair in the other corner.

"I convinced the coroner to bring in a verdict of suicide."

My breath catches in my throat. We're safe.

Thank you, Lord. That's what I call a real miracle.

"Greg, when I marry Mark next week, please will you give me away?"

The detective inspector smiles and nods.

***

One week later, I don a white dress, made for me by Brie and Tina. Emily holds Emma, her goddaughter, as they watch me prepare for my wedding.

As I stand still, allowing Tina to fasten the intricate buttons at the back of my dress, I pray again, thanking the Lord that everything has worked out so well. I do feel guilt for committing murder and 'getting away with it', but from things Dr Griffiths has said to me following on from the letter, I gather Dominic's mental health was very indicative of suicide. So I'm now gowned and veiled, with my red hair vibrant against the white dress, I lean lightly on Greg's arm, as he leads me towards Mark in the small church half a mile from the Abbey.

A short while later, I'm finally wed to the man I love most in the world. I carry our beloved daughter in a purple papoose that seems to clash with everything, and we return to the Abbey, where a catered feast awaits us. I look around at the familiar faces in the front row of our reception: Tina, Brie, Jimmy, Greg, Dr Griffiths and Emily – our friends and family.

Somehow we've survived the Apocalypse and arrived safely on the other side. Damaged, but alive, and strong, and together.

THE END

Fantastic Books
Great Authors

CROOKED
CAT

Meet our authors and discover
our exciting range:

- Gripping Thrillers
- Cosy Mysteries
- Romantic Chick-Lit
- Fascinating Historicals
- Exciting Fantasy
- Young Adult and Children's
  Adventures
- Non-Fiction

Visit us at:
www.crookedcatbooks.com

Join us on facebook:
www.facebook.com/crookedcatbooks

31115780R00148

Printed in Great Britain
by Amazon